THE ALPHA AND THE MAIDEN

LYNN BRANCH

To my friends who selflessly devote their time to making these books possible.
And,
To love in all its forms; may its light forever embrace those who seek its warmth.

CONTENTS

PROLOGUE

ERIS

B UILDINGS CRUMBLED AROUND ME, and the fire roared, making me
feel like I ran through a thundercloud. Sheer terror and thick
smoke constricted my throat while I weaved through the streets of the
pack's village where I had lived my entire life, tears streaming from my
burning eyes.

Mere minutes ago, I'd been a mostly normal teenage shifter. Mostly
normal, since the firstborn child of the Alpha is groomed their entire
life to succeed their father or mother. My upbringing differed from
a regular wolf shifter pup. Always training. Always studying. Always
improving. The fate of the pack depended on my devotion to my
development, and I felt the pressure to rise to the challenge as my
father bypassed age-old laws that required a male heir and chose me
as his successor. We both expected I'd face opposition for the title,
and I would be ready to defend my right.

This afternoon, I'd been in a sparring lesson at the edge of the forest
for longer than planned. We were finishing as dusk turned into night,
when the chaos started. My father's Beta, or second-in-command, had
linked me through the pack bond in a panic. *'Eris, we're under attack.*
You need to return to the pack house and find your mother!'

By the look on the warrior's face with whom I'd been training, I
knew he had received similar news. We ran back together, and just
before we crested the small hill into the valley where our pack lived, I

smelled the smoke. My mother's soothing voice linked me. *'Eris, your sister is at Holly's. Please find her and return to me.'*

I picked up my pace. Holly was a girl the same age as my sister, Enid. The warrior peeled away towards the West Forest without a word. It seemed like everything was already burning. I entered the chaos and tried to sniff through the smoke. Who could be responsible for this unwarranted attack? The packs were at peace. The entire realm was.

I tried to link with Holly's mother but received no reply. Enid was still a young pup, only eleven years old, and would not join the pack link until she was fifteen. I turned down the street to Holly's home and cried out when I saw the building completely engulfed in flames. I squinted through the smoke and saw a small figure standing at the front gate. Enid.

I ran to my sister, getting close and yelling over the noise, "Holly?"

Her eyes were wide as she pointed a shaking finger at the wreckage behind me. I flinched away, feeling the intense heatwave as the roof caved in and crashed through both levels of the home. No one could've survived. I grabbed Enid's hand and ran towards the pack house, dragging her behind me.

Sudden pain ripped through my chest, and I howled, dropping to my knees. The pack members around me stopped their mad scurry and did the same, a symphony of agony filling the night air as we all wailed. My sister sobbed, crying for our mother.

Next to us, a woman screamed, "The Alpha is dead! Goddess, help us all!"

No! It wasn't possible. I felt for my father through the pack bond and found a black void where his energy should be. I tried to remain calm, but the surrounding screams turned from pain to horror. The metallic scent of blood invaded my nostrils, accompanied by the smell of rot. A glance over my shoulder and I caught sight of our attackers.

I'd never actually been in their presence. I was too young to go on patrols, but I recognized these creatures as vampires. Pallid skin, elongated claws, and glowing red eyes. As the night provided their cover, they snarled and ripped at the throats of those around them, drinking and squealing in the bloodbath.

I didn't see a leader, knowing they would be in control of their urges and aged to amber in the eyes. This was a chaotic horde, slithering and clawing over each other to get to the murdered wolves and fight for a sip of blood. Inhuman strength and agility allowed them to crawl like insects along the sides of any buildings that weren't on fire.

Panic erupted, chasing my heart into a painful sprint, and I scooped my sister into my arms and ran. We wouldn't make it. They descended upon us, a wave of reeking death. I wished I could shift to my wolf, but I still had two months until my nineteenth birthday when I would see my first change at the full moon.

A sob escaped my stubborn lips as I felt those wolves running close to us being pulled back and the subsequent sounds of the slaughter behind me. I squeezed Enid, bracing myself for the fiends to grab me, but the hands never came.

Instead, a vicious growl sounded, and a large brown wolf leaped into the fray. It was Thad, my mother's personal guard. He was a fierce warrior and had been a constant in my life for as long as I could remember. Mother must have sent him to aid our escape.

He turned, his eyes locking with mine, and his burly voice rumbled into my head. *'Run, little wolf. Don't look back.'*

Thad threw back his head and howled. Other adults, although not warriors, rallied to his call and shifted into their wolves. They battled for their lives, tearing limbs and heads from the vampires. Despite their bravery, the disparity in numbers was too great. They would all be slaughtered.

I screamed, "Thad!" begging him to come with us.

'Run, you foolish girl! Run!'

I spun on my heel and did as I was told. My throat was tight with grief. He and the others would die for our chance to survive.

The pack house was just ahead, and I focused on it, running as fast as my legs would carry. Enid's weight tested my strength, but I refused to put her down. I clutched her tightly, but gently, like a prized little egg, and she buried her sobbing face into my chest.

'Mother? Mother!'

I sobbed with relief when she answered, *'To the stables now. Hurry, Eris!'*

Our pack was one of the few remaining that were too stubborn to embrace the technology that leaked over the borders of the realm from the human world. Although I'd seen pictures, we did not travel with vehicles. Father said that the grand pack of Gold Moon, our neighbors, had many of them driving on their roads. Our horses were seldom used because adult shifters were faster in second form, as their wolves. The stables stayed occupied because my mother loved horses and insisted every child learn to ride.

I rounded the corner into the center aisle, flanked by stalls. They were all open, allowing the horses to escape. Mother was tightening the saddle on my favorite bay gelding, Ollie. She turned and opened her arms for me, and I dove into them, sobbing.

"Mother! Father, he—" I choked on the words, unable to finish.

Mother stroked my hair and soothed me. "I know, baby. I know."

Her voice was broken by tears, and the hollows under her eyes were like deep moors. Losing a true mate was the most painful experience a wolf shifter could endure. The ever-present shine in her eyes was dull, and the instinct to protect her pups was the only thing driving her past the grief.

She gripped us for a heartbeat longer before she pushed me away from her and looked into my eyes. "You need to take your sister and ride, Eris. Go and don't look back. I have to stay. I am the Luna, the mother of this pack. I cannot abandon them. He wants me."

"Who does?"

She nudged me toward Ollie, not offering an answer. "Get in the saddle now, my sweet girls. Come on."

My head whipped back and forth, tears flying. "No, no! Please, Mother, don't make me go! I can fight! I can fight!"

It was my duty as the future Alpha of this pack. When I felt through the pack bond, I gasped. Mere minutes, but there was hardly anyone left alive. I could sense a few flickering life forces, and flinched as each one was snuffed out.

Mother opened her mouth to answer, but a shaking boom interrupted her. I thought the pack house must've collapsed because the ground quivered beneath our feet. Her eyes grew wide, and she stepped in front of us, holding her arms out protectively.

I braced for a monster to enter the stables, but a smiling man rounded the corner instead. Close to seven feet tall, he was the largest man I'd ever seen. I didn't recognize the scent—like fresh cinders. He was certainly no wolf.

Hair danced on his head like fire, varying shades of reds and oranges, and his unsettling yellow eyes set on my mother.

Thin, pale lips lifted in a vile smirk as he stalked towards us, saying, "Oh, my sweet Ceres, I've finally found you, darling."

Mother screamed, "Stay back!"

He wasn't perturbed, and my mother's hands shook as she turned and threw my sister into the saddle, forcing me up behind her.

Tears streamed down her cheeks, but when she spoke, her voice was steady. "Never forget that I love you both more than anything in this world. Be strong, okay? Take care of each other."

My sister wailed, reaching for her, but Mother slapped Ollie's haunch, and he jumped into a run, exiting the stable away from the red-haired man.

I handed the reins to Enid and turned in time to see her shift into her beautiful white wolf. The color was so rare we didn't know of another in any of the surrounding packs. The man cackled, and I lost sight of them as we ascended a hill into the forest. Enid stopped the horse, and we both turned to watch.

Sometimes I wished I could go back to that moment, and not turn. Not stop. Many nights, I wished my memories of my mother could be pure.

The man stepped out of the stable, and we gasped, Enid screaming, "No! Mother! Eris! Go back!"

He held her by her neck, still in her wolf form. She struggled in his grasp, her teeth clacking as she tried to get a bite. I couldn't understand how he could restrain her in his human form. It shouldn't be possible.

My heart jumped, filling with traitorous hope when she got a latch on his arm and ripped at the skin, tearing it in a spurt of blood. A wail tore up my throat when he grabbed her scruff and ripped her head from her body as if she were a paper doll. With the Alpha and Luna gone, the pack bond dissolved. Eliminated.

I snatched my sister's head into my chest to hide her eyes, my stomach churning while I watched him lift Mother's body and drink her blood. What was this creature? Not a vampire. Not a wolf. Not a fae. Then what?

"Ride!" I screamed, digging my heels into Ollie's sides.

The gelding was wild-eyed, and he kept a sprint as long as he could. He ran at his own discretion because I didn't direct him. Enid and I sobbed, blinded by tears. We were orphans now, lost and afraid.

CHAPTER 1

ERIS

MY EYES SNAPPED OPEN, and I took a shaking breath as the familiar nightmare released its claws. Our tiny window was black, informing me it was still early morning. Enid stirred, and I stilled, not wanting to wake her. Neither of us slept well. Piercing yellow eyes loomed over our lives like a gloomy cloud.

Enid's cat opened one eye to glare at me. He was the only other survivor from our pack. I went back once, a few days after we found the abandoned cabin that we now called home.

There were no survivors. Every ounce of life in our pack had been sought out and destroyed by the man with the red hair and his vampire horde. The smell of decay was stifling as I walked up and down the streets, seeing the drained husks of everyone I had ever known.

My father's head was mounted on a spike in the middle of the slaughter, and I buried it in the cemetery, marking the spot with a large stone. I looked in the stables, but my mother's body was nowhere to be found.

The rest were drained and rotted beyond recognition. I could still feel the sweat that slid down my lower back as I dragged my pack mates to the center of town and burned them in a mass funeral pyre, releasing their souls to run in the grasslands with the Goddess. It was the closest thing to a proper burial I could give them.

As I walked out of the town, I had noticed I had a stalker. This midnight black cat. Odd, as wolf shifters rarely kept cats and cats hardly enjoyed our company. He had hopped up onto the back of the saddle blanket like he owned the horse and had ridden all the way back to the cabin with me.

An odd cat indeed. He took to Enid right away and rarely left her side, barely giving me a sideways glance. She'd named him Hades, something I found macabre. When I asked why, she'd told me that was the name he liked.

I extracted myself from our shared bed and went to stoke the low-burning fire. I liked to wake up early and go to bed late. Every day, I worked as hard as I could in search of exhausted, dreamless sleep. Still hadn't found it, though. Maybe someday the dead would stop haunting me.

We had been lost and desperate for four days after our pack had been decimated. Starving and cold, we'd stumbled across this neglected cabin. Canned foods, long expired, had been our saviors. I would never forget the taste of old beans and sour corn. We'd made them last until my birthday, when my wolf could take over and hunt.

Satisfied with the strong flame, I dressed and loaded the pile of furs I'd been collecting into my backpack. The cabin rested on the border of shifter and fae territory. It was only a twenty-minute walk to an eclectic fae town that honored the old ways of their people. The major fae city, Ceanna-Bhaile, was said to hold millions of people, but I never ventured that far. I sold furs in the small outskirt settlement once a month to earn a little money for supplies.

For wolves, the pack was life. The pack was sacred, and nothing else mattered. The Fae, however, welcomed all species into their folds. I thought it was because many of them were tricksters and cheats and allowed outsiders because they had a much easier time running their cons on species unwise to their ways. Something I'd learned the hard way.

I tried to be quiet as I clicked open the first of the ten locks I had on the door. Excessive maybe, but I never felt safe. The logical part of my brain often teased me, assuring me that silly little locks wouldn't stop the red-haired man, anyway.

"Can't I come with you today?" my sister's soft voice asked behind me.

I sighed, hoping to sneak away from this conversation.

"You know you can't, Enid. You must stay here, where it's safe. I won't even be gone half of the day, I promise."

She nodded and looked down at her fidgeting hands. I never let her go, but she never argued with me. She was such a good girl. An innocent child. And it was my job to keep her safe.

The other occupant in my head asked, *'Keep her safe or keep her prisoner?'*

I frowned and felt a familiar pang of guilt. My wolf, Calliope, or Calli, didn't like how I kept Enid here. Part of me knew it was cruel to isolate her, but I couldn't bring myself to loosen my grip. I was too afraid of losing her. Enid was special. We both were, but her unnatural power was too noticeable. I could at least pass as a normal wolf.

I walked over and lifted my sister's chin, giving her a smile. "Do you want to bet you can finish it before I get back?"

She glanced at the thousand-piece puzzle sitting on our old table. Whenever I was out, I tried to buy fun things for her. Puzzles, books, and seeds for the garden were her favorites.

Enid had the greenest thumb I'd ever seen. Our entire cabin was a testament to it, filled with various plants and flowers. She grew much of our food, tea, and medicines. We both did our part to keep each other alive, taking care of each other just like Mother wanted.

Enid wasn't convinced by my positivity and shrugged without returning my smile. My heart pinched as she shuffled with drooping shoulders to the kitchen stove and put water on for tea, a small sniffle floating back from her. Hades sashayed after her, giving me a look as if to tell me I was a wicked wretch.

I sighed and turned back towards the door, stepping out into the morning chill. The sun greeted me through the needles of the pine, and Ollie nickered from his pen.

"At least someone's happy to see me this morning," I muttered, letting him out to roam. He never went far past the garden, as attached to us as we were to him.

CHAPTER 2

ERIS

EVEN THIS EARLY IN the morning, the market street of Snowwhistle was bustling. Classic fae architecture reflected their silly and mischievous attitudes alongside their harmony with nature. Many of the shops and homes were large mushrooms in neon colors, growing and twisting in unpredictable shapes.

Other homes were enormous trees, carved out to house several rooms. I didn't understand how the trees were not harmed during this process. They seemed to thrive, and they were so wide I thought a hundred people could link hands and still not encircle them.

I walked through the crowd shoulder to shoulder with haggling merchants and squabbling customers. Almost anything imaginable was for sale here. Witches peddled everything from hexes to love potions for those searching for revenge or for their "happily ever after." They failed to mention the unpredictable side effects if the spells were used incorrectly, which happened often.

The Fae viewed life as one big party and their booths sold elixirs and powders that were used to alter the mind and spirit. I even saw a sketchy man claiming to have a djinn in a bottle for sale. I kept my eyes forward, not interested in their wares.

My only stop was a clean, quaint shop with a small sign on chains reading *Double Trouble Spells & Market*. This was the place I trusted. When I walked in here three years ago, the witches that owned it, named River and Rhia, recognized my struggle, and took pity on me.

They always gave me a better than fair price. I hoped I could repay their kindness someday.

After some friendly conversation, I left the shop with flour, sugar, several packs of seeds, a block of cheese and a new puzzle for Enid. I was adjusting the items in my pack when I noticed the most enticing smell. Calli shifted, suddenly restless in my head. It was fresh rain with a hint of peppermint. I loved peppermint, and I searched the crowd, wondering if it was a candle or incense. There was a little extra money. I could buy it.

I saw him before he saw me. Standing taller than those who moved around him, he wasn't jostled by the shoving, with a thick body that showed discipline and dedication to training. My mouth ran dry, and I swallowed, knowing this wasn't the average rogue wolf. I could feel his dark, powerful aura and knew he was an anointed Alpha. His black hair shifted softly in the breeze while his nose was up, sniffing and scanning the crowd. Our eyes met and the golden hazel flashed like a lightning strike, his nostrils flaring.

'Mate!' Calli celebrated in my head, and her joy erupted, mixing with my spiking fear. I shoved everything in my pack and pushed through the crowd. Calli whined in my head. *'Mate! It's our mate. What are you doing? Go back!'*

'No, no, no, Calli. I don't want a mate.' I ducked down a side street and broke into a full run.

'The Goddess decides such things, you foolish girl.'

'No! A mate means a pack, and a pack means too many people I can love and then lose.'

She whined louder and pawed at the front of my mind.

I had known for a long time that Gold Moon was south of Snowwhistle, but I never went. It was likely they would accept us if Enid and I asked to join them, but I never asked. His aura. He was the Alpha.

'I am certainly no Luna!' I snapped at Callie. They were the heart of the pack. The mother. Nothing in my life had prepared me for such a role.

We were better off alone. I could keep Enid safe by myself, and we wouldn't risk joining another pack that the red-haired man could obliterate in one evening. The more people you loved; the more you had to lose. Love wasn't harmless. I'd learned that the hard way.

I thought of shifting to my wolf to run faster, but I didn't trust Calli not to turn around and go back. I still made it home in record time, slamming the door behind me. My chest heaved, but was tight, like the air couldn't actually enter my lungs. The farther I ran, the stronger the mate pull was. He was following me. The fated mate bond was a powerful force, nearly impossible to resist.

There was no question I would reject him when he found me. I knew he would chase me until he did. An Alpha wolf would not so easily give up on finding his mate.

Callie barked at me, *'What? You cannot reject the mate given to us by the Goddess! He's here for a reason; she has a plan. It's your fate.'*

'I just want to be left alone! Is that too much to ask?'

'He will help us. A wolf needs a pack, Eris. You cannot hide here forever.'

'Do you want to bet on that?' I hissed, and I slid down the door, resting my head in my hands and trying to calm my erratic breathing. I sat up with a start when I realized my sister hadn't greeted me yet.

"Enid?"

Instead of Enid, Hades confronted me. He was stressed, and me-owed as he trotted towards the bed. Enid's slight frame was unmoving under the blanket.

"Enid!"

Since her fifteenth birthday, she had been having these sudden fever seizures. I was always afraid she'd have one when I was gone, and today, of all days, it had happened. I touched her, and she was burning hot. Knowing I would be vulnerable, I rested my hand on her forehead and sang our mother's lullaby.

"Under the silver moon's embrace,
The wolves all gather in a secret place.
Their eyes aglow with an ancient fire,

They sing our lullaby, Goddess-inspired.

Sleep, little one, in the forest's bed,
Where shadows dance and dreams are bred.
The stars above are your silent guide,
As the Goddess watches you with pride.

Dream of running through moon-kissed snow.
Of wild adventures where spirits flow.
The pack surrounds you, hearts entwined,
In this enchanted world, find peace of mind.

Our moon, our guardian, watches above,
As the wolves chorus their lullaby of love.
Close your eyes, my precious child,
And let the wolf song keep you wild.
In dreams, you'll run with paws of grace,
Embraced by the moonlight's tender embrace."

As I sang, a soft illumination blossomed under my hand where I touched Enid. Singing was the only way I had found to activate my ability. She and I had discovered my power by accident during one of Enid's first seizures when I had simply been trying to calm her with the gentle lullaby.

I felt the familiar pull of my energy draining as her fever calmed. She whimpered, and I laid down next to her, closing my eyes. Healing her exhausted me. A man with black hair and hazel eyes drifted into my thoughts as darkness took over.

CHAPTER 3

GIDEON

I REFRAINED FROM ROLLING my eyes while my Beta, who was also my younger brother, made another cringy joke. We were eating at a restaurant in the fae town close to our pack and discussing borders with a representative of the Fae King. I didn't enjoy traveling into their massive city if I didn't have to because it smelled like piss.

Unfortunately for me, very little business was being done. This was a waste of my time. The representative was a pretty woman and my whore of a brother, Finn, was all too happy to take over the conversation. Fortunately for him, this girl was eating it up.

He went on, "I know there have been a few scuffles and some fighting on the border, and we'll take care of that, I promise. Right now, I'm fighting the urge to take you home and make you the happiest woman on Earth, Poppy."

Finn added a wink at the end, and I actually rolled my eyes this time, muttering, "My gods."

Poppy blushed all the way to the tips of her pointed ears and giggled, the color of her cheeks nearing the hue of her flaming red hair.

I linked him. *'You make me want to vomit.'*

'Then go away. It's not my fault I ooze sex appeal from every pore. These fae women love it!'

'You'll regret sleeping around when you find your true mate and she rejects you for it,' I scolded, knowing he didn't care. We'd already had this conversation a million times.

He rolled his eyes. *'Get over it and accept we're not finding our mates. We're old maids, or whatever the male equivalent of that is. Might as well just have some fun.'*

I sighed and stood up. *'I'm taking the car. You can run home after you're done.'*

I looked at Poppy, who was squirming from whatever Finn was doing to her under the table. She blushed, trying to maintain some kind of professional decorum.

I tried not to be too curt with her. "Poppy. Thank you for meeting me. Let the king know I will work toward a solution on the border that benefits us both." Her eyebrows lifted, and she bit her lip, giving me a half-hearted nod. I sighed. "Well, I think I'm done here—"

My train of thought derailed when a potent scent wafted through the open door. Like a vanilla cookie. My wolf, Ivailo, was restless in my head, pushing me to pursue it.

I thought I knew what it was and concluded I was probably dreaming again. When I stood, I pushed my chair back clumsily, knocking it over before stumbling toward the door.

"Gideon? You alright?" Finn yelled behind me.

I felt like I couldn't breathe. I loosened my tie as I ran outside and stopped, inhaling the scent, and surveying the crowd. The street was packed, and it took me a moment to find her. My eyes scanned, but my nose led me to a woman kneeling by a backpack on the ground. We made eye contact, and my heart kicked into a race.

Ivailo confirmed what I already knew, barking, *'MATE!'* in my head.

We'd finally found her after all this time. After I'd all but given up. Loose strands of ash blonde hair floated gently in the breeze, framing her tan face. Soft pink lips that I would soon kiss were pulled in a slight frown while bright amber eyes regarded me with intense... panic? I started towards her but, to my surprise, she ran.

'Mate! Go! Follow her!' Ivailo reminded me, growling because I wasn't already pursuing her. I found my legs and moved, but a firm hand grabbed my arm.

"Earth to Gideon! What's going on with you?" I looked over and found my brother staring at me with raised eyebrows.

Yanking out of his grasp, I shouted, "My mate!"

"Holy shit, no way," he said, looking past me and searching for her with his mouth hanging open. I ignored him and turned, not seeing her in the crowd.

'Let me out! I will find her!' Ivailo growled in my head. I obliged, my suit ripping as I shifted to my second form, the large black wolf eliciting several screams from people standing close by.

Ivailo pummeled through the crowd with disregard for anyone but her, following the sweet vanilla scent as it turned down a side street and headed out into the forest, back toward Gold Moon.

We trotted down a worn footpath until we came to a small cabin. At least I thought it was a cabin. It was absolutely smothered by greenery. The plants defied nature, blossoming, and putting on fruit even in the cold autumn air. A bay horse lifted his head, eyeing me with disinterest, before returning to his grass.

I was sure her scent led here, and I began to shift back before I realized I had ripped through all of my clothes earlier. On cue, Finn joined me, also in his wolf form, and dropped the clothes he'd been wearing at my feet.

"Thanks," I said, pulling them on.

'No problem, Brother. Do you need me to do anything? This looks like a witch's hut, doesn't it?'

He was wary, and so was I. I'd met a couple, but I had little experience with witches. They were private creatures, and so were wolves. They could be dangerous, too, with their command of the elemental world.

'Just wait here,' I told him, making my way to the front stoop.

'Gladly. I hate magic.'

I knocked lightly on the door and waited. No one answered, and I didn't detect any movement inside. Feeling a little creepy, I moved some vines and peered in through a window. My heart skipped when I recognized her lying motionless on the bed, her hair spilling over the edge and brushing the floor.

Finally, my gods, it was her! After a decade of torment and praying every night for my miracle, I'd discovered it in the most unlikely place. I knocked on the window, but she didn't move.

'Something is wrong with our little mate,' Ivailo whined.

I nodded and went back to the door, checking the knob. Locked. With no time to waste, I ripped the door off the hinges and tossed it aside.

Finn scoffed and chuckled from somewhere behind me, saying, *'Subtle.'*

I ignored him and strode over to the bed, trying to quell my panic. Ripping the door away hadn't even caused her to stir. I brushed the hair from her face, treasuring the sparks that shot through my fingers at the touch. She moaned and her lips twitched with a small smile. Ivailo, normally steady for an alpha wolf, was impatient in my head, already pushing me to wake her up to mate and mark her right here. I closed my eyes, taking a deep breath to calm him and myself.

'She was frightened when she saw us in town. She ran. Now she's unconscious in a witch's hut. We need to take it slow and figure out what's going on,' I reasoned with him. He whined but backed off.

"Who are you?"

I nearly died of a heart attack at the small voice. I had been so focused on my mate that I hadn't even realized there was a young girl snuggled into her chest.

They were sisters or maybe cousins because of their face shape and features, but I shifted away, stunned by the eeriness of this petite girl. She was ethereal in an unsettling way. I couldn't tell what she was, exactly.

I placed her in her early teens, maybe younger. She regarded me with wide eyes. They were stunningly green, and the color seemed to swirl in on itself like a whirlpool. Hair so blonde it was white fell in long waves around her face. Combined with skin so pale I could see purple veins running up her neck and temples, she appeared ghostly.

Even as an Alpha, my wolf whined at the power radiating off of her. There was no fear in her gaze, only curiosity. Apparently, a strange man breaking into her home wasn't enough to frighten her.

"I'm her mate," I blurted, and she giggled.

"Oh, wow. She won't be happy about that," she replied wistfully, running her finger over my mate's cheek.

"What's her name?" I whispered, wanting to run my finger over her cheek like that.

"Eris," she said. "And I'm her sister, Enid."

'Eris,' Ivailo hummed happily, already in love. I chuckled under my breath, and I wanted to kiss her so badly.

Enid extended her hand to me.

"It's nice to meet you, uh..." she left the last syllable hanging, waiting for me to fill in the gap.

"Gideon," I said, grabbing her tiny hand like it was porcelain. She was a petite girl and seemed so fragile. "I'm Gideon Greenwood, the Alpha of the Gold Moon pack."

A furball flew from the corner of the bed and attacked me, hissing like a cobra. I jumped back, stunned, and studied my hand. The four bleeding scratches were already healing, but I glared at the perpetrator. It was a black cat, and I could tell he wasn't normal either. He was strange, staring at me too knowingly for an average house pet. I growled at him, and he hissed again before rubbing his nose across Enid's chin and settling in her lap.

Enid giggled, stroking his back. "Sorry about him. He is protective."

I wrinkled my brow, unsure of what to think.

She addressed the cat, stroking his head and whispering, "Don't worry, Hades, this is the part in the story where Prince Charming saves us from our dismal existence." Enid smiled at me and added, "Right, Gideon Greenwood?"

I arched my eyebrow and grinned, sensing I had an ally in her. "Something like that, Enid."

Chapter 4

Gideon

FINN WENT BACK FOR the car, and we were all loaded in and heading back to the pack. Our pack. Where she would be my Luna, and we would have beautiful pups. A dream I'd dreamed a thousand times. Unable to let her go, I sat in the back with Eris in my lap. I kept my arms under her, alarmed at how badly I needed to have her, and shifted to hide the straining bulge in my pants. It was overwhelming. Her scent, and her delicate features, and her soft body. I couldn't stop staring, knowing I'd go mad if I ever had to take my eyes off of her again. I tapped my toe on the floor mat, eager to get started. Never had I felt emotions so strong as I did from simply cradling her. It could only be summed up in one word:

Mine.

Ivailo hummed happily in my head, the brute more blissful than I'd ever known him to be.

I knew he wouldn't be calm for long when he pushed his possessiveness into my veins. *'When she wakes, you will mate with her and mark her. We must complete the bond.'*

He was jealous. Worried that someone else might swoop in and steal her. It was uncommon, unheard of in the current day where our kind had evolved with the rest of society, but wolves were wolves. I tightened my grip. *Mine.*

I brushed my thumb over her cheek, wishing she'd wake. Enid assured me this comatose state was normal, but I wasn't any less concerned. I was curious, too, at why this would be a normal occurrence.

My thoughts were interrupted by Finn. *'What is this girl, man?'*

I glanced at Enid in the front seat with Hades in her lap. The cat sat and stared menacingly at Finn, daring him to make a move. Enid didn't seem to notice and beamed as she alternated between fiddling with the dials and staring in awe at the moving window. I knew Finn felt it too; her aura was intense and stifling in this small space.

'I don't know. Something powerful.'

'I can't handle her aura. Maybe I'll just...' He trailed off and reached over, rolling down his window. Enid glanced over and he offered a polite smile. "I just love that fresh air, you know?"

"Oh, yes, Finn, it's wonderful," she chirped, grinning wider.

He nodded, but in the link said, *'Well, that didn't help.'*

'She's a witch, maybe?' I suggested.

'Gods. I hate magic. And how about the devil cat? He's murderous, isn't he?'

I chuckled. *'I don't know about him either. Enid assured me they would explain everything when Eris wakes up.'*

"So, Enid," Finn started, "have you ever been to Gold Moon before?"

"No," she said simply. "This is my first time in a car."

She ran her hand up and down the armrest and fiddled with the window button again, making it go up and down. Finn arched an eyebrow.

"My pack were traditionalists," she explained. I furrowed my brow at the past tense wording and Finn and I both opened our mouths to ask more, but she spoke again first. "How long until we get to your pack, Gideon Greenwood?"

"Just a few minutes now. Why?"

Enid smiled, a mischievous curl to her lips, and giggled over her shoulder at me. "Because she is not going to like this."

Eris was no longer breathing evenly in my arms, and I looked down, shocked to find her glowering at me. Before I could react, her fist connected with a crack to my jaw, and she pushed away from me, plastering herself against the opposite door.

I rubbed my chin, stunned, impressed, and aroused at the force she'd inflicted. Finn barked out a laugh, and she scowled at him before glaring back at me.

"What do you think you're doing?" she demanded, reaching over the seat and squeezing her sister's shoulder. "Are you okay?"

Enid patted her hand like this was nothing out of the ordinary, and smiled, looking back. "It's okay, Eris. Your Prince Charming is here."

ERIS

"My what?" I hissed, my mouth falling open. "Who do you think you are? How dare you take me from my home?" I asked, glaring at him. I didn't need a Prince Charming.

As I waited for his answer, I focused on steadying my ragged breath. His touch had been powerful, electric, and addictive. I had to fight not to crawl back into his arms and ask for more. A lot more. I'd never been a sexual person—I'd never had time for it—and now I wanted to lick every inch of this man's body.

Calli sighed in my head, followed by a husky little growl. *'Yes, please. Oh, a big strong Alpha. We are blessed.'*

My body flushed with a strange heat, courtesy of my wolf.

'Thanks for your help.'

'What's his wolf's name? Who is my beau? Ask him.'

'No! Shut it.'

She snickered but, thankfully, quieted.

My hand hurt from the punch, but I refused to give any sign of the pain, maintaining my harsh expression. My mate just stared at me, struck dumb by my unorthodox behavior.

"Well?" I demanded, trying to sound more confident than I felt.

He gushed, "Gods, you are beautiful."

The man in the front seat laughed, and my cheeks were hot when I lifted my fist like I'd be throwing another punch.

My mate blushed, and it was the sweetest, sexiest blush I'd ever beheld. He held his hands up defensively, stuttering, "Who am I? I am your mate... in case you didn't notice. And I-I thought you needed medical attention, so we were taking you back to my pack. Enid said it was okay."

The man in the front seat guffawed at the explanation, and my mate's cheek colored a deeper red, making the dusting of freckles on his face stand out. He ran a hand through his hair. Through our connection, I felt his emotion, his embarrassment at shifting the blame to a teenage girl. *Gods. Why did I want to run my hand through his hair now?*

"Well, I'm fine, so you can take us back," I said, a stubborn frown pulling my lips down.

His jaw set, and he said, "That will not happen."

I narrowed my eyes. "What's your name?"

"Gideon Greenwood, Alpha of the Gold Moon Pack."

"I, Eris Oakenfire, reject you, Gideon Greenwood, as my mate."

I blurted it as fast as I could before I lost my resolve. A sharp pain cut through my chest as the words left my lips, and I gripped my shirt tightly, sucking in a breath. Gideon's eyes widened, flashing with disbelief. The man in the front seat gasped as if he were listening to a horror story.

Gideon's brows lifted. "I reject your rejection."

I glared at him.

"Second, did you just say Oakenfire? Like the lost Ice Moon pack Oakenfires?"

I pressed my lips together.

To my dismay, Enid chimed in, "Yes, we're the only survivors of the massacre of our pack. The two daughters of Alpha Gaylon and Luna Ceres."

The man in the front seat arched his eyebrows in the mirror, and what he said next left me reeling. "Well, not the only survivors."

"What?" Enid and I both yelled as we pulled through the gates and up a long drive.

She reached out to grab the driver's arm, and my heart pinched when he pulled away from her, wincing. My heart galloped into a run. They could tell. Her aura was crushing in this tiny space.

Gideon reached for me, and I could feel his concern about my sudden spike of anxiety.

I scowled at him so he held his hands up again, and I tested if I could block the bond. It worked, shutting off the mixing of our emotions. My head cleared, but Calli whined in protest.

He frowned. "Don't do that."

"I do as I wish, *Alpha*," I hissed, earning another chuckle from the driver. "Now, who is this survivor? I don't believe you."

"Open the bond and I'll tell you."

I narrowed my eyes. "I think maybe I'll hit you again."

He smirked. "I think I'll be ready this time."

I pursed my lips and stayed stubbornly quiet. So did he. We stared at each other until I heard a delighted gasp from Enid. We stopped in the circle driveway of the most luxurious pack house I had ever seen. It was a mansion, with white pillars framing a large stairway leading up to the front doors. The yard was perfectly manicured, and deciduous trees surrounded the building, boasting their beautiful fall colors.

I remembered learning about Gold Moon when I was training to be Alpha. They were a large pack, one of the big three in the realm, followed by Diamond Moon and Ruby Moon. Their pack lands were lush with natural mineral deposits, including gold and silver, hence the name. Our tiny pack was their ally before we were destroyed, and I could remember being advised that it was best to always keep it that way. They were very rich and powerful.

"I've asked him to come down," Gideon told us.

Enid and I looked at each other and jumped out of the car, staring at the massive front doors. It took agonizingly longer than I expected, probably because of the enormity of this exorbitant building.

'Excessive, isn't it? He'd better take good care of his pack, living in luxury like this,' I mumbled to Calli.

'I have a feeling he does. He seems very capable, doesn't he? Let's find out,' she purred, rushing me with another wave of fervent desire.

I cleared my throat and took a step away from Gideon, only to sigh when he took a step toward me.

The doors burst open, and a familiar, round face emerged, colored a deep red from running. I strangled a sob, feeling lightheaded. He seemed as stunned as I was, mouth opening and closing like a beached fish as he searched for words.

Gideon placed a hand on my back to steady me, and I let him, enjoying the comfort of my mate that I had just tried to reject five minutes ago. This mate bond was something else.

Enid was the one who spoke as she walked into his waiting arms. "Oh, Thad, we've missed you!"

I stumbled forward, his other huge arm catching me and pulling me in with a familiar squeeze. I allowed myself, for the first time in years, to sob into his shoulder.

CHAPTER 5

GIDEON

I HAD TO QUIET Ivailo's jealousy as we watched our mate hug another male. He was old enough to be her father, and I could tell the love she had for him was not romantic. Thad was a bear of a man with an untamed mess of curly hair and a large beard. His soft, kind eyes were teary, and they crinkled deeply at the corners with his smile.

He was saying, "Oh my Goddess, be blessed," over and over, staring up at the sky to make sure She heard him.

Thad had come to me after his pack was annihilated and relayed the story. It had been disturbing, to say the least. I accepted him into Gold Moon, and he quickly climbed the ranks to become an elite warrior. Now, he trained the newest warriors and was a valuable asset to our pack.

When I could handle it no longer, I stepped to them and said, "Thad, you told us there were no survivors."

His eyes widened. "I thought there weren't, Alpha! I swear it. I thought everyone was dead, and I couldn't feel the bond anymore with the Alpha and Luna both gone."

Finally, Eris pulled back and shook her head, confused. "I came back, Thad. I searched the pack. You weren't there."

His face fell, his brow knitting. "Oh no. You went back to that cursed place, child? I am so sorry you witnessed that."

"It's okay. I had to see," she said quickly, crossing her arms over her chest.

"I was probably already gone when you returned, little wolf. We made our last stand on the bridge, but I'm ashamed to say I was knocked into the river instead of dying with my people. I floated downstream, unconscious, and when I returned, everyone was... gone. I didn't see your mother or your bodies among the dead, so I hurried here, hoping you'd found your way here as well."

I'd heard the story but was suddenly suspicious of how neat it all sounded. Fell into the river. What if he had something to do with the downfall of the pack, and now he was going to be around my mate? Even though it was unnecessary worrying, I had to be sure he was trustworthy. Nothing mattered except her.

Using an Alpha command, something I didn't do unless absolutely necessary, I compelled him to tell the truth. Ivailo's deep, throaty tone colored my next words. "That's really what happened, Thad?"

Thad's eyes lit with shock, but he blurted, "Absolutely, Alpha."

Eris turned, her mouth falling open, and snapped, "Of course it is!" like she couldn't believe I'd even suggest otherwise.

"I had to be sure! I can't have him around you if he's no good."

She set her jaw and turned away with a humph.

'You keep upsetting her. You're terrible at this,' Ivailo said, huffing.

'Well, this isn't how it's supposed to go!'

It was said to be the easiest decision a shifter would ever make. Instant love that couldn't be shaken. Voilà, here's your happily ever after.

Thad glanced between us. "Oh, you're... I see. Mates. Well, congratulations."

"None are necessary," she hissed, crossing her arms again. "I'm sorry he would accuse you of such awful things on my behalf, Thad."

"It's okay, little wolf," Thad said to her, and looked at me. "I promise I'll tell you all the truth, Alpha. I would never hurt these girls. They're the last family I have."

His eyes grew distant as he remembered the horror of finding his entire pack decimated. Suddenly, he perked up and looked behind me at the car, searching for someone.

"Your mother? Please tell me she's survived as well."

Eris shook her head, and he closed his eyes.

Enid shuddered and spoke into his chest, her voice muffled, "He killed her in front of us. The red-haired man tore her head from her shoulders."

I balked and looked at Finn, who had his hand over his mouth. His eyebrows lifted.

'We will kill this red-haired man. He hurt our wonderful mate. He's hurt her heart,' Ivailo seethed in my head.

'We will,' I agreed.

Thad's features tightened, and he whispered, "I failed her, and you. I will never forgive myself."

"You couldn't have done anything to help," Eris said, shaking her head. "He was a monster. Too powerful for even the strongest wolf to handle. I don't think even my father and all of his warriors could've done anything to stop it."

Thad nodded. "He was there for her—your mother. I think it's time to tell you what I know because, Miss Enid, with that aura, I'm guessing he could come for you next."

Eris' back went rigid, and I interjected, "Let's all go to my office. We can talk in private there."

ERIS

My mind reeled like a broken fishing rod as we, myself, Enid, Thad, Finn, and Gideon ascended to the fourth floor in a contraption I'd read about in books. An elevator. It was a strange sensation in my gut, like jumping from too high of a branch.

I peeked over at Enid and found she was coping better than I was. Hades was wrapped around the back of her neck, and she smiled as she stroked him. He kept a watchful eye on everyone, as always, purring and kneading his claws into her shoulder. She grabbed my hand and squeezed it. I returned the gesture, trying to get my emotions under control.

I glanced to my right. Why I did that when I was trying to calm down, I wasn't sure, since Gideon stood next to me. My heart jumped at the sight of his profile, and my palms were suddenly slick with sweat.

When I faced forward, I realized I could examine him in the reflection of the metal doors. His hair, which I thought was black, was actually a dark auburn, short on the sides with some length on top. It had been styled earlier but was mussed from when he ran his hand through it. A dusting of freckles softened his look, giving him a youthful appearance despite the thick shadow of a beard that darkened his cheeks.

My eyes had a mind of their own, drifting down his body. He had a white t-shirt on, and it was fitted. They traveled lower, to the zipper of his jeans, and I swallowed, trying to wet my dry mouth. An unfamiliar sensation, like a tingling in my thighs, was accompanied by a tight twist in my lower stomach.

I heard his soft inhale, and I felt him stiffen next to me.

Oh, no. Oh, gods.

My gaze snapped up to his face in the reflection. His eyes were hazel fire, and my face burned as everyone filed off of the elevator in front of us.

I went to move, but his arm shot out, blocking my way. Still, I refused to look at him. It had already gone this far simply from studying his reflection.

He leaned close to me. "Open the bond, Eris. Please."

"Why?" I asked, finding only a whisper of my voice.

There was a pause, and I jumped, his lips nearly touching my cheek. "Because you're the sweetest thing I've ever smelled, and I want you to know what that does to me."

His breath kissed my ear with the words, sending a shudder down my spine. The coil of desire in my stomach spun, making it hard to breathe. I wanted to turn and find his lips, so I ducked under his arm, hurrying to find the others and hoping no one would notice my glowing face as I entered the office.

It was a beautiful room. Ornate dark-oak furniture with dark green leather upholstery. A painting hung on the wall, a younger Gideon with two older people who were obviously his parents, plus a teenaged Finn, and a smaller strawberry-haired boy who must be their little brother.

I chose the seat between Enid and Thad so Gideon couldn't sit next to me. He sat behind his desk instead, and we all looked expectantly at Thad.

"I don't know the entire story," he started, turning to look only at Enid and me. "Just what I was told so I could do the best job possible."

We nodded, urging him to continue, and Enid took my hand.

"Your mother was a special wolf. An Ancient One was what she called herself. I don't understand exactly what it means, but it's some kind of mix between a powerful witch and a wolf. It's an archaic bloodline that lies dormant until it combines with an Alpha, like her father, and your own father. Only shows up if a daughter is born. Your mom could compel people to do as she wanted as long as she was touching them skin to skin. The weaker the person, the better it worked. She didn't like to use it, though. It made her feel treacherous, and her heart was gentle."

"So, the bloodline continued in us," Enid said, obviously less surprised by the news than I was. I was slack-jawed, staring at Thad.

He nodded. "As far as I understand, that's how it works. Enid, your aura is very intense."

"Eris heals when she sings," Enid said, as if I needed to be called out in the open with her.

Thad nodded thoughtfully, as if that wasn't too much of a surprise, but I noticed Gideon and Finn exchanging stunned glances.

"And you, Enid?" Thad asked.

She shrugged, playing with Hades' toe pads on one of his paws. "I know there's a power in me fighting to get out. If I don't let it go, I get sick and hot. I have those seizures. I don't know exactly what I am, though."

"What does this all have to do with the red-haired man?" I asked.

"When I took over your mother's guard, I was told an evil person sought that power. I didn't know what that meant then, and I still don't know. I only know she wept both times you were born, having prayed for sons so they would not face the same fate as she. Your father hoped she was safe here since your mother was originally from the northeastern realm. Our pack was small. We didn't think he'd find her. Obviously, that was not so."

We sat in silence, letting the information sink in. I felt tired, even though the sun suggested it was only mid-afternoon.

Gideon broke the silence. "We should all get some rest. Tomorrow we can look into exactly what happened at Ice Moon and hopefully find some clues. I wasn't Alpha yet, but I know my father sent people to the scene, and they collected some files of evidence. How helpful it will be, I don't know."

I looked up, surprised, and he answered the question in my eyes. "Ice Moon was our ally, and it would always be pertinent to know what or who is going around destroying entire packs in one evening."

"I can show you ladies to a room together," Finn said, standing. "Unless you want to..." He indicated towards Gideon, and I gasped when I realized what he was suggesting.

I knew it wasn't unusual. Once upon a time, I'd believed I'd find my mate, and we'd complete the bond as expected. Which, bluntly, meant sex and then marking each other with a bite on the neck. Most couples did it as soon as possible, within hours of meeting each other. Minutes even. Everyone dreamed of the day.

My pulse throbbed at the thought of his mark, that wicked coil returning to my stomach. But this was not once upon a time or happily ever after. It was now, after I'd experienced what it meant to have everything to love and then lose it all. There was a wall around my heart, and I wasn't willing to tear it down for anyone.

Hearing Thad's explanation, I knew I'd been correct all along. Enid was special, and because of that, she wasn't safe. I couldn't afford any distractions. She had to be protected, and it was my job to take care of her.

My mouth opened and closed once before I made my voice firm. "I'll stay with Enid."

CHAPTER 6

ERIS

W E RODE WITH FINN up one level on the elevator to the fourth floor. He opened a door and ushered us inside.

"I'll have them bring some food and clothes up for you both."

"So, you are brothers," I said, more than asked.

They had many of the same facial features, including hazel eyes, but Finn was fairer with lighter auburn hair. His was styled in an undercut with the length on top pushed to the right, and the trimmed sides flowed down into a short, well-maintained beard.

He grinned. "Yes. I'm the fun one and he's the boring one. Leo, our baby brother, is the angsty one."

Enid giggled, but conflict brewed in my soul. I was so sure Enid and I would live in our little cabin and hide from the world for the rest of our lives, but she'd hardly stopped smiling since we'd been in the car.

"What's he like?" I asked before I could stop myself.

Finn smiled and looked up, like he was searching his brain for the explanation. "To me, he's too serious, too stubborn, and too bossy. Typical older sibling." He winked at Enid, and she giggled, hiding her smile in her hand and looking at me with mischievous eyes. "But all those things make him an outstanding leader. He cares for the pack and treats all members equally, regardless of status."

"No Omega discrimination?"

Omegas were shifters without Alpha blood, which was most of the population. Historically, Alphas treated them like lesser beings, especially in larger packs like this one. As if they were there to serve. My father hadn't liked that.

Finn peered at me and smirked. "You should find out for yourself. He's waited a long time for you, Luna. We didn't realize we were looking for Jane of the Jungle."

I recoiled at being called Luna, but Enid smiled and snapped her fingers. "*Tarzan of the Apes!* I read that one!"

He chuckled and asked if we needed anything else. I declined, and Enid was already exploring the room. Decadent was an understatement. I watched as she ran her hand over the silk bedding and examined the small Dresden dolls on the dresser. A philodendron sat in the corner, looking slightly wilted. She frowned when she saw it and hurried over, placing her hand on one leaf. I saw the green glow of her magic as the plant perked up and lifted.

I was smiling when Enid turned to me, crossing her arms over her chest. "We should stay."

I arched an eyebrow. "Oh, really?"

She sat on the bed and patted the spot next to her, beckoning me to come over. I obliged and wrapped my arms around her, pulling her close.

"Come on, Eris, you can't tell me you want to leave this and go back to the cabin. I was going crazy there! You can relax now. For the last three years, you've focused only on my survival, but you were suffocating me. I think this is where we're supposed to be. The Moon Goddess guided us here. He tore the door off to get to you!"

Tears pricked my eyes, and I hugged her close. "I don't know if I can do this."

She rubbed my arm. As always, she seemed so much older than fifteen. "Give Gideon a chance to be your mate. Give me a chance to show you I'm stronger than you think. We both deserve to have a happy life. You have help now, and you don't have to do this all by yourself. Won't you at least try? Please?"

I shrugged and cleared my throat, unable to give her an answer. My heart ached to find Gideon. To be with him and feel the comfort of his magical touch. Before I could talk myself out of it, I removed the block

I'd placed on our bond. His feelings returned. Our anxieties mixed, but relief from him followed, and then a warm feeling, like his arms were wrapped around me from another room.

My eyes drifted shut, and I jumped when Enid shouted, "Holy Hades, come look at this! You could swim in this bathtub!"

We were exploring the bathroom when a knock at the door signaled the arrival of our dinner. Our mouths watered at the smells rising from the cart. I elected to take a shower before I ate, and Enid dug in with a ferocity I hadn't seen from her in months.

I held my hand under the warm water, marveling at how nice it felt. We'd been bathing in an icy stream for three years. When I saw myself naked in the mirror, I winced.

This lighting left little to the imagination, and I looked exactly like I felt. Large black circles surrounded my tired eyes, and my cheeks were slightly gaunt. I could see most of my ribs and the curve of my collarbone. Even if we had food, I never ate much, and neither did Enid. Stress and worry curbed the appetite.

Would this pack protect a girl they barely knew? Memories of the decay I'd found when I returned home pushed their way into my mind. I did not want to bring that horror to these innocent people.

Calli chimed in. *'We are the Luna of this pack. The Goddess has deemed it our fate. I think our mate would fight to the death to make you happy. He will be as devoted as you are to Enid's safety. I'm sure of it. Eris, we cannot return to the cabin. We alone could never fight the red-haired man.'*

I felt it again, his push of comfort, and knew he was eavesdropping on my feelings. Sighing, I looked at the heap of my clothes on the floor, suspecting that this would be the last time I took those worn, hand-stitched garments off. Shedding my old life and embracing the unknown.

GIDEON

I paced the floor in my room. My mate was just three doors down, and it took everything in me to remain here. Ivailo was annoyed with me. He wanted me to go to her, and I did, too. But her feelings had been tumultuous all afternoon. I needed her, but I didn't want to pressure her.

I glanced at the clock. It was almost midnight, and I didn't know if I could even sleep. Surrendering, I collapsed on the bed and stared at the ceiling. Closing my eyes, I was immediately back in the elevator, surrounded by the scent of her arousal. Blood rushed to fill my shaft, and I groaned, running my hands down my face.

Ivailo chuckled. *'At least we know she finds you attractive.'*

I smirked, followed by a frown. *'How will we ever earn her trust?'*

I jolted out of sleep and jumped to my feet. Fear surged through the mate bond and my heart erupted with it. Ivailo was in a panic in my head, demanding to be let out, but I ran down the hall to her door and stopped, listening for movement or any sign of trouble. When I heard nothing, I pushed the master code into the keypad on the door. It clicked unlocked, and I snuck in, glancing around.

There were two beds, but Enid and Eris shared one. Enid was awake, stroking Eris' hair. She was in a fitful sleep and cried out in distress. I jumped at the sound, hurrying to the bedside.

Enid's electric eyes were heavy with sadness, and she whispered, "She has lots of nightmares."

I reached but stopped my hand. She had clarified that she didn't want me to touch her. Enid snatched my wrist and placed my hand on Eris' forehead. She sighed and stilled, leaning into my touch. The electric tingles were there, and I bit my lip.

Enid grinned up at me before hopping out of the bed and going to the other one, followed closely by her cat. She crawled under the covers and deliberately turned her back to us. The cat curled around her head and purred like a motor.

I stared at the spot Enid left open and took my hand from Eris' forehead. She moaned softly, frowning, and leaned toward me like she searched for my touch.

'She needs you,' Ivailo assured me, and I pulled the covers up, lying down next to her on top of the duvet.

'It feels a little wrong. Maybe? I chastise Finn constantly for taking advantage of women.'

'Stop holding yourself to human standards of conduct. It's not what we are. She needs you, and she's your mate.'

I placed my hand on her back and took a deep breath. We were in bed together, and I repeatedly reminded myself that a young girl was present.

I was happy to lie like that, with my hand on her back, but Eris turned into me. My chest was bare, and she hugged me, nestling her face into my neck. My pulse thundered with her mouth so close to my marking spot, and the tingles of her touch buzzed through my veins. She sighed, followed by a soft moan that made my mouth dry.

Oh, my gods, help me.

I forced my mind away from the sex that would not be happening, and breathed in her scent, focusing on the joy of holding her. Her weight in my arms gave me profound peace, allowing me to drift away into bliss.

CHAPTER 7

ERIS

RAIN AND PEPPERMINT GREETED me upon waking. A smile lifted my lips, and I felt more rested than I had since the raid on our pack. Abruptly, I noticed a warm embrace that certainly did not belong to my sister. I stilled and peeked with one eye open. Gideon was in bed. My bed. With me.

Calli panted in my head, pushing a powerful wave of desire into my veins. I looked over his shoulder at the other bed and saw it had been slept in, but that Enid was not in the room. Panic churned in my gut, and I started extracting myself from his arm to find her.

Gideon's voice was thick with sleep. "Your sister is with Finn and Thad." He groaned and added, "Gods, stop wiggling like that."

I stilled and my eyes went wide when I realized what I was feeling against my lower stomach. The mate bond was overwhelming, and as an alpha male, he was being pushed to mate and mark me. I was an alpha, too, and Calli was relentless, my head spinning with intoxicating desire.

'It's okay. This is how it's supposed to go,' she assured me.

'But Enid—'

'Enid is fine. She doesn't want you to follow her around like a shadow, Eris. Remember, someone has to go through Hades to get to her.'

His hand drifted up and down my back, stopping to squeeze my neck and shoulders, rubbing the tension from them. Everywhere our skin touched, there were tingles, the electric pleasure of his touch. Warmth twisted in my stomach, coiling with the awareness that I was in only underwear and a silk nightgown.

Oh, gods, help me.

Swallowing, I braved a look up at his face, only to find him staring at me. His pupils were dilated, eclipsing the hazel, and I glanced at his lips, stunned to realize I wanted to kiss him.

Reading my thoughts, he brought his thumb to my lips and traced them. Those sparks of pleasure erupted, and I closed my eyes, my next breath shaky.

"Can I kiss you, Eris? Would you like that?" I nodded my head, but he said, "Please, I want you to say it. I want you to trust me."

My face heated another degree, and I opened my eyes, looking at him. My heartbeat thundered as I leaned forward, whispering, "Yes. I want you to kiss me, but that doesn't mean I trust you."

Our noses touched, and he groaned, closing the small gap between our lips. The spark from the contact pulled a moan from me, and I blushed everywhere, my entire body flushing with warmth.

He took advantage of my parted lips, his tongue pressing, so I opened further, allowing him in. His fingers pushed into my hair, and my hands bracing on his chest traveled up, lacing around his nape. I let my tongue copy his movements, intrigued by the intimacy of his taste.

I moaned when he pushed his hips forward, grinding the hard bulge of his sweats between my thighs. It was like nothing I'd ever felt, the intense sparks tightening around that coil of desire. There was a throb, a need for more, and I pushed my hips into him.

He muttered, "Eris," into the kiss, and we pushed together, grinding.

My lips rolled in, trying to suppress my whimpers, but he shifted us, his weight pressing my back into the downy mattress. The roll of his hips intensified; he was hard, and I was soft, giving and needing. I wrapped my legs around him and gasped his name when he kissed my neck, sucking on my marking spot until my head swam with a slow, drugging heat.

The grinding didn't stop. It grew more intense with the pull of his lips, and the increased friction washed a wave of carnality through me.

Having never been touched before, never even venturing far down that road by myself, I gasped, tension curling my toes and clawing up my legs.

I managed, "Oh, my gods..." but my breath hitched. My hips lifted of their own accord, arching to search for more when it was already too much.

My body was stiff, pulled tight like the string of a bow. He said, "Are you?" and a low groan rumbled in his chest to finish the question.

His hand grabbed my backside, and he pressed harder, holding me still while I felt this unfamiliar eruption reach a point of no return.

My fingers dug into his back, and he moaned, "It's so good... that's a good girl. Come for me."

I couldn't even breathe, but I was saying, "I'm, I'm, I'm..." over and over. I didn't know what I was doing, but I needed it.

His lips found mine again, muffling the words. With one more pass of his hips, I fell over an edge I didn't know existed. He kept grinding, and my body rolled with waves. I was lost to them, drowning in bliss, and clinging to him. Never in my life had I experienced such a dissociation from reality. It was just us, and the world melted away.

My hands clamped down on his hips, stopping the grind when the pleasure became so intense my body twitched, and I couldn't help but giggle. Such a womanly sound; I wasn't used to it bubbling from my lips.

He was breathing hard in my neck, and said, "I want to touch you, Eris. I need *you* to touch me."

I wished I knew how to touch a man, but that conversation with my mother had never happened.

Blushing, I whispered, "How?"

"However you wish, as slow as you want to go. I just need your hands on me."

Knowing it was far from where he desired, I put my hands on his cheeks. He liked it, though, kissing me deeper. Emboldened, my hands drifted down to his chest. The muscles moved beneath my fingers, hard and soft at the same time. I brushed my nails down his sides, stunned when I felt him grin and snicker into the kiss.

I smiled with him, and he leaned away from me so I could touch lower. The way he looked at me—his eyes half-mast and his lips glistening from my kiss—I felt truly feminine. Maybe for the first time in my life. My heart quickened as my fingers drifted over the dips and valleys of his stomach.

He looked down, and so did I, my chest leaping. I could see the outline of his hard length in the sweats he wore, and a stain of moisture colored the gray material at the tip. From me or him, I wasn't sure. My panties were wet, I could feel it.

My thumbs came to a rest under his hips, just above the waist of his sweats, and we looked at each other again. Doubt snapped through the haze of desire.

Is this happening? Am I ready to commit to this? There are things I'd wanted to discuss first.

He felt it and said, "Eris, I—"

A knock stopped his words, and his nostrils flared. His eyes glazed, which I knew meant he was linking with someone, but the thought of my sister standing on the other side of that door made me jump. I pushed him away and scooted back, my face blazing.

Gideon took a deep breath, and started, "It's okay," but his eyes drifted down my body and widened.

I followed his gaze, my heart stopping when I realized the nightgown had shifted when I pushed away. My nipple was showing through the armhole. His hands clamped down on my thighs, squeezing hard enough to make me gasp.

I almost hit him out of instinct, but I wasn't sure if that would spark more aggression, so I sat still, saying, "Get your hands off of me."

"Gods, I can't—" he muttered, and I heard his wolf pushing forward, his voice guttural. His eyes shifted to golden brown before he slammed them shut.

I snatched the sheet and covered myself while Gideon shook his head like he was trying to clear it. His face was plum red, and a vein bulged in his forehead. He jumped off of the bed, running his hand through his hair and striding across the room toward the door in a hurry.

With his hand on the knob, he looked down at himself. Sighing, he grabbed the floral runner from the table next to him and wrapped it around his waist.

Without looking back at me, he asked, "Would you go out with me today? To see the pack?"

"Yes."

"Thank you. I'm sorry. I'll be back in an hour."

"I'll be ready."

CHAPTER 8

GIDEON

I RETURNED TO MY room, passing Enid, Finn, and a group of pack staff members with shopping bags. They snickered at my floral skirt, positioned to hide my stained sweats. It took serious self-control not to grab my brother and toss him out the window. He'd ruined that entire moment with his stupid knocking.

'Just link me next time, unless you want to die,' I said on my way by, and he laughed as he passed me.

To Ivailo, I scolded, *'You need to calm down. That almost went badly.'*

'We were very close. I got excited.'

I was horrified at my near loss of control, courtesy of my wolf. We'd held it together that entire time, just to nearly commit an unredeemable act at the sight of a breast. A beautiful, perfect, must-have-been-crafted-by-Aphrodite breast.

'Don't push me like that. She'll never love us if we force her, my gods!'

'Eris understands. She feels the pull, too. Her wolf pushes her, too.'

'She understands? She was a heartbeat away from busting my nose.'

'True, but the mating still might've happened after that.'

'Gods.'

'But she likes you. She wants to go on this date.'

'Just don't interfere. I'll handle it from now on, and you shut up.'

'Hm. No promises.'

I sighed at his flippancy. Obviously, he didn't understand the gravity of that situation. Her consent was important—vital—to me. In the past, male wolf shifters weren't well known for their patience in mating, but I was better than that. Those moments before, when she'd been enjoying my touch, had been bliss. When she'd touched me? It must be what crossing the golden gates into Elysium felt like.

I turned the shower on as cold as it would go, and still ended up having to masturbate for the first time in a long time, thinking of her. Imagining her there, joining me in the shower in an unexpected and unrealistic turn of events, and trying not to think of the venom in her voice when she told me to get my hands off of her.

I chose a simple white t-shirt and jeans, hoping to keep today as casual as I could. It had been a long time since I'd had a casual day.

Alpha was a demanding role. My presence was required in meetings, my counsel was needed on issues with other packs, and every tiny thing that happened around here needed my approval. Once I had my Luna, it would be balanced. She would control most of the inner-pack dynamics while I focused on relations with the human world and outside packs.

My attention was all for her today. No business. Well, that wasn't true. I had one thing to take care of before we left.

I linked Finn. *'Cancel everything I have planned today. I am spending the day with Eris. Also, gather some experts to look over the files from Ice Moon. And contact those witches we consult with to see if they can help us figure out why Enid is having those fever seizures. Maybe they can help her.'*

'Sure thing. So, I'm guessing you couldn't seal the deal this morning?' I could feel his humor through the bond and growled at him in response. There was a slight pause and then he continued. *'You're going to contact Alpha Owen today, right? You have to.'*

I sighed. *'Yes, I am going to call him right now.'*

'Good. I told you that was a stupid thing to do. I'm just happy it didn't go any further than it has.'

Regret rang like a bell in my chest. *'It seemed like the right thing to do. I need a Luna to run this pack properly and I never thought I would find my mate. I'm twenty-eight. It rarely takes this long.'*

'Well, good luck, Brother,' he said before severing the link.

I stared at the phone, not excited to make this call. It had been part of the deal, though, that if I found my fated mate, the wedding was off with no hard feelings.

Rallying my nerves, I snatched the phone and dialed. "Hello, Alpha Owen? Yes, it's me. I'm good. Actually, I need to discuss my engagement with your daughter."

ERIS

Enid returned after Gideon left, followed by several ladies bringing dozens of shopping bags with new clothes. I noticed none of the price tags were left on, making me worry about the cost.

Enid was beaming. "Eris! Finn took me shopping. Oh, you should see it out there. Everything is so big and beautiful!"

After I thumbed through a fraction of the beautiful garments, I returned her smile and asked, "Why don't you pick something for me to wear today while I shower?"

Her brows lifted, and she grinned. "What's the occasion? A date?"

"I think so, yes. Nothing too fancy, okay?"

She squealed and started digging in the bags. My heart pinched seeing her happiness, and Calli said, *'See? Things are good here.'*

In the shower, I noticed Gideon had closed the bond and knew it was because he'd almost lost control a few minutes ago.

'But he didn't,' Calli reminded me. *'It's not a simple thing to keep an alpha wolf under control like he did.'*

'I know, trust me.'

'You think I am bad? Try having one of those brutes in your head. Testosterone turns males into idiots.'

I chuckled, inhaling the sweet scent of the rose soap. His desire for my consent and his patience were lovely. My soapy hands floated over my skin, and I lost myself in a daydream where he replaced them with his. I wondered what it would feel like to have him touch me. My breasts, and my stomach, and between my legs. When I ventured there, I found a slick wetness unfamiliar to me, and bit my lip, remembering the climb to bliss and the climax he'd brought.

Enid wanted me to wear a yellow sundress, but in the bathroom mirror I'd noticed the mark of his kiss low on my neck. She'd obviously noticed, too, and had a white shawl with a high collar ready for the cover-up. Callie wouldn't explain why she wouldn't heal the mark.

Enid offered to help braid my hair, but we decided to let it be free for the first time in years. It hung in a wavy curtain to my lower back, having not been cut since the day we rode away from our pack on Ollie. I froze when I remembered our horse was still back at the cabin.

"Oh, Goddess, I'll have to remember to ask Gideon about Ollie. He is probably worried sick about us."

"I already told them when we were leaving yesterday that we need-ed to bring him. Beta Finn assured me this morning someone was on their way."

I turned and hugged her, kissing the top of her head. "I love you, Enid."

My heart was racing under her ear, and she giggled. "Don't have a heart attack! I love you, too. Just relax. Have some fun for the first time in your life!"

"Hold on! I have fun!"

"Oh, really? When?" she teased.

I scoffed, smiling dumbly because I couldn't think of an example, but a soft knock on the door saved me from having to admit that I didn't have a personality anymore.

I hugged my sister again and took a deep breath while I was still able. He made it hard to breathe. Feeling much more self-conscious in this dress than I had in my dirty rags, I checked myself in the mirror again.

Looking over my shoulder, I said, "I'm going to have so much fun today, just to prove you wrong."

Enid giggled. "A wrong I will gladly endure."

I chuckled, turning the knob. Gideon was waiting, and he was running his hand through his hair as the door opened. His brows lifted when he saw me, and he closed his eyes over a sheepish smile.

"What?" I asked, looking down at the dress again.

"I suppose I'm just feeling lucky today. You are beautiful. Have I told you that?"

"You have," I whispered, swallowing. Enid cleared her throat behind me, and I blurted, "And you. You look quite nice as well."

He responded by opening the bond, and my cheeks heated when his feelings crashed into me. His eyes opened, and there was a long second where we looked at each other, saying nothing and saying everything.

When I could bear no more of this tension he brought, I asked, "Where are we going?"

He blinked. "Are we going somewhere? I forgot everything when you opened that door."

I smiled, *pretty* sure he was joking, and I heard Enid giggle behind me.

Gideon offered his hand, and I reached for it. He seized the opportunity, pulling me out into the hall so our chests were touching.

The door clicked shut behind me, leaving us alone.

Flirting, which I'd never done, came naturally with him. "You had something to show me. *Alpha.*"

He chuckled. "Don't say Alpha like that."

"Or what? *Alpha.*"

My answer surprised him, but I felt his excitement in the bond. "Or I might have to kiss you again."

He reached up, pulled my collar aside, and grinned when he saw the mark from his kiss.

I arched my brow. "Admiring your handiwork?"

"I do enjoy it, but I'm actually imagining what the real thing will look like."

"And who says you get to mark me?"

"You do."

"That's right." I leaned closer, so I could feel his breath on my lips. "Don't forget it. *Alpha.*"

He smiled and tried to press our lips together, but I ducked him and started down the hall, still holding his hand. "Do you think you can kiss me anytime you like now, Alpha, just because you've done it once?"

He sighed, and I could feel how surprised he was by that entire interaction. "Where did this vixen come from?"

I didn't know either, so I shrugged, grinning over my shoulder. "It was recommended to me to have some fun."

CHAPTER 9

GIDEON

S HE LED ME DOWN the hall, and I was speechless at this sudden shift in attitude. Not complaining, though.

Obviously, she wasn't upset by the morning's events, but when we boarded the elevator I said, "I am sorry, Eris, for earlier. When I grabbed you. My wolf was—"

"You stopped when I asked. That's what matters."

"Well, still—"

She interrupted again, adding, "Good thing, too. I don't want to have to kill you."

I looked over at her. She was petite, underweight even, but said the words with such confidence. Her lips curled into a small smile, and she stared ahead, her fingers toying with the material of her dress.

"Do you think it would be so easy to kill me?"

"Yes," she said simply. "I am quite skilled."

I blinked and smiled, chuckling, before I changed the subject. "I just want to show you some of the pack. I want you to know me and I want to know you, too. Plus, these will be your people when you're my Luna."

She smirked at our reflection in the elevator doors. "Who says—"

The doors dinged open, and we ran right into Leo, my baby brother. I smiled at him, happy to get this introduction underway. "Eris, this is my youngest brother, Leo. Leo, this is Eris, my mate."

"Hello, Leo, nice to meet you."

Leo nodded at her and mumbled, "You too," but otherwise looked bored, adding, "I need to go up."

He pushed by me and got on the elevator. My anger flared, and I was about to say something, but Eris grabbed my arm, stopping me.

"Is he okay?" she asked when the doors slid shut.

I shrugged. "I don't know. He's only sixteen and, uh, pretty committed to teenage angst. He's really struggled since Dad died five years ago and Mom..." I trailed off, feeling unsure about the situation with my mother. "Never mind. He'll warm up to you."

I smiled again, and, emboldened by this little game we were playing, grabbed her waist, and walked her toward the garage. She allowed it, but I knew she was toying with me when she stepped closer and slung her arm around my waist. Humor danced in the bond between us.

We entered the garage, and she eyed my car with interest. "Can I drive that thing?"

"Have you ever?"

"No."

"Well, we're going to be in town, so maybe not today." I felt a flash of disappointment, and said, "But I'll teach you, I promise."

"Have you ridden a horse?"

"Uh, no."

"Okay. You'll teach me to drive, and I'll teach you to ride a horse."

"Oh, certainly," I said, opening her door for her. "Or I could just teach you to drive."

Teasing again, she said, "I see. So, you're frightened of horses, Alpha?"

"Oh, yes. They absolutely terrify me."

She blinked, a wry smile pulling her lips, and answered, "I hope that's not true, because if my horse doesn't like you, I don't think this is going to work out."

ERIS

He kept looking at me as we drove through the streets, trying to read my reactions even when the bond was open between us. I was in obvious awe, not trying to hide it.

Gold Moon was at least ten times larger than my old pack, and it was beautifully crafted and arranged. The city was a work of art in itself. I remembered a book I'd read years ago on architecture and knew these gorgeous homes were Victorian style.

Main Street was bustling, lined with charming pubs and restaurants. It was a vast change from the simple, rustic decor I had grown up in. I decided he was wise for not letting me drive, considering the street was packed with cars and innocent bystanders. Running a bunch of people down with this steel beast probably wasn't the best introduction to the pack.

Gideon showed me the city, pointing out some of his favorite places like the movie theater, something I was intrigued by, and he showed me the school, driving around so I could see the football field and the championship banner with his name on it.

"Do you like football? I don't remember your pack having a team."

I shrugged. Kids had played it around the pack, but it wasn't official. "We were too small to field actual sports teams, but I was a two-time champion of catching the greased pig at our fair when I was a child."

He clicked his tongue and chuckled. "It's cruel to crush my hopes when I thought I was impressing you."

I leaned my elbow on the armrest between our seats and put my chin on my knuckles. "Don't feel too bad. It's almost the same thing. You're good at catching a pigskin, and I'm good at catching a pig."

"Throwing. I was throwing the pigskin."

"Ah. Maybe we would make a good team, then."

"Certainly we would." Gideon put his elbow on the armrest, so our forearms were touching, and our faces were a few inches apart. We grinned at the sparks, and he said, "You know what kids came back here to do when I was in high school?"

"I might be able to guess, and to discern your true motives for showing me this banner."

"Oh, this was only to feed my Alpha ego, believe me," he teased.

"Oh, silly me, and here I was, about to kiss you." I leaned away and added, "But there's probably much more to see."

He didn't move, and sucked air through his teeth. "You are actually a wicked woman, aren't you?"

I tilted my head, stunned at how calm I felt in his presence, even when my heart raced with excitement. "What's wrong? Am I just torturing you?"

He leaned back into his seat and moved what I now knew was the gear control, or shifter. "If sitting in this car with you is torture, you can chain me to the steering wheel."

After about an hour of driving around, he pulled up to a quaint bakery called *The Crumble and Flake* and stopped the car, indicating this was our first stop. I could smell the baking bread and pastries as soon as I opened the door.

He walked around the car and offered his hand. I accepted, and he escorted me towards the door. Several people stopped and stared, and despite the earlier playfulness between us, I felt unnerved at the attention. They couldn't be blamed. I'm sure they would be surprised to see their Alpha out in the city with a strange woman.

'Hold your head up and be proud. He's our mate. We're not doing anything to be embarrassed about,' Calli encouraged me.

'I'm not embarrassed by him. I'm just not used to people. Maybe I've forgotten how to interact with them.'

Gideon didn't seem to notice anyone except me, holding my waist and guiding me. A small girl stared up at me with doe-like brown eyes, and I waved slightly. She grinned and waved back, giggling up at her mother.

A robust, rosy-cheeked woman with silvering hair held the door for us. "It's good to see you again, Alpha. And who is this beautiful young lady?"

"Afternoon, Berta. This... well, this is my mate, Eris," he said, as if he couldn't believe he was actually saying it. The boyish smile on his face made my heart flutter.

Berta's eyes grew three sizes, and she beamed at us. "Oh, Goddess, be blessed! The Alpha found his mate!" She shouted it, her excitement boiling over as the whispers behind us intensified. "It's so nice to meet you, Luna. Please come in and sit. It's an honor to have you in our little bakery."

I didn't correct her about the Luna title, nodding and smiling as we walked by. "Thank you, Berta. Everything smells incredible."

"Oh, we do our best."

Gideon sat down across from me and said, "She's being humble. This has been my favorite place since I was a kid. Berta is probably the best baker in all the realm."

She took the praise by teasing him. "The Alpha single-handedly keeps us in business."

"A sweet tooth, Alpha?" I asked.

He looked at my lips and answered with a wistful, "Absolutely."

Heat tickled my cheeks, and I glanced around to escape his charm. It was a small place with only six tables on one side of the room. The other half was dominated by a large display case full of pastries, muffins, cupcakes, cakes, and more. My mouth watered, rallying my stomach so it rumbled with aggression.

Berta walked behind the counter and tapped the shoulder of a tall man who was kneading dough. His hair poked out wildly beneath his chef's hat and he bobbed his head with the music that floated softly from an old record player behind the counter.

"Oh, Claude, guess what? Alpha Gideon found his mate! Isn't she lovely?"

Claude looked around at us, grinning. "Ah, yes, she is! Congratulations kids, there's nothing better."

He gazed lovingly at Berta, stooping to kiss her cheek, and she giggled. They were both in their late seventies, an adorable couple. A testament to the beauty of the bond.

"Can you make us something to go, Berta? I want to show Eris the lake before we head..." Gideon looked at me and finished with a smug smile, "Home."

Berta nodded. "Of course. Give us a few minutes."

I reached for his hands, and he rubbed his thumbs over mine, igniting more sparks between us. A love like Berta and Claude. It was right here in my grasp.

'Be brave, Eris,' Calli said. *'Trust the Goddess.'*

'You mean the same Goddess that allowed my family to be butchered?'

Calli whined. She didn't like it when I questioned divinity, but I often did. My mother had been staunchly devoted to the Moon Goddess, and it earned her no mercy.

I didn't expect her answer, my brows knitting when she said, *'Well, maybe he is Her apology.'*

CHAPTER 10

ERIS

WE DROVE UNTIL WE reached the edge of town and then walked down to a large, deep blue mountain lake. I marveled at its beauty and watched the autumn sunlight dance in orange sparkles across the surface. The air was crisp, but being a shifter had its perks, and I felt comfortable in my dress and short-sleeved shawl.

We were interrupted several times on our walk down to the water by people wanting to say hello to Gideon. I noticed his behavior was very casual for an Alpha. His aura and demeanor commanded respect from his subjects, but he was kind and tried to give everyone his time and attention, and I could tell his pack members loved him. The wall around my heart I'd been so sure of only a day ago cracked, the mortar softening and the brick slowly crumbling away.

'Our mate is a good leader,' Calli said, still intent on her campaign to convince me this was the right thing to do.

I smiled as I watched him talk animatedly to a young boy, maybe thirteen years old. *'He seems perfect, doesn't he?'*

'Look at him. He'll be an excellent father to our pups, too.'

'My gods, Calli!' I snapped, and my flush of embarrassment was so intense his brow furrowed, and he glanced over at me.

I smiled like I didn't know what had gotten his attention, and he narrowed his eyes, returning my grin before he was pulled back into the conversation.

Finally, he could get away, and we walked to the quieter side of the beach. Berta had arranged a beautiful spread, complete with a picnic cloth and a pitcher of lemonade. I recognized meat pies and several types of Danishes.

We chatted while we ate, and it felt like I'd known him forever. I wasn't good at talking to people, and I wondered why I couldn't shut up with him. My voice almost felt tired, so used to speaking only to Enid.

He appeared to be suffering the same issue and was blunt about the problems he was facing as Alpha. Having been trained to be an Alpha someday, I understood the dynamics of the position and I could tell he was impressed by my knowledge.

We discussed our siblings, and I laughed. Authentic laughter, as he described Finn as a self-proclaimed womanizer who had a hard time being serious about anything. Gideon admitted he was still an excellent businessman who thrived as Beta. Leo, he said, was a withdrawn and serious kid who would rather draw in his sketchbook or play his guitar than do "normal" shifter activities like fighting or training.

I could tell that he was worried about his youngest brother, and I assured him that Enid was similar. Even when we lived in the cabin, I couldn't get her to train with me or learn any self-defense. She preferred gardening, books, and puzzles.

"I worry about her so much," I whispered, a single tear slipping down my cheek. "I worry he'll come for her, the red-haired man."

Gideon slid closer, and I stared at my bare toes wiggling in the sand.

"You don't have to fight alone anymore, Eris. I will never allow anything to happen to you or Enid. You're my family now, and anyone that tries to harm either of you will die."

I could feel his resolve through the bond and hear the confidence of an Alpha in his voice. It sent a shiver up my spine, and I was pretty sure my wolf would fan herself if she was able.

Looking over, my voice was thick, asking, "You promise she'll be safe?"

The corner of his mouth dipped, and I was aware I was asking for something he couldn't guarantee. So, I was surprised when he answered, "I promise."

"How can you promise such a thing?" I demanded, shaking my head.

He grinned, and he teased me, but he was serious, too. "Because I'll have to be dead for anything to happen to her, and if that's the case, I won't be worried about broken promises."

"That is horribly morbid!" I scolded, but laughed, unable to deny the logic.

The tear lingered at my jawline, and he cupped my face, wiping it with his thumb. The mood shifted, the surrounding air growing heavy with the tension of desire. It had been like this all day, but this time I wouldn't joke my way out of it. I didn't want to.

He gazed at me with a contradictory look, hard longing and soft affection, and brushed his thumb over my lips. For some odd reason, I kissed it as he did, and he sighed, leaning into me.

GIDEON

Finally, after a wonderful day of her coy teasing, I could press my lips to hers. They were perfect, and silky, and they were mine. I'd never known perfection until today. But it was here, on this sunny beach with me, and returning my affection while I wondered what I did to deserve such a thing.

Eris grabbed my elbow, pulling closer to me until the curve of her breasts pressed against me. Ivailo put his foot on the gas, a thick wave of desire coursing through my veins.

Not wanting whatever happened next to be a public affair, I broke the lock of our lips and looked around, feeling her disappointment through the bond. There were only a handful of people milling around in the area, and I spotted my salvation only a couple dozen yards away. An abandoned boathouse was slowly sinking into the lake; sucked in, just like me.

I grabbed her hand and pulled her to her feet, hurrying towards the boathouse. To my relief, the door was broken, the lock disabled, and I jarred it open, bringing her inside after me.

My head spun when a thick wave of understanding, and then desire, flowed from her. An elixir of madness to my wolf, who pushed, saying, *'Now. Now it's time.'*

She gasped when I laced my fingers in the hair at her nape and pulled her to me. I took advantage, connecting with her lips and immediately invading her open mouth. Her arms wrapped around my neck, and she deepened the kiss, our tongues sliding over each other. With the breeze gone, I could smell her desire, and I pinned her against the wall, grinding against her. She moaned in my mouth and responded, pushing her hips into me.

I growled, trailing kisses down her neck, and saying, "Gods, you're beautiful. I need you so bad. I've wanted nothing as much as I want you."

She pushed out a sharp breath, and I felt her embarrassment mixing with a fresh current of desire. I sensed she wasn't accustomed to compliments, but she liked them. It made me grin against her skin. I would make sure she never wanted for them again.

The high collared shawl got in my way, and I grabbed it and pulled, so the large single button came free from its loose hold. I had to take a deep breath to calm my wolf at the sight of her neck, and I traveled instead to her chest, kissing the soft swell of her breasts.

She whispered my name, and the scent of her desire grew stronger. "I can't stop thinking about how you must taste."

Her shy confusion muddled the hot current of the bond, and she said, "But... you already know."

She thought I meant her mouth. Her lips. *Why does that turn me on so much?* I muttered, "Gods, you're a contradiction," and my cock throbbed against the too-tight fabric of my pants. The sweet innocence of her naivety walked hand in hand with her death threat from this morning, running roughshod over my self-control. I grabbed her waist and lifted her, so swift in my actions that she didn't know what to expect until I had her knees over my shoulders.

I wrapped my arms around her, pulling her close and pressing my nose between her thighs. Inhaling, so my head swam like I was drugged. I was at her mercy.

Moaning, I said, "Oh, my gods." Her desire and embarrassment hit me like a runaway train, and I looked up, feeling I'd elaborated enough, but adding, "I want to *taste* you."

I closed my eyes, trying to get myself under control. She could say no—she probably would—and I'd need to find the strength to respect that.

I felt her dress move and opened my eyes. She was pulling it up toward her stomach. Her hands were shaky, and her breath fast, but, suddenly, the only thing separating me from bliss was a pair of wet, white underwear. The trust she was extending was heady, another dose of ecstasy. I couldn't think of anything more personal to a woman than letting a man see her like that.

She toyed with my hair, and I pressed my lips to the inside of her thigh, kissing, so she jumped. My lips moved higher, and her legs clenched, a little giggle bubbling in her chest. Looking up at her, I deepened that kiss, sucking on the soft skin to give her a hickey only she would know about this time.

She moaned and tightened her hands in my hair when I pulled away, like she thought I might stop.

"No. Keep going."

My heart paused to check if I'd heard correctly, and then raced, encouraging me to hurry. Slow. Control. I wanted her to want it as bad as I did.

I kissed her over her panties first, pressing where I knew she'd be sensitive. She whimpered, and the small sound made me throb. Unable to stop myself, I pulled the white cotton aside and moaned at the sight of her, never having seen a woman so intimately. It was intriguing, like peeking behind the curtain in the land of Oz.

My arms were wrapped around her hips, so I could use my fingers and spread her, revealing the pink bud I couldn't wait to get acquainted with.

Just one lick, one pass of my tongue all the way up from her entrance, to start. Oh, gods, the way she clenched, and how her hands tightened in my hair. I looked up, and she was staring down at me, her mouth half open. I did it again, not looking away, and then again.

She was slick, wet just for me, and the taste was incredible. Intoxicating. I knew it could be good, but it was better than any dessert I'd ever had.

I groaned, "Fuck," and my control slipped away.

Her clitoris became my focus. I sucked on it, too hard at first because she squealed and pulled away. She was so sensitive; so untouched. I was gentler, applying less pressure as I drew my tongue in slow, measured circles.

The sounds she made were gasoline to this fire. Hot. She was still trying to be quiet, so it was whimpers and moans and little whines that inflamed something carnal in me, and in my wolf.

Ivailo was annoyingly present, pushing me to hurry, and I did my best to ignore him. The pressure against my zipper was painful, and I adjusted myself with my free hand so the head of my cock could find some relief, pushing up and out of my waistband instead of pressing into my pants.

She was peaking, growing more excited, and I wanted to finish her. I wanted her to think about this often, and for a long time.

Maybe all these years of listening to Finn would pay off. I'd heard him talk about it once, and I made my lips into a little "o," closing them over her clitoris and sucking it into my mouth. Gentle as I could.

She squealed again, but grabbed my hair and held me there, her thighs closing around my head like silk pillows.

"Oh, no! Oh, *gods...* Oh." The last word was drawn out, and her body went slack and then started rolling, until she was twitching in my arms.

I licked her, lapped at her, wanting to taste her pleasure. All of it.

My wolf was on edge, saying, *'Enough play. Just do it!'*

I looked up at her. Her eyes were still closed, and we were both breathing hard. She had been biting her lip; it was swollen, glistening.

But I said, *'No,'* and adjusted my pants again to hide my erection.

His shock hit me like a cold splash, followed by the fiery burn of anger. *'What?'*

'I still have things to tell her. And I will not have her for her first time in some moldy old boathouse.'

All the talking we'd done today, and I still hadn't admitted the engagement to her. It was severed, but only a few hours ago.

I closed the bond to hide my guilt, and to staunch her desire. She would've let me have her, I was pretty sure. It was confirmed when I let her down, and she kissed me with a new passion, even though my lips and chin were still wet.

I had to pull away. The taste of her kiss and her pleasure had me reconsidering.

"Let's go home," I whispered, imagining something more romantic.

She fisted the back of my shirt, hugging me, and buried her face in my neck. Her lips pressed to my marking spot, and my wolf jumped, excited.

'See? She's ready.'

"There's more to discuss first," I said to her, running my hand down the curtain of her beautiful hair.

She whispered, "Okay," but turned her face up and kissed me again.

I buried my guilt and opened the bond. To lighten the mood, I asked, "How was that?"

She smiled into the kiss and nodded her head, making a loose claim of exclusivity. Implying she desired more, and that she wanted to stay with me. "I could get used to that, Alpha." I could feel her curiosity, and she asked, "Did you enjoy it like you thought you would?"

"Did I like it?" I grinned at the question, wanting to push her boundaries. "I've waited a decade for the perfect woman. Now that you're here, I promise I'm going to bury my face in your pretty little pussy whenever I can."

She gasped, her cheeks immediately pink, and then giggled, but it was huskier. Thicker. Another pulse of embarrassment and desire skipped hand-in-hand down the bond between us.

"That blush is lovely on you," I said.

"Is that why you say such vulgar things to me?"

"I say it because you like it."

Eris fisted the material of my shirt in her hands and pushed up on her toes, pressing her lips to mine. We kissed a while longer, and I fixed her clothes while we did, buttoning the shawl and adjusting her dress.

Finding the willpower to stop, I grabbed her hand. "Let's go home. We can talk in my office."

Maybe I'd have her there on my desk, after I'd relieved my guilt and told her the truth.

CHAPTER 11

ERIS

I STARED OUT THE front window and watched the houses flow by in a blur of color, mixing with the oranges and yellows of the deciduous trees. It felt like a dream, and it had been a long time since my dreams were of the pleasurable variety.

Gideon held my hand, caressing my thumb with his in small circles. He'd blocked the bond again, and I wasn't sure why. I sensed that, suddenly, he was the one holding back. The way we'd been in that boathouse, I thought we were going to take it the entire way. I'd wanted to bite him, to mark him, and to have him take possession of me.

My cheeks heated at the thought, but Calli encouraged me, *'There's no shame in loving our true mate, little one.'*

The warmth in my cheeks deepened, and I looked out the side window. *'No one has said anything about love.'*

'Don't you feel it? Like a vine wrapped around your heart, spreading its tendrils of warmth into your soul?'

'Maybe I do.'

She continued, *'I'm sure that's why he's blocking us now. He's probably feeling it, too, and thinks you aren't because you've been so difficult.'*

'I have not!'

'Most wolves don't even wait two hours! Ivailo and I should receive awards for our unmatched patience.'

We turned into the drive, a slight incline, and I turned to him, blurting, "I would've done it, you know? The mating and the marking."

He shook his head. "In that old boathouse? You deserve better."

"Things like that matter little to me. I did not grow up in such a place where every sheet is silk." I grinned, adding, "I'm quite sure my mother and father were on a bed of pine needles. She'd mentioned some splinters in some very undesirable places."

He winced, chuckling, but sobered. "It's more than that—"

I was looking at him, but he stopped, tensing in his seat. My eyes followed his, and my brow furrowed.

An unfamiliar car, one that hadn't been here earlier, was in the drive. A tall, black-haired woman was screaming at Finn on the steps leading up to the house. She waved her arms erratically and stomped her high-heeled shoe like a child. When Finn noticed us, his eyes went wide. The girl turned at the sound of the car approaching and narrowed her eyes.

She was lovely. Curvy. Her breasts bounced in the tight dress she wore, and she had a generous flare at her hips. Certainly not underfed and not underweight.

I asked, "Who is that?" She clicked down the steps in a huff, and I felt uneasy. I didn't think I would like the answer. There was an edge of ice in my tone when I glared over at Gideon. "Why don't you open the bond? *Mate.*"

He looked furious, his eyes glazing like he was using the link or talking to his wolf.

GIDEON

Unable to believe my idiot brother, I shouted in his head, *'You could've warned me!'*

'Don't blame me! I've been trying to link you for the last thirty minutes and your stupid phone is off.'

He was right. I had blocked the mind link during our moment in the boathouse, not wanting to be interrupted, and hadn't opened it again. My phone was turned off, sitting on the console.

'Who is the idiot? Huh? Not Finn!' Ivailo ranted in my head, his guttural voice growing to a bellow in my head. *'You should've sealed her with a mark at the boathouse! Now she will leave us because you don't deserve a true mate! Fool! Idiot! Stupid boy!'*

I turned to Eris, and the look she offered was so cold, it felt like someone ran a finger of ice down my spine.

"Who is that, Gideon?"

I held my hands up. "Please, just wait here for a moment and let me handle this. Then we'll talk, okay?"

She offered no answer, and her expression did not soften, but I hopped out of the car. "Why are you here, Sophia? I talked to your father this morning, and he told me he'd talk to you."

I heard the passenger door open and knew Eris was standing outside. It was stupid to assume she'd actually wait in the car.

"I don't care what my father said!" Sophia screeched. "We had a deal, Gideon Greenwood! I am the Luna of Gold Moon! Me!"

Sophia had rejected her true mate three years ago because he was an omega, or a low-ranking wolf with no alpha heritage. Rejections of the bond did not happen often, but it was not unheard of, especially if an alpha desired to mate with another alpha and produce pureblood pups. She had her eyes on bigger prizes.

Her father, Owen, was the Alpha of the Ruby Moon pack, and Sophia was his only heir. Ruby was the third largest behind Gold Moon and Diamond Moon. When I believed I wasn't ever going to find my true mate, I entered into an engagement with Sophia. I would have a Luna, and the merger of Ruby and Gold would put us well above the other packs in terms of size and power. Sophia and I had been using each other, and we were aware of it.

Owen hadn't been angry when I called this morning. He understood the true mate bond, but I supposed I was stupid to assume this was all dealt with.

"You know the deal is off," I hissed under my breath, and I couldn't even look at Eris.

Sophia scoffed and leveled her eyes at Eris, having no problem spilling the beans. "Did he tell you we are engaged?" She held out her left hand and wiggled her fingers so the diamond ring she wore glittered in the fading evening light.

I interjected, "Were! We *were* engaged!"

Sophia talked louder, and I considered grabbing her and putting my hand over her mouth.

"The wedding is right around the corner! Two weekends from now!" She put her hand on my shoulder, and wrinkled her nose at Eris, spewing her vile words, "He's already picked me to be his Luna, so you can go home to whatever Podunk you crawled out of. *Trash.*"

My mouth dropped open. Sophia and I hadn't shared an intense connection, but she'd been sweet in my presence. An act, all of it.

"That is enough," I hissed, shrugging her off and trying to get a handle on my wolf, who was ready to kill her. "Apologize. Right now."

Gravel crunched, and I looked over to see Eris was not interested in an apology. She was walking away toward the tree line, her hands fisted at her sides. I dropped the block I had on the bond, but she'd erected her own.

I stepped into Sophia's face and growled. It got her attention, her smug smirk disappearing as Ivailo pushed forward, so my voice warbled with his guttural inflection. "Get in your fucking car and leave my pack. Never return. I don't care who your father is. I'll kill you if I ever see you here again."

Her eyes were wide, but she was determined to push her luck, clinging to my arm. "Gideon, wait, please. Can't we discuss this? On second thought, you can have her as your mate. I'm okay with that. You can have two! They've done that in the past! I'll-I'll marry Finn, even! I don't mind being the second lady!"

"I'm good on that, thanks though," Finn muttered, and I scoffed, pushing Sophia away from me harder than I was intending.

Finn caught her, his lip curling, and escorted her, more like dragged her, towards her car. She was screaming profanities at me, but I turned away, running after Eris.

My heart pinched to see that pretty yellow dress ripped to pieces from her shift just inside the tree line, and I let Ivailo free so he could follow her sweet scent.

CHAPTER 12

ERIS

I GAVE CALLI CONTROL, and she ran on, the forest passing beneath our paws.

'We should go back and kill her for touching our mate,' she growled.

'Why?' I asked. *'She didn't lie. I don't think a man can do what he did in that boathouse without a little practice. Now we know where it came from, hm?'*

It was strange. Maybe others would sob. Not me. I felt the cracks and crumbles of that frozen wall around my heart filling with bitterness. This was why I didn't need people. Love always led to pain, like the two feelings had a contract, and insisted on defrauding everyone that ever lived.

Calli whined. She was hurt, too, and couldn't find excuses to justify what we'd just witnessed.

We ran and ran until Calli's tongue hung out of her mouth, panting despite the cool evening. I'd made her cross several streams to hide the visual evidence of our passing, and turn in circles, backtrack, and anything else to throw his wolf off our trail.

I knew he'd be coming after me, but I wanted to make it as hard as I could to find me. I'd have to face him, but I didn't want to see him. My heart lurched and the day we'd shared played in my mind's eye for the hundredth time. Our passion in the boathouse and the idea I was entertaining of love on our drive home. I felt sick and stupid for trusting so quickly. Just like a silly girl who was tricked once again into believing fairytales.

I finally let Calli stop at a spot where a small stream bubbled from a mountainside into a geothermal pool. It was just deep enough for wading, but I didn't go in. I shifted and sat by the edge, pulling my knees to my chest, and watching the steam curl off of the water.

The moon was almost full, and it rose in the sky, reflecting on the water in a dance of glowing ripples. I soaked the beams into my naked skin, hoping the magic might fill this hollow ache in my chest.

"Was I just awful in my past life?" I asked the moon. "Is that why you punish me like you do? Could you give me a estimate on how long your vengeance will last? It'd be nice to know how much more I have to endure."

She didn't answer. That bitch never did.

For the first time in a long time, I let a familiar grief rock me, ripping at the old wound in my chest. I wanted my mother. I needed her to explain to me the intricacies of men and tell me what I should do.

My mind shifted to that girl, Sophia. *Girl*. Silly to call her that. She was a woman, and a strikingly beautiful one. Slate-gray eyes and black hair. Not an underfed hermit with a suitcase full of emotional issues. *Trash*.

Calli and I basked in our sorrow until she growled. My ears perked up at the crack of a stick, and the hair on the back of my neck prickled with awareness.

'We're not alone, little one,' she warned me. *'And it's no wolf that's found us.'*

I nodded and listened, smelling the air. Decay and rot slapped my nostrils, and I nearly gagged.

'Vampires,' I concluded, and she growled in agreement.

"Well, well, well. What luck!" a nasally voice crooned to my right, a figure stepping into the moonlight. "A lone little wolf, how sad."

A cackle sounded behind me, and I stood, rolling my neck so the bones cracked. A female showed herself this time, sniffing excitedly, her nostrils flaring. "She smells good, too. Young and fresh."

"I bet she'll squeal good when we bite her, like a fall piggy at the chopping block," another voice said, stepping from the woods behind me. He chomped his jaws, making his teeth clack. "Pretty too! I'll fuck her hard while I drain her."

I stood and stretched. "Thank the gods you've all come." Their brows knit, and they glanced at each other, their sharp smiles faltering. I clicked my tongue and said, "I've had an awful day, and I really, really need to kill something."

GIDEON

We ran, stopping all the time to let Ivailo sniff and search. She was clever, making it nearly impossible to track her down. I'd crisscrossed so many times already I was damn near dizzy.

Finn's voice broke my concentration. *'Gideon?'*

'What?' I growled, trying to find the scent again.

'There's a big problem. Reports from the scouts. Several small groups of vampires pushed the borders tonight. Some may have gotten through.'

I stopped in my tracks, a cold chill running down my spine. *'Where? The west border? The north?'*

Those were the two most likely locations, but it could be anywhere.

I could hear the concern in his voice. *'The eastern forest.'*

Panic blossomed in my chest and Ivailo threw back his head, howling. He intensified his search, running as fast as we could track her scent.

We growled together when the smell turned from her scent to a mixture of rot, decay, and fresh blood. Her blood.

'They've killed her!' Ivailo howled in my head.

'No! Don't say that!'

I was so fearful of what I was about to find, I almost stopped my pursuit. Ivailo's feet felt like they were made of lead.

We bounded into a small valley and put on the brakes. She was waist deep in a warm pool. I shifted back, trying to make sense of the scene.

However, she was naked, making logical thought almost impossible. I sucked in a breath, staring at her bare back.

The pool was only for wading, and I could see the heart-shaped curves of her backside, and the water dip at the top of the cleave between them. Her wet hair glistened in the moonlight while steam rose around her like tendrils of the night, caressing her. For a moment, I wondered if she was actually the Moon Goddess in the flesh.

She was washing her face and chest in the water, rusty red blood dripping from her hands. Instincts told me she was aware of my presence.

I glanced around the clearing and realized a small massacre had occurred here. Disembodied limbs were scattered around, and, by my count, she had dispatched at least three vampires. Relief washed through me, followed by intense pride. When I thought I couldn't desire her more.

Ivailo was panting in my head. *'Our little mate is stronger than you thought.'*

'What? Me! You're the one who thought—'

'Now fix your stupidness, stupid,' he growled. He'd never been okay with the engagement, insisting we wait for our true mate.

"Are you hurt?" I asked.

"Yes."

My concern peaked again. "Where?"

She was still facing away, and I watched her arm bend, knowing she patted her chest over her heart while she whispered, "Right here."

"Eris," I started. "Please let me explain."

"No," she said, and turned, giving me a full frontal. "Let me explain something to you."

She strode out of the water, and I threatened my eyes that I'd pluck them out if they ventured anywhere aside from her face. Eris didn't look down either, her lips in a tight frown.

She stuck a finger into my chest and hissed, "I don't have the patience to be made a fool, and I don't have time for silly games. Let me make something clear, *Alpha*. I'm no damsel in distress, and I don't need, nor have I ever wanted, a Prince Charming."

My eyes traveled around the carnage of the clearing. "That is crystal clear, trust me. But I promise I wasn't trying to make you the fool. I only wished to protect myself from looking like one."

Her jaw tightened, and she walked past me.

"We have to talk about this," I reasoned, trying to hold her arm.

She ripped it from me. "Well, I need to check on my sister." Stopping to glance around the clearing, she hissed, "You should hold your borders better, Alpha. Someone could've been hurt."

Eris shifted, and it was my first time seeing her wolf. Calliope was a decent size, obviously an alpha, and her beautiful silver fur almost sparkled in the moonlight. I'd never seen such a color before.

She left me standing there naked and alone with a cold ache in my chest, my pride hurt by her last words. Ivailo refused to speak to me or shift, so I walked the entire way home in the dark, wearing nothing but my shame.

Chapter 13

Eris

Sunlight streaming through the window broke my fitful sleep, and I glanced over at the other bed, surprised to find Enid and Hades gone again.

My head was pounding. I couldn't remember ever in my life suffering a headache, and a hollow pain rang in my chest.

'It's the incomplete bond. You'll weaken away from him. You'll feel ill,' Calli explained.

I rubbed my temples. *'Can't you fix it?'*

'I can't heal heartbreak, little one. I'm sorry.'

So, I was facing the inevitable confrontation with my mate. Today.

A decadent breakfast was laid out on the table, untouched by Enid, and I nibbled halfheartedly at a couple of things. After I gave up on that charade, I went and took a long, steamy shower. No matter how hot I turned up the water, the cold hole in my chest wouldn't abate.

I finally dressed, something a little more practical than yesterday. Pants and a long-sleeved shirt. Once my hair was braided, I had nothing else to use as an excuse, so I headed for his office, meeting Finn in the third-floor hallway.

"He's not there," he said, realizing where I was going.

"Can you direct me, Beta? He and I are due to have a conversation."

Finn looked contemplative, like he was unsure if he should share that information.

I bristled. "Are you joking? He's with her, isn't he? That vile woman, Sophia."

Anger seared in my heart, and I balled my fists. Finn blanched, holding up both of his hands to stop me.

"No! No, not her."

I stared at him. "What do you mean, not her? My gods, is there another?" I turned on my heel, annoyed at the tears stinging my eyes.

He followed, sputtering, "Woah, woah, woah. I swear, Luna, he—"

I spun again, shoving my finger into his chest. "Do *not* call me that. Please."

"Eris," he said, holding his hands up again. "He's with another woman, but it's not what you think."

"Why are you playing riddles with me, Beta?" I demanded, my brow furrowing.

"He has no other romantic ties, I assure you."

"Then where? What other secrets is he keeping?"

He cleared his throat and looked at the floor. "He's with Mother."

"Then I'd like to be directed there. Immediately."

He hesitated, and I arched an eyebrow at him, crossing my arms over my chest. Finn scrubbed his hand down his beard. "Come on, I'll escort you. She's in a different wing of the house. You haven't seen it yet."

I nodded and followed him to the elevator.

Finn took advantage of my inability to escape, and looked over at me, his gaze serious. He rushed his words while I frowned at my reflection in the elevator doors.

"I told him it was stupid, you know, the engagement. But he felt obligated. He thought the pack needed a Luna, and he hadn't found his mate. Gave up on finding her—well, *you*. I can relate. I'm twenty-four and every day that passes, I feel like I won't find mine either." I let out a long, loud sigh, but Finn continued. "He didn't have feelings for Sophia. I don't think he even liked her. It just seemed like a good business deal to him."

"So, he's a user? Good to know. Thank you, Beta."

Finn blanched. "No! No, that's not—uh. I'm not doing well, am I? It was more of a mutual using of each other. Don't feel bad for her! She only wants Gideon because he's the Alpha of the biggest pack, and being his Luna carries a lot of power."

"I respect your loyalty, Beta, but he can plead his case to me." The doors dinged and slid open, and Finn sighed. "I'm sure you'll find your mate someday, and I'm sure she'll be wonderful," I said, patting his shoulder.

"Yeah. Thanks," he muttered, running his hand down his beard again.

We walked in silence until I realized we were in some kind of hospital wing. "Beta, is your mother... unhealthy?"

I had picked up that Gideon did not want to talk about her yesterday, and Finn's earlier hesitation at bringing me here suddenly made sense.

"Our dad, Henry, was her true mate, and he died a few years ago, unexpectedly. She's just not the same; dementia is what the doctors tell us. It steals her memories. Her light." His voice thickened, so he cleared his throat before he continued, "It's a human disease, but losing her mate left her vulnerable to it. We can't even speak to her wolf, and she hasn't shifted since Dad's death. Gideon has spent millions flying in doctors and summoning witches from all over the world. They all say the same thing. There's no cure and nothing they can do."

"I'm sorry, Beta. That is truly awful to hear."

Lore taught us that mates were two halves of one soul. The true mate bond was special and sacred, and that she was still alive was a testament to her strength. Many true mates died shortly after losing their other half, often by their own hand, or sought comfort with a chosen bond, but those were notoriously difficult relationships.

"She likes Gideon to sit with her. She thinks he's Dad because they look so similar. I'm a little too ginger," he said, running his hand through his hair. "She doesn't know who any of us are. It, uh, has really taken a toll on Leo. Our little brother." He cleared his throat again. "It's like saying goodbye every day."

"I am so sorry for you all, Finn."

"Thank you. Here we are," he whispered, and opened a door, allowing me inside.

Gideon sat at a large bay window holding the hand of a woman. Her hair was a long curly mane. I could tell at one time it had been strawberry blond like Leo's, but white streaks were taking the majority. I was at her profile, and could see her watery eyes were light blue, almost a gray color, and freckles dusted her face.

Gideon turned when he heard the door, and when he saw me, he jumped, shooting to his feet. Finn hadn't informed him we were coming.

"Eris?"

I didn't think he'd slept. Dark bags drowned his eyes, and a five o'clock shadow showed clearly on his face. The shirt he wore was unbuttoned and wrinkled, and he ran his hand through his hair, unsure of what to do.

"Who is it, Henry?" his mother asked, looking confused.

"This is Eris," he said, offering nothing else. I didn't mind that he didn't introduce me as his mate. It would've confused her and broken her heart since she thought he was her mate.

"A new pack member? Hello, dear. Oh, you're lovely. Lovely. Look at that eye color. So unique. I'm the Luna, Diane. This is Alpha Henry, although I think you've met." She tsked her tongue at him, and scolded, "You know I like to meet all the new pack members."

He smiled sweetly and squeezed her hand. "Won't you forgive me?"

She nodded and smiled. "Well, don't be shy, dear. Come and sit with us. Tell me about yourself. My, aren't you just lovely! Look at her eyes, Henry, so unique!"

"She is so lovely," he agreed, looking at me with a sad smile.

"It's wonderful to meet you, Luna," I said, taking her hand when she extended it to me.

We chatted. I had little to share that was happy, but I told her the good parts. I gushed about the beauty of Gold Moon and complimented her for her hard work. The inner workings of the pack were the duty of the Luna, so all this beauty was to her credit.

Gideon watched me the whole time, his eyes blank, like he was somewhere else, and I noticed Finn stayed by the door.

I studied Diane, trying to understand her ailment. Finn had called it a disease. It was a physical illness, harming her brain.

'Calli, do you think we could heal her?'

'Maybe. It might be a lot, though. I don't know if we're strong enough.'

'I'd like to try.'

'Of course.'

"Could I sing to you, Luna?" I asked, taking her hand again.

She was taken aback, but then smiled sweetly. "I'd love that, dear. Isn't that nice, Henry?"

"It is," he said, more of a question than a statement.

I grabbed her hand and took a deep breath, starting my mother's lullaby. My cheeks warmed at my audience, but I closed my eyes, focusing on Diane.

My hands grew hot, and I knew they were glowing when I heard Gideon stand. I could feel the sickness, like a dark cloud in her blood, and I pulled it to me, continuing the song. Diane moaned like she was in pain, and I heard shuffling from Finn's direction.

He intended to stop me, but Gideon whispered, "Just wait."

It was taking more energy than healing Enid ever had, and I could feel myself waning, but I had to clear it all away. Just a bit more.

My brow was slick with sweat, running down my temples. A hot trickle of thick blood leaked from my nose, sliding over my lips.

"Eris!" Gideon said. I heard his steps, and he kneeled next to me.

"Almost there," I said, pushing the words through gritted teeth.

Calli agreed, *'We can do it.'*

I pulled the last of the darkness away and Diane sighed, slumping back in her chair, and breaking our contact. I fell forward, and Gideon caught me.

"Are you okay? What do you need? Can I help?" he said, almost all at once.

"Just a rest."

The blackness was trying to take me, but I wanted to see if I'd done it. Finn was with Diane, stroking her hair. He looked worried, and I knitted my brows, my heart dropping. Gods, had I harmed her? Maybe it was too much.

Her eyelids fluttered, and she sat up with a jolt, confused. "Finny?" She grinned up at him. "Why are you petting me, darling?"

His voice was thick, and a tear rolled into his beard. "Mom? You know who I am?"

She laughed. "Well, I birthed you! I think I would know my own son."

Gideon gasped. "My gods. Eris?"

I shrugged, but I had to submit to the blackness invading my vision.

CHAPTER 14

GIDEON

I WALKED INTO *THE Crumble and Flake*. Eris was in some kind of deep sleep, and Enid was with her, suggesting she may not wake for a long while. She'd convinced me to find something to eat, and maybe sleep. I knew sleep wouldn't come, so I went for a walk, and of course found my way to the bakery.

"Alpha!" Berta cried, her brow furrowing when I entered. "You look awful."

"And you're as lovely as ever," I muttered and sat at the same table Eris and I had been at only yesterday.

She came around the counter and sat with me. "What's wrong? I don't know if I've ever seen you so down. Where's your Luna?" She paused, her eyes falling to my neck, exposed by the sloppy collar of my unbuttoned shirt. "Where's your mark?"

"It's complicated." I sighed. "I messed up. With that engagement to Ruby Moon's daughter."

"Ah," she said, sitting back and pursing her lips. "Don't tell me you didn't tell her."

"I meant to. I wanted to."

"Fool," she said curtly, shaking her head.

"Eris is complicated," I mumbled, picking at the yellow plaid table-cloth. "She's been hurt. A lot. She's untrusting. I think she's afraid... but she's also incredibly fierce."

"A tough one to crack?"

"Yes. It hasn't been like they said it would be. It's not been easy."

"I've never known you to be one to whine and pout," Berta said. "Although I imagine it's tough for you to be told no, Alpha. Not used to not getting your way."

My brows lifted, and I glanced up at her. I opened my mouth, but a loud buzzer interrupted me.

"I'll be right back," Berta said, and stood, hurrying around the counter. She returned with a fresh plate of croissants and set them on the table.

When I didn't take one, she clicked her tongue. "It's Pain au Chocolat! One of your favorites!"

The chocolate croissants usually wouldn't last long in my presence, but I couldn't even muster my appetite for them. "Not hungry."

She sighed, running her finger along the edge of the plate. "This is a difficult dessert, you know?"

"But you make dozens every week," I said, holding my hands open.

"Well, practice and wisdom can't be beat, but in the beginning, oh, I hated them. Croissants are so picky." She shook her head. "The dough is handled too much. There aren't enough folds, or there are too many. The kitchen is too hot or too cold. You've added too much water." She threw her hands up. "And trust me, the dough wouldn't lie. It's so fine, it would always show your mistakes. Gods, I'd be in tears over pastry!"

"Why are you telling me this?" I asked, a curious smile curling my lips.

She leaned forward. "Because one day, Alpha, I pulled out of the oven a perfect tray of croissants. Fluffy and beautiful with a nice golden crust and melted chocolate filling." Berta smiled, sighing and putting her hand over her heart. "That was over fifty years ago now, and I still remember how good I felt that day." Taking my hands, she patted my fingers. "Don't you see? The difficult ones, the victories you really have to fight for, those are the sweetest. The best rewards always cost a little more, but they're worth it."

I stood. "Thank you, Berta."

"Of course." She stood and offered me the plate. "One for the walk back?"

"No, thank you," I said, already at the door. "It's going to be more like a run."

I took the path straight up the hill through the forest, normally only used by deer. My legs burned by the time I reached the level ground of the pack house lawn, and I ran up the stairs. I knocked softly and clicked in my code on the guest door when I received no answer. I frowned when I found the room empty. My heart sank. Had she gone?

'Finn? Do you know where Eris is?'

'Uh, yeah. She's here in the training room.'

'The training room?'

'Yep,' he said, and I could hear amusement in the word. *'Says she's waiting for you to get here.'*

'I'll be right there.'

The training gym was on the first floor. As usual, several warriors were present, training on their own time and spread out at various stations. Her scent was a magnet for my nose, and my eyes followed it easily. She was at one of the punching bags, unloading what looked like years of frustration on the unfortunate thing.

'She's probably pretending it's you,' Ivailo said, and I tilted my head, watching her.

I couldn't argue with him, so I said, *'She's no amateur, that is certain.'* Her punches were crisp and trained. She was deadly; I knew that already, and I approached with caution. "I heard you wanted to see me."

Eris stopped, pausing before she turned to face me. Her hair was plaited in two braids, and she was in exercise gear, a tight tank top and spandex shorts. I looked down at her chest when she drew in a deep inhale, watching her nipples harden through the thin material of her sports bra and tank top.

When my eyes trailed back up to hers, she tilted her head, and I asked, "Do I smell that good?"

"You know you do." I smirked, and she said, "I did want to see you. I want to fight you. In that ring."

"Excuse me?" I asked, glancing over at the sparring area.

"I want to fight you," she repeated, "and if I win, you must accept my rejection."

My head whipped to study her face, and I practically shouted, "No!" Her brows lifted, and I repeated, "No, I won't do that."

"Why?"

"I don't want to fight you. Or hurt you."

"I'll heal," she said, scoffing.

"That's not the point."

"Afraid you'll lose, Alpha?"

"Not even a little. Can't we just talk?"

"I don't want to talk. I want to break your nose."

My lips parted, and my brows lifted.

Ivailo said, *'Well, Berta said the things we fight for.'*

'I don't think she meant literally.'

Eris sighed and said, "Don't be a coward. It's unbecoming of an Alpha. My nipples may even soften in your presence," and looked down at her hands, adjusting the tape on her knuckles.

'Coward?' Ivailo spat, nearly choking on the word.

I knew what she was doing and frowned. Alphas didn't cope with challenges to their valor well, and even my level-headed wolf would take offense.

"Don't call me a coward."

"Then don't be one."

"Eris," I said, with a tone of warning that made her smirk.

"Gideon?"

"I don't want to hurt you."

"You already have. Worse than any physical blow you could deliver me in that ring."

"Well, I'm very sorry. I would like to talk about that."

She stepped past me toward the ring. "I told you; we're not talking, we're fighting."

I followed. "So, if I agree to this, and I win, then what? You'll take my mark?"

She whipped around after she ducked under the ropes, narrowing her eyes at me. "No. I'll take your mark if I ask for it."

"Then what?" I asked, entering the ring after her and tossing my overshirt off.

"Then we'll talk."

"Fine, but I won't hurt you."

"Then you're going to lose," she said, putting her hands on her hips.

"Don't count on it."

CHAPTER 15

ERIS

'*WHY ARE WE DOING this?*' Calli asked. '*He's an anointed Alpha. He's got the strength of the pack behind him. You're a lone rogue.*'

I watched Gideon slide his shirt off and toss it aside, leaving him only in jeans. Studying his well-formed body, I said, '*I don't think that's fair,*' in place of an actual answer.

'*Definitely not. So, why are we fighting a battle we can't win?*'

'*I just want to hit him once. One good one and I'll be satisfied.*'

She cackled her wolfish laugh. '*Really? That's it?*'

'*And to see how badly he wants me.*'

'*You want to see if he'll fight you, for you?*'

'*I want to see what he's made of, you know, if I'm going to be his mate.*'

'*I see. A test to determine if he's good enough for you and our future pups.*'

'*No. A test of whether he's good enough to trust with the safety of my sister.*'

"Are you ready, or are you going to stand there conversing with your wolf all day?" Gideon asked, tilting his head.

From the corner of my eye, I noticed Finn wander over and act like he was placing weights on a press up bar. I fisted my hand over my heart and offered a slight bow at my waist to Gideon, and he did the same, signaling that the fight was beginning.

He surprised me by stalking across the ring when I expected him to let me make the first move. I threw a purposefully lame punch, which he stopped, grabbing my fist and using my arm and my momentum to spin me into his tight embrace, my back to his chest. The sparks of pleasure erupted, sending a wave of gooseflesh down my arms and legs.

His breath tickled my ear. "I know you can hit harder than that." His free hand landed on my waist, wrapping around to flatten on my stomach and pull me into him. "Is this what you wanted, after all?"

"Yes," I whispered, gritting my teeth. This might hurt. Him more than me, hopefully.

With a tight cry of aggression, I threw my head back into his face as hard as I could. He hissed, his nose breaking under the force, and he tried to back away, but I tightened my grip on his arm and threw my elbow into his gut, stealing his breath. The heel of my boot came down on his toe, crushing it inside his shoe. Finn's raucous laughter echoed in my ears as I used the corner pin of the ring as a launching pad, pushing against it with my feet to send us both flying backward. I landed on top of Gideon, reveling in his pained grunt, and rolled away, turning and bringing my fist down to punch him in the face.

The element of surprise had gone in my favor, but that was over, and he moved his head, leaving me to yelp when my knuckles crunched against the hard floor. For such a large man, he was quicker than I expected, launching at me and grabbing my wrist. I winced when he twisted my arm behind my back, and knowing I needed to move before he got me wrapped up, I tossed my weight into him. We both rolled to our feet, but his shoulder was already lowered, coming to catch me at my waist. I let him grab me, but swung my legs up, wrapping them around his neck in a reversal that earned me some cheers from the gathering crowd. Using his momentum against him, I folded myself around his body, to his opposite shoulder, and got him off balance, successfully flipping him to his back. I took hold of his arm as I did, twisting it into a straight arm bar and wrapping my leg around his neck on the way down. His wrist cracked in the hold, but he was grinning, his teeth laced with blood.

Gideon looked down at his chin, where my crotch now rested, and said, "This is the best seat in the house, I promise."

"It was alright, I guess," I said, remembering what he'd done to me in that boathouse.

His expression turned serious. "I should've told you about my previous engagement, Eris, and I'm sorry. I was working towards it. That's why I didn't have you by the lake when I could've."

My brows lifted. The unexpected guilt he'd experienced that day. That's why he'd blocked the bond. "You should have told me before—"

He took advantage of my distraction, bringing his knees up to push me off-balance, and then tossing me in a roll over his head. I tried to crawl away, but his weight pinned my legs. Before I could counter, he was on my back, his meaty forearm wrapping around my throat. I strained to get free, but he was like a bag of bricks, proving unmovable.

He didn't tighten his arm and put me out, just restrained me, and hissed, "That's it now. You're mine. Yield."

I would never admit what those words, *you're mine*, did to me, but I said, "I..." and trailed off. When I felt him relax to hear the rest of my surrender,

I let Calli have some fun, my teeth elongating. I sank them deep into his forearm, and I nearly cackled at the stunned gasp it elicited from him. Throwing my shoulder, I tried to shake him off, but I didn't get far, only able to roll onto my back before he recovered. This time, he tangled my legs with his. His arm ratcheted around me like a steel viper, pinning hands to my sides, and his free hand wrapped around my throat. We were nose to nose, and his nostrils flared, his pupils dilated.

I grinned, tasting his blood in my mouth, and he hissed, "Biting, now?"

"Did it hurt that bad?" I asked, sticking out a mocking pouty lip.

"There's little honor in it!"

I couldn't move anything except my fingers, my toes, and my lips, finding it hard to even laugh with his weight on my chest. "Oh, please, I'm a wolf. Plus, there's less honor in losing."

"Yield, Eris." A smug smirk lifted his lips. "You have lost."

"Make me yield, Alpha," I taunted.

His nostrils flared again, and he shifted his weight on me, tightening his hand on my throat for just a second, so the blood gathered in my cheeks. I snickered when he softened his grip.

"I said I wouldn't hurt you. Yield, so we can talk."

"Why? I forgive you."

"Because it's complicated." He paused. "Wait. What?"

"Finn already pleaded your case yesterday. It's not that complicated. You're old."

He recoiled, blinking. "That's rude. I'm not that old."

"Nearly thirty, with no mate and no Luna, and a pack this large to manage. You were trying to do the right thing by your people. I understand. I was supposed to be an Alpha myself. Duty to the pack above all else, even your own happiness."

His face flattened, and he sighed. "I was already forgiven before we did this, wasn't I?"

"Yes."

"Then why?"

"Because you lied to me—omitted the truth, anyway—and I wanted your blood for it." His brows lifted, and I whispered, "Ever do that again, and I'll kill you after I cut your balls off. That's an oath, Gideon Greenwood."

He cleared his throat with a slight shake of his head. "You're not quite right in your mind, Eris Oakenfire, you know that?"

"I know you like it," I teased, trying to lift my hips into him, where I could feel the tight bulge of his jeans. I let the bond fall open, and I was rushed by his relief and his arousal. He sucked air through his teeth, and I said, "Kiss me."

He narrowed his eyes. "You'll bite me again, I know it."

"You do sample better than expected," I admitted, smacking my lips. He tasted like he smelled. Rain and peppermint.

"I haven't heard a yield from you yet."

"And you won't ever hear it. But what if I promise to make the reward worth the risk, Alpha?"

He made a dark sound, a growl that was part man and part wolf, and looked down at my lips before taking them. His mouth closed over mine with a fierceness that I hadn't experienced yet. Something different from the first two times, mirroring the intensity of our sparring match, as if he finally realized I didn't need to be handled gently like some fragile maiden. I could feel it in the thread that tied us, and in it, his need not to just have me, but possess me. The wolf and his incontestable claim. I sucked his lower lip into my mouth, and he froze, his body tensing. I laughed low in my chest, knowing he awaited my bite. Instead, I sucked on his lip, running my tongue over the soft ridges.

He huffed, like he was trying to catch his breath, and pulled away from me. I blinked, jumping when he barked, "Leave!"

The hurried shuffling of feet reminded me there were others here. Finn whooped a cheer, and clapping started. I looked over, watching them file to the exit with haste. The group left us with the echo of their applause, punctuated by the click of the door.

I turned my attention back to Gideon and said, "So bossy, Alpha."

"Well, I am the boss."

"Are you—" I started, teasing.

"I am!" he snapped, getting close to my face and then growling in my ear. I quieted, a flush of excitement blossoming in my belly. He asked, "Do you want me to call them back? Do you want an audience? Because I don't care." With a grunt, he released the tight grip he had on my legs, only to shove them open with his knee and sink against me. I gasped, moaning at the shot of electricity that ripped through my veins when he dropped against the soft flesh between my thighs. I wrapped my legs around him, squeezing his waist and trying to relieve the tension in my lower stomach.

Gideon still had his hand on my throat, and it tightened. He turned my chin with his thumb and hissed against my ear, "I am the boss, and you are a feral, bloodthirsty, vicious, *wild* woman."

The reverent way he spoke made the words sweet like honey, and I turned, nipping his jaw hard enough to prove his point. He growled again, low in his chest, and I asked, "Are you going to tame me? Is that what you think? I am more wolf than woman most days."

"Of course not. I want you to stay wild." He leaned away, releasing the clasp of his arm on my upper body. His hands seized my wrists and lifted them above my head, one holding them there while the other dipped, his thumb tracing the line of my cheekbone. His hazel eyes were swimming, blending to wolf gold and back again. "I just want to love you. I want you to be my wild woman. *Mine.*"

My pulse fluttered. "It takes a brave man to claim a woman like me."

He kissed my cheek, just a brush of his lips, and then muttered in my ear, "I am no coward. You are mine. I claim you."

CHAPTER 16

GIDEON

OUR FEELINGS WERE LAID bare in the bond, and the raw, feral need to be together burst the dam of any resistance from either of us. I kissed her, needing her more than oxygen. Her nails dug into my wrist and hand where I secured hers above her head, but I didn't relinquish the hold, still not trusting that she wouldn't try to best me. She hadn't admitted to my victory yet.

Both of us were breathless, and I kissed her cheek down to her neck. I licked her, running my tongue from her collarbone to just under her ear. Her body quivered, and I reveled in it, my head buzzing from the taste of her, the light salt of her sweat and the sweetness of baked vanilla. I stopped at her marking spot and sucked on it. I could feel her pulse beating under my tongue and I groaned, pressing my teeth to her. The sound she made, a vulnerable little whimper, made my blood rush.

I didn't relent, sucking on the spot until she was writhing beneath me, and she gasped, "What are you waiting for? Take me. If you're going to insist on holding my wrists, then rip these clothes off and have me!"

It took profound willpower not to oblige, and she was fighting to free herself from my grasp.

My voice was rougher than I expected when I got in her face and answered, "Then fucking yield, and admit you're mine! I want to hear you say it."

She stared up at me, her amber eyes swirling with the brighter yellow of her wolf. Surprised by my aggression, I considered an apology, only to feel a fresh pulse of her desire in the bond. Naughty girl.

I don't know why I expected her to oblige so easily. She asked, "Why do you want to hear it?"

I frowned, unsure exactly why. I did want to leave her wild, but part of me wanted just a taste of her submission. "Why are you so stubborn?"

"Because it's so fun."

"You will say it. You will say you're mine."

"I will? Why is that?"

"Because I won't fuck you until you do." Her eyes widened, and I chuckled, going back to torturing her neck with my kiss. Against her hot skin, I declared, "I can play your wicked game. I know you want me to give you that relief again, that only I have ever given you. I can smell how slick you are for me." I didn't even need the pulsing bond to know she liked it, the things I said. Her breathing hitched, and her back arched into me, begging for the friction. I reached between us and cupped her, providing pressure with my palm that made her whimper. "You want me to slide my hard cock into your tight, quivering sheath and take your maidenhood and make you moan and make you mine, don't you?"

"Gods, yes, I need it," she gasped, writhing under my hand. I was sure she'd drawn blood with her grip on my wrist, but it only heightened the high.

My willpower was fraying, so I relented. "Then I'll be generous. You don't even have to yield. Just admit you're mine. Declare it to me and I'll make it so."

Eris giggled, her body rolling with light, feminine laughter. I stopped my assault at her neck, huffing a growl before I was in her face again, studying her to discover what she found so funny. Her cheeks were flushed, and her pupils were so dilated they nearly took the entirety of her irises.

She leaned up as much as she could and nipped at my chin. "If you want to pull words of submission from my lips, Alpha, you'll have to earn them."

I narrowed my eyes and sat back abruptly, earning a gasp, at least, when I released her wrists and ripped her shirt up, catching her sports bra with my thumbs. Her breasts sprang free, the peachy-pink tips already at attention. I cupped them in my hands, a deep moan in my chest, and gave a firm squeeze before I dropped my head, taking one of her nipples into the heat of my mouth.

Her hands slapped the mat beneath us, and her hips lifted against me. When I increased the pressure, she cried, "Oh, gods!" and I sucked harder still, pulling a sharp moan from her.

"I'll do more than earn the words. I'll make you scream them," I rasped. "The entire pack house will hear you."

I took my time, letting my tongue roam her breasts and stomach, kissing and sucking and licking until she panted my name, her entire body quivering beneath me. My lips stopped in the center of her chest, and I gripped the waist of her spandex, reminding myself to only take her with my mouth when they came off. I would loiter there between her legs, bringing her to climax after climax until she said the words. I didn't care if it took all night.

A throat-clearing sound felt like a slap, my ears telling me it came from my left and not from Eris. My eyes flew open, blinking away the haze of desire, only to be replaced by the red curtain of rage. Ivailo rushed to be let out, furious at the intrusion, and I threw my body over Eris to conceal her nudity. It certainly wasn't uncommon to be nude as a shifter in front of others, but this was intimacy, and she hadn't consented to be.

"I am going to tear you to pieces!" I snarled, feeling my face perform a partial shift, and I looked over to see who was going to die.

A stern woman in her usual black robe was unperturbed, her answer steady. "That would be very ill-mannered, considering you've summoned us here, Alpha." It was the witch I'd asked Finn to contact, and with her was her wife.

"Ill-mannered?" I snapped, ready to rage at them until they left.

"River, is that you?" Eris asked beneath me, pushing on my chest to give her room.

"It is. Hello again, Eris. How are you?"

"I'm... well, I'm well," she stuttered, and to my dismay, pulled her shirt down.

"I can see that, and I am happy for you," River said, and I thought I detected a slight smirk on her stony face. "However, I need to speak to you and Enid. It's important."

An icy fear gripped the bond, sprouting from Eris's side. She sat up, trying to wiggle away, and I grabbed her arm. "Nuh-uh."

I glared at the witches. "We need a minute." Glancing down at Eris, I corrected myself. "We need an hour."

River clasped her hands at her waist. "I do not have an hour. I do not have a minute. Like I said, it is of utmost importance I speak to Eris and, more particularly, Enid. It is of *dire* importance."

Eris slid away from me, offering a sympathetic smile.

"Eris," I pleaded, grabbing her hand even though I knew I wasn't getting my way.

She leaned forward and pressed her lips to mine. "We will finish this as soon as possible, I promise. Enid and I may finally get some answers." Her hand slipped from mine, and she ducked under the ropes, hurrying to meet the witches.

"I may die first," I muttered under my breath, leaning back to sit on my feet and drawing a deep, purposeful inhale to calm myself. I climbed out of the ring, snatching up my shirt and pulling it on as I trailed them, my wolf grumbling his displeasure the entire way.

CHAPTER 17

ERIS

G IDEON WAS HORRIFIED AT being interrupted. I was too, honestly, but I was too overwhelmed with curiosity and concern for Enid. River, Rhia, and I were walking at a brisk pace, but Gideon still caught up to us, and he took my hand, lacing our fingers. We rode in the elevator and stopped on the office floor, not going to his office like I expected, but to a door at the end of the hall. It was a windowed room with a large oak table and several seats. Thad, Finn, Enid, and Hades were all present, as well as two other shifters who I assumed were the ones investigating the death of my pack.

Gideon went to the open chair at the head of the table and said a curt, "Move, please," to the wolf in the chair to his right. The man didn't argue, standing and moving down next to Thad while Gideon offered me the now open chair.

I went to take it, leaning into him and whispering so only he could hear, "And here I was, willing to sit in your lap."

His brows lifted, and his lips twitched, but he muttered back, "I honestly don't think I could handle that at this moment."

I cleared my throat to hide a snicker while he took his chair. His heel hooked the leg of my seat, pulling me closer until his hand rested on my bare thigh.

River and Rhia had taken their seats, and River said, "You've done the right thing by asking for our aid in this matter, Alpha."

She always did the talking. Her wife, Rhia, was reserved. She was always observing, always watching. They were both beautiful and looked to be in their late twenties, but I knew it was impossible to tell a witch's age. I assumed they were a lot older just by the way they carried themselves. River was a sharp-featured woman with platinum blonde hair. Her makeup was always applied to perfection. Black eyeshadow, dramatic eyeliner, and black lipstick were all flawless while Rhia went without makeup. Her smooth ebony skin didn't need it. Her hair was left free to its natural curl and held back from her face by a thick purple headband. They were opposites and complemented each other perfectly.

I'd only ever seen them wear long black robes. Rhia had a large hawk that sat on her shoulder, his beady eyes always watching everything that happened. He usually made people sidestep, giving her a wide berth, something she didn't seem to mind. Finn sat closest to the bird now and was doing a terrible job of hiding his discomfort.

River had a monarch butterfly the size of a dinner plate that followed her everywhere. Right now, it rested softly on the side of her head, looking like a giant hairpiece.

I smiled, comforted by their familiarity. "I'm so glad to see you again, and thank you for coming."

"How do you know each other?" Gideon asked.

"They're the only people I've spoken to in the last three years besides Enid."

His brows lifted. "That's an odd coincidence."

River chuckled, and he looked at her, but she offered no explanation.

Gideon turned to the wolf he'd booted from my current seat. "First, why don't you tell us what you've found, Lucien?"

"Based on what we saw in the wreckage and the testimony from Enid, we believe the man who did this was a dragon. In fact, there's no other explanation."

Gideon stiffened, his hand squeezing my thigh.

"How is that possible?" he asked, looking at River. "No one has seen a dragon for over two centuries."

Lucien nodded. "We know it's unbelievable, but it's the only answer we keep coming back to. Enid said this man seemed to be there for her mother, who was a special wolf. Dragons are notoriously greedy. They like to hoard things, taking anything that piques their interest, including treasures and rare items. We think he wanted to, well, collect her." He said the last part with a little disgust in his voice and my stomach lurched as well. "We can't figure out why he killed her, though."

"I don't know if he intended to that day," I said, thinking back. "She bit him, and I think he just snapped. He drank her blood, though. I was never sure why."

I hadn't ever told Enid that detail, wanting to spare her, and I looked at her apologetically. She smiled gently at me, understanding, of course, because that's what she always did. Lucien's eyebrows shot up, but he didn't offer an answer.

"Many creatures, including dragons, enjoy bloodletting. It provides a euphoric high. Better blood provides better results," River said. "He wouldn't have wasted something so unique."

"Will he come for Eris or Enid?" Finn asked. "They're of the ancient bloodline as well."

River nodded. "Most definitely. We understand Eris must be a special witch called The Mother's Maiden. A name given to the one true healer that is gifted by the Goddess Hecate at rare and crucial times in history. If the dragons are returning, it makes sense that she would send her Maiden to us now."

An intense rush of anxious rage passed through the bond, and I wasn't sure if Gideon realized how tightly he held my leg.

River went on, placing her hand on Enid's. "As rare and incredible as Eris is, Enid is the absolute. She is the Pythonissum Viridi. The Green Witch. Only told of in the most ancient books. She is said to be sent by the Mother at the end of times to stop the destruction of all light in the world. Signified by iridescent green eyes, she possesses the ability to master and control all four earthly elements: earth, fire, water, and air. As you know, most witches can possess only one element in a lifetime. I am an earth witch, and Rhia is an air witch. Witches also mature to power much earlier than wolves, at fifteen. I assume you've come into your first element, Enid?"

"The plants," I said, looking at my sister and thinking of our garden at the cabin. "That's why you can manipulate the plants."

River nodded, continuing, "Earth is the first element, then. It's only a matter of time before the others manifest in her as well. This also explains her fever seizures. She needs to use her powers to relieve the magical proliferation inside her. To possess all the elements in one vessel is extremely strenuous. That's why, to aid her in her trials, she was sent a powerful familiar to help guide her path and protect her." River reached over and scratched Hades' head. I expected his normal aggressive reaction, but my mouth fell ajar when he leaned into the touch, purring.

"How can you be sure?" I demanded. "That she is this Green Witch."

"I suspected it by reading Beta Finn's message. A child with eyes of neon green and," she looked at Finn, "an absolutely wicked aura. Sitting in this room with her was all the confirmation I needed."

A heavy silence fell over the group. I was trying to gather my unruly thoughts. My delicate baby sister, who likes puzzles and gardening, possessed unimaginable power and was expected to stop the apocalypse.

Gideon broke the quiet. "How do we keep them safe? That's all that matters to me."

River tilted her head. "The easiest way for now is to find and dispose of this dragon. He will not be easy to kill. He has to be stabbed through the heart with a special sword. The witches who made it called it Dragonsbane. When it fell into human hands, they renamed it Excalibur. But it has been lost to history, unfortunately."

Finn arched an eyebrow. "Excalibur? Like King Arthur and the Knights of the Round Table?"

"Precisely, Beta," River said, inclining her head.

Finn scrubbed his hand down his face. "Well, that's a new one. Can't you just make another?"

River shook her head. "No one alive knows how Dragonsbane was created, so it cannot be replicated. It has been decided that I will stay with Enid and guide her on her path. Rhia will go out and locate the sword."

I was more worried about the task laid before Enid. "And if we kill him, what about the end of days? When and how will that happen?"

She frowned, and her lip curled in disgust. "I'm not sure. Vampires are allied with the dragon. No surprise considering they're both vile; leeches love mud. The bloodsuckers could be our first piece of the puzzle."

My heart sank. "So, we know nothing."

"That's not true. We know where to start," she said, and laced her fingers on the table.

The silence thickened the air in the room, everyone staring at each other.

Gideon asked, "Anything else?"

River shook her head. "Not right now, Alpha."

"You'll let me know if I can help in locating the sword, or with anything else?"

"Of course. Right now, I need only time with Enid."

"You're both free to stay in the pack as guests."

Gideon ended the meeting but went for a brief word with Lucien. I walked over to Enid, trying to understand how she remained so calm.

I hugged her. "How're you doing?"

She laughed into our embrace. "Better than you, as always. It gives me peace to know who and what I am."

"I imagine so. It's a lot of pressure, though, huh?"

She shrugged. "Mother always said you can't plant the field in a day. Focus on the row in front of you. I'll just take it a day at a time. With River's help, I'll figure it out."

I felt tears prick my eyes. "Well, I'm here, you know? You'll never fight alone. I know I've been distracted these last few days, but I will always be here when you need me."

"I'm happy to see you distracted, so I can actually have a little fun."

I sniffled, chuckling, but squeezed her tight. She said, "I always know where to find you, Eris. Right by my side."

Gideon's presence appeared behind me, and he added, "Don't worry. You are family now. I will use every resource I have to guide our path, Enid."

Enid smiled and squeezed my hand before sliding away to join River.

Gideon grabbed my hand. "We missed dinner, and you haven't eaten since yesterday."

My stomach rumbled, assuring me he spoke the truth.

Calli casually chimed in, *'Good idea. He's an Alpha. You need your energy for the mating. It can be very strenuous, especially if he's got stamina and a big—'*

'Thank you, Calli!' I shouted, my cheeks flaming.

I knew he could feel my embarrassment, and he asked, "What about dinner has you so mortified?"

"My wolf. She's..." I trailed off, unsure what to say.

"Looking forward to our after-dinner activities?"

"Yes."

"That makes three of us," he said, referring to himself and his wolf.

"Four of us," I admitted, grinning up at him.

His expression shifted, his eyes flashing. He motioned to the door with a tilt of his head. "Kitchen. Now. Unless you'd like to torture me longer."

"Well, I have enjoyed tying you in knots, Alpha. Maybe too much."

"I'd be lying if I said I haven't enjoyed it myself," he muttered, putting his hand on my lower back and giving me a gentle shove toward the door.

CHAPTER 18

GIDEON

I RUSHED ERIS TO the kitchen and slapped together some bread, cheese, and ham like I was going for the fastest sandwiches world record.

"This odd little thing really makes coffee?" she asked, bending and studying the machine.

"Yes, would you like some?"

Eris nodded, and I moved behind her, reaching into the cabinets above us. Unable to help myself, I molded my body against hers. She slayed me with the heated look she threw over her shoulder, pressing her hips back.

"Like this," I said, and had to clear my throat because my voice was rough.

My hands guided hers to open the filter port and pour the grounds. I had made coffee many times in my life, but I was struggling to focus, amazed at how she could make a mundane task purely erotic; at how she could change a musty old boathouse into its own piece of Elysium.

Standing there was a positive feedback loop, with every brush of her ass making me harder and more sensitive to the next moment of contact, and so on until I was straining to have her.

I pressed the start button, and the coffee pot gurgled like it was dying.

"Don't we need water to make coffee?" she asked.

Whoops.

"Yes! Water."

After I filled the tank, I picked her up, placing her on the counter. We kissed, her hands around my head and her nails digging into my scalp while I moved against her, the denim of my jeans creating friction for both of us. The scent of fresh coffee mixed with the smell of her arousal, and I knew I would never again have coffee without thinking of this moment.

"You're supposed to be eating," I mumbled into the kiss when the coffee maker beeped, breaking into the haze.

She smiled against my lips. "You're keeping my mouth busy."

I pulled myself away and retrieved the sandwiches. We ate and had our coffee in heavy silence. What we'd learned in the conference room was life altering, but we didn't talk about it. We did a lot of looking at each other, both of us grinning each time like we were teenagers, but neither of us could find a word to say that was important enough to surmount the tension in the room.

I took her hand and pulled her into me, asking, "Do you want to have a race?"

Her coy little smile appeared. "Only if you're ready to lose. *Alpha*."

"Keep talking to me like that and maybe I'll have you here on the counter."

She chuckled. "Where are we racing?"

"The pool where you tore those vamps to pieces."

I felt the sharp splash of her surprise in the bond, but she smiled. "Why there?"

"It's where I witnessed beauty for the first time."

"That's not true. You've seen a sunset, and a full moon, and a lush green spring."

"All lovely, sure, but I thought you were the Goddess herself. I'm still not convinced you aren't one."

"You like your goddesses covered in the blood of slain enemies?"

"Is that wrong, my shield maiden?"

That she could protect herself was not only a relief, but it made me want to throw her down and fuck her until we broke my bed frame.

She had her bottom lip held in her teeth, but shouted, "Go!" and *shoved* me hard enough that I stumbled and had to catch the fridge to keep from falling.

"Hey!" I turned, but she was already out the door. Gravel crunched under her feet, and I tripped to catch up, shouting, "Have you no honor, Eris Oakenfire?"

A taunting yip answered me. She was her wolf, and her clothes were in a line, spandex and tank-top and bra leading me to salvation. I didn't waste time undressing. I just shifted like she had, ripping through my clothes.

Ivailo was taking the challenge personally, and he was desperate to catch her. He did, nipping her heels just before we got to the clearing with the pool. Watching from my view inside his head, I shouted, *'Ivailo!'* when he leaped on her, causing both him and Calli to go into a tumble that ended at the edge of the water.

I didn't want the brute to harm her, but the bond thrummed with excitement, and Calli returned his aggression, growling and biting at his neck.

It was rough, but they were playing, doing their own courting. It was sweet, but I said, *'Okay, my turn, then you can have yours.'*

He growled, *'Hurry up, my Goddess. If you don't get it done this time, Calliope and I will.'*

Eris realized I was shifting back, but she didn't do the same. I ended up with a giant silver wolf in my embrace, her yellow eyes looking through me with a glazed expression, so I knew Calli was speaking with Eris. A burst of nervous energy rocked the bond when I stood, offering my hand.

ERIS

From inside Calli's head, I watched him shamelessly stand, and I received a quick education regarding the form of a naked, excited man. If I'd been in my human body, my mouth would have fallen open. My nerves fluttered. I knew that shifter bodies were crafted for their mates—so *everything* would fit—but, seeing him, I said a quick prayer to the Goddess, anyway.

'Oh, now you're a believer?' Calli asked, snickering, and trying to force the shift back. I fought her, hiding a few more seconds and searching for all of that confidence I'd had in the training room.

Gideon chuckled, retracting the hand he'd extended for me. "Suddenly shy. Really?" He turned away and waded into the pool up to his waist, keeping his back to me and saying, "I promise I won't peek."

I changed to my human form, feeling his desire pulse when he heard it. The shift had ruined my braids, so I ran my fingers through my long, wavy hair, feeling his impatience ratchet with every second that passed.

He didn't look, but he said, "Come here. Please, gods, I *need* to touch you. And I'm going to hear those words from your lips. I haven't forgotten."

Neither had I. The water was warm as I entered, an embrace on my shins and then my thighs. When I was standing behind him, I whispered, "How about I touch you?" and placed my hands on his back.

He groaned, his muscles tensing and then relaxing under my hands. I stepped closer, pushing against his back with my naked body. It was electric, those tingles of our bond dancing as I ran my hands around his body and over his chest, feeling the hair beneath my fingers and following its perfect line down to his navel.

He reached around and rested his hands on the sides of my hips. My thighs were tingling; the sensation traveling so it rested low in my stomach. This ache threatened to tear me in half, and I knew only he could mend me.

Swallowing my nerves, I dropped my hands, grabbing his cock. I was so stunned, I blurted, "It's *so* hard!" I mean, I knew it would be, but I was shocked—and how soft it was, too. How *weird*.

That broke the tension, and he barked out a laugh, turning to me, and saying, "Well, I *want* you."

We kissed, and it was the same aggression as before, an instant invasion of his tongue in my mouth. The tight string of desire in my core twisted when I felt the pressure of his erection on my stomach, and the slide of his rough hands on my body. My skin jumped at every touch, and he picked me up, setting me on the edge of a flat, cool rock so he was standing between my legs.

I gasped, my head dropping back when his mouth encased my nipple, sucking until I whimpered, and kneading my other breast in his hand.

"Are you going to make me work so hard this time? Or will you just admit it, that you're mine?"

He was kissing down my stomach, and a moan rattled through me when his thumb traveled between my legs, finding that little bud of nerves and pressing, traveling in slow circles.

My next words were breathy, riding on a shaky exhale. "I love it when you work hard."

His hand dropped lower, and I tensed when I felt his fingers at my entrance. He only ran his finger through the folds of my core. It was slick, and Gideon leaned up, kissing my neck, and asking, "Do you feel that? How wet you are?"

I nodded, resting my cheek against his temple and whispering, "Yes, I do."

"I know you're hurting for some relief. Do you want my mouth on you again?"

"Yes. *Yes*," I said, the second one with emphasis to let him know I more than wanted it.

"Then I'm going to taste you again. You're going to come, like you did in the boathouse, so you're ready for me. Then you're going to tell me who owns your heart, and I'm going to fuck you in this beautiful moonlight."

I nodded and whispered, "Yes, Alpha," my breath short.

Gideon made a sound in his chest at those two brief words, almost a laugh, and he tilted his head, his eyes sharp. The bond was heated, pulsing with desire, and I knew his control was frayed. He dropped between my legs, and his mouth was on me again. My toes curled, and I stared at the top of his head, his dark hair tickling my inner thighs. Like before, I couldn't understand what he was doing with his tongue to make me feel this way, but I flopped on my back and relaxed into the sensations, letting my voice go free to echo in the forest.

My breath caught when I felt his finger at my entrance again, but he said, "I'll be gentle. May I?"

I nodded, but realized he could not see me, and said, "I trust you."

He squeezed my thigh and said, "I savor those words."

There was pressure at my entrance, and he moaned, but I could feel he was shallow and gentle, like promised, moving his finger slowly while his mouth went back to its rhythm. I was overcome with need and curiosity. I wanted him to press more, to find out what it felt like to have him inside me, but the thread of desire was coiling, spinning and turning so I grew louder, my moans lost to the trees around us. It was happening again, that tight sensation, and then the breaking of the dam of bliss.

I was still moaning, the last waves passing, when I heard the break of the water, and his body weight pressed me into the rock. He grabbed my hand, guiding it to wrap around his shaft. This time, he moved it, showing me how to stroke him up and down.

His voice tight, he said, "Yes, yes... *fuck*. When you're ready, guide me where you need me."

I swallowed, grabbing his nape and pulling him to kiss me again. He returned the affection, but his mouth dropped open, his breath shallow and rough against my lips with each pass of my hand.

My body ached, wanting him. Needing him. My wolf was present, quiet, but offering her confidence. I knew this wouldn't be the most pleasant part for a maiden, but we could get it done and get to the better.

I wrapped my legs around his waist and shifted my hips, guiding him and saying, "I am yours. My mind, body, spirit, and heart. They serve no one but you and I."

Gideon groaned and lifted his head from my shoulder, lacing his hand in my hair and tugging so I opened my eyes, meeting his ardent gaze. His wolf was there, his voice raspy and guttural, when he agreed. "You are *mine*." His tone softened around the next words. "And I am yours. Let our souls never part after tonight."

His hand clamped down on my hip, and he was pressing forward. He still held my hair, and my eyes stayed open, locked with his. My breath hitched, stunned by the stretch when he pushed past my entrance. His eyes rolled back in his head while mine grew impossibly wide, and his mouth dropped open around a deep moan while my teeth gnashed together. It reached a point where I thought there was no way, but he flexed his hips, and I was so stunned by the sudden rush of pain I cried out, tightening my legs around him and bracing my hands on his stomach. I felt betrayed by that enticing, twisting desire in my core because it shattered, the sharp strikes of pain slicing it to pieces. My hand traveled up to his throat, digging my nails in until I could feel his pulse under my finger pads.

He froze, his chest heaving, and he dropped his mouth against my marking spot, kissing, and saying, "I'm sorry about that part. Are you going to rip my throat out?"

"Considering it," I gasped, still trying to reconcile his filling presence in my body.

"Well, I'm yours to command when you're ready."

We stayed like that for a few long moments, while my wolf healed the worst of it. Finally, I said, "Keep going."

He started rocking his hips, moving in centimeters while I breathed, unable to believe the pressure. The sharp pain slowly trickled away, but the stretch was too intense. There was an echo of something that told me it would get better, but I could hardly breathe.

Gideon still had his lips on my neck, and I felt the brush of his teeth. He wanted to mark me, and as was tradition, he was waiting for me to ask. The woman always asked. That was the rule. I remembered being told that the first time would be painful, but the marking was euphoria.

It was also the seal. An irreversible commitment to each other, where our souls melded into one.

He wrapped his arms around me, holding me off of the rock, and his thrusts were still slow, but deeper now. I whimpered, turning my face into him, and he answered with his lips. Intertwined intimacy, where our bodies couldn't be closer, my hand still resting on his throat.

I slid it away, lacing my fingers in his hair, and when the kiss paused, I said, "Mark me."

It was a primal request that received an equal answer. His wolf pushed forward with a growl, and he bit me, right where my shoulder meets my neck. I cried out, feeling cheated because it hurt, but it was only a heartbeat before a forest fire of pleasure burned through my veins. The coil of desire was back and then some, and he responded by picking up speed.

The blissful pressure returned, building and then exploding in a matter of seconds. I held on tight to his back, feeling like I might float away from this world as my body tightened, my core clenching around him while waves of pleasure washed over me.

"Oh, my gods!" I cried when it was ending, lost in the sea of bliss, while he licked the wound, which closed it.

"Me. Mark me. You feel too good. I want to come," he whispered, and Calli helped me find my wits, pushing forward so my teeth elongated.

I bit him on his left, the mirror spot to mine, and he moaned, saying like I did, "Oh, *gods*."

His thrusts were jerkier than they had been. When I felt a flood of heat, I realized he was coming. Filling me. My heart fluttered, and my wolf was satisfied, our happiness mixing not only with each other, but with his and Ivailo's. I'd felt nothing like it, a true peace, as if we floated together on a cloud.

I licked him, tasting the tang of his blood, and then he kissed me.

The marking sealed the bond, and his voice was in my head, repeating, *'I love you. I love you. I love you.'*

My chest was tight. I had a link with someone for the first time since losing my pack. Not just someone. My mate. My heart and soul.

'I love you,' I answered, and we kissed under the moon, having found a new reason to be alive.

CHAPTER 19

GIDEON

THIS ROCK WAS NOT the most comfortable thing to lie on, but I didn't care. If she wanted to relax on my chest for the rest of forever, then fuck my back, it would have to suffer.

I understood why my ancestors and those before me spoke so fondly of the mate bond. Talked about it. Worshiped it. Wrote about it. Sang about it. The marking and the completion of the connection were one of those things that couldn't be understood until you'd done it yourself. Poetry and stories and songs couldn't come close to putting it into words. Nothing could.

The high was wearing off, though, and my mind tracked to what we'd learned in the conference room. A dragon might want Eris. My arms tightened around her. The gods only knew what he'd do if he got his hands on her. He'd drunk her mother's blood, for fate's sake. There were worse things, too, and I stopped my mind from wandering there.

Ivailo growled. *'No one will hurt her. She's ours. We'll rip apart anyone who tries.'*

I wanted to agree with him, but for the first time in my life as an Alpha wolf, I had to face a reality where I wasn't the most powerful being in the equation. A one-on-one fight with a dragon would not end in my favor.

Ivailo whined at the thought. Historically, dragons ruled the supernatural world. They were the apex predators of our food chain. Over two centuries ago, the rest of the supernaturals united against them and put a stop to that terror. With the help of the other races, witches locked them away in warded prisons deep beneath the Earth's surface, never to be released. We needed to find out how this red-haired dragon had escaped his dungeon, and, worse, if others were free as well.

Eris shifted her weight so she could look up at me. "What's wrong?"

My anxiety had wriggled its way into the bond and ruined our peace. I tightened my grip on her again and kissed her. "I just can't ever lose you."

She sighed. "That's why I didn't want a mate. The pain of losing a loved one is just too much." I could feel her shame, and she muttered, "I treated Enid unfairly, too, keeping her locked away. I just wanted her safe."

I stroked her hair. "You were just doing the best you could, Eris."

Her guilt thickened, and she whispered, "Tell that to Enid."

"You know she's already forgiven you."

"I know, and that makes it worse."

I rubbed her arm and tried to inject confidence into my voice. "We'll figure this out."

So many details were in the hands of others. Our fates hinged on their success, and I did not like it when I didn't have control. Rhia needed to find the lost sword, and Enid had to become some kind of witch-warrior when she seemed so delicate. I couldn't picture her harming anything, or anyone.

"We will," Eris agreed. "We don't have a choice."

I nodded, and she pulled herself up to my face. No surprise, but we were kissing again, the bond pulsing with desire. I felt my body react, and I knew I would never have enough of her.

I was trying to turn her, to have her under me again with hopes this time would be pain free for her.

She sighed, stopping my movements and breaking the kiss. "As much as I want to continue, Calli is insistent that it is her turn to have control."

Ivailo perked up from his sullen mood. *'I couldn't agree more.'*

'I'm sure,' I said dryly.

He huffed. *'I have been patient with your bumbling idiocy through-out this entire ordeal.'*

'You made me walk home naked in the dark.'

'Tell me you didn't deserve it and make yourself a liar.'

I said nothing and sat up with her still in my lap. We kissed until Ivailo started howling incessantly in my head, something that gets annoying after about three seconds.

Eris laughed when I told her about his antics and shifted. Calli was a true silver wolf. Gray was a common color, but she certainly wasn't gray. Her fur had a strange blue undertone and shimmered in the moonlight. Her yellow eyes stared at me, waiting for Ivailo.

I reached up and stroked her head. She leaned into my hand, and I said, "You are the most beautiful wolf I've ever seen, Calli."

Ivailo whined impatiently in my head.

'I love you, Luna,' I told Eris, and retreated deep into my mind, allowing Ivailo to take complete control.

The wolves ran, played, killed some poor unsuspecting forest crit-ters, and, of course, mated. As the sun bloomed on the eastern horizon, they bounded home.

I showed Eris a spot in the tree line where clothes were stashed for situations like this. We shifted to our human forms. She wasn't shy about her nakedness anymore, and I growled, picking her up and pushing her against a tree. Now that I had her, I wasn't sure how I was going to get anything done ever again.

ERIS

Maybe Gideon was an exhibitionist; our first day in the boathouse, the warm pool last night, and now sex against a tree when the pack house was only a hundred feet away. I'd had to cover my mouth to keep from being too loud. The pain was only an echo, replaced by the sensation of fullness, and I thoroughly understood the hype of physical intimacy.

He placed me back on my feet, and, still breathless, I asked, "Should I even put clothes on?"

He chuckled, kissing the top of my head. "Luna, if you don't put clothes on, our pack will fall into ruin because we'll get nothing else done."

There were only gym shorts and white t-shirts in the bag, so we both wore the same thing as we walked into the pack house holding hands. We passed several others on our way up to the room, and they all greeted us as Alpha and Luna. Some were professional, but some grinned at our appearance and gave us the, *I know what you did last night*, look. Neither of us cared. I was proud to be marked by my mate, and so was Gideon.

We got back to his room and collapsed on the bed together.

Around a yawn, I mumbled, "I need a shower."

He shook his head and pulled me into him. "Sleep first."

For the first time in a long time, no yellow eyes waited for me on the other side of my closed lids.

CHAPTER 20

GIDEON

I WOKE IN A panic when I didn't feel Eris in my arms but calmed when I heard the toilet flush. The shower turned on and I grinned, tossing the duvet and practically tripping over myself to get to the bathroom.

Her silhouetted figure behind the glass was enough to make me hard, so I stepped in, pulling her to me and pressing my desire into her lower back. She let out what sounded like a combination of a laugh and a moan and leaned her head back on my shoulder, giving me a perfect view of my mark on her neck. A surge of pride shot through me, and I sucked on it, eliciting another moan.

"Gods, that is beautiful," I said, kissing it. "You are." She shook her and chuckled, so I asked, "You're not tiring of me yet, are you, Luna?"

She smiled. "Never, Alpha."

"Then I'll have you in this shower now."

She chuckled, lacing her arms around my neck. "The first of many times, I'm sure."

"We'll be just in time for dinner. I cannot wait to show you off, Luna. To the pack. To the other Alphas when it's time. It's not been fun being the only one unmated."

"I'm sorry I was hiding in the woods like Jane of the Jungle."

"It's okay, wild woman. Fate turns how it does for a reason. Now may they all rot in their jealousy because I may have waited the longest, but the Goddess gifted me the most beautiful mate. My golden Luna."

ERIS

Last night while we were out, someone had brought all of my new clothes and organized them into what was now our shared closet. I wasn't used to having so many choices, and it took me a ridiculously long time to choose dark blue jeans and a simple lavender shirt for dinner.

Gideon wore a white shirt and black jeans, pushing his hair back while he watched me finish the bottom of my braid. It was odd, like we already had some kind of routine together. The bond was intense, and I felt I'd known him my entire life.

A memory, so lost and fuzzy it was barely there, surfaced and I smiled into the mirror.

"I watched you once, Gideon Greenwood. You were fighting in the tournament when I was a young girl... at Obsidian Moon, I think."

The tournament was a yearly competition held in July to celebrate the Union of the Packs. It was for high school aged youth, and everyone was invited. I'd won one year. The year my pack died.

His brows lifted. "You did? My gods, please tell me it was a year I won."

"You didn't win every year?" I asked, teasing him.

He sucked air through his teeth. "I wish I could really impress you and say yes. I can't think of anyone who won every year. That would be truly impressive."

"I see. I do remember your form needing some work," I deadpanned, and he stopped tying his shoe to look at me.

"Excuse me?"

"A little sloppy," I said, shrugging.

He shot to his feet and grabbed my waist, tickling me. I squealed at the unfamiliar sensation.

"Stop it! I'm kidding! I hardly remember it at all!"

"You're going to give me a complex!"

We were still laughing in the hall and then kissing in the elevator. I was unsure if we'd ever fall from this cloud we were floating on together.

We approached the dining room doors and Leo stepped out, walking towards us. At sixteen years old, I could tell he was going to be bigger and taller than either of his brothers. Gideon had mentioned he didn't like to train as much as he and Finn and I could see that he was huskier than them, lacking the cut definition most shifter warriors have.

His hair was the same strawberry hue as his mother's, and he let it grow out longer than either of his brothers. He had the same nervous habit as Gideon and pushed it back out of his face as he approached us. Like the first day we met, he wore all black.

His hooded sweatshirt had the logo of something called *Slipknot* and I had the feeling it had nothing to do with an actual knot. The black jeans he wore were so ripped I wondered if he'd been attacked by another wolf, and he slid what I now knew to be a cellphone into the front pocket after fiddling with it. He pulled white things out of his ears and stopped in front of us.

"Are you having dinner?" Gideon asked, obviously surprised to see him.

"Uh, yeah. I just got done actually. Everyone else is still in there, though. I was just heading back up." He stopped and chewed at the ring adorning his bottom right lip. A nervous tick. To my surprise, his light blue eyes turned to me. "Luna Eris?"

I glanced at Gideon and then smiled. "Yes, Leo?"

Surprising me even more, he enveloped me in a tight hug, dwarfing me. I felt him sniffle into my hair. "Thank you for saving my mom."

Tears pricked my eyes, and I squeezed him back. He broke the hug and shoved the heel of his hand up his cheek to catch an escaped tear. Then he glanced at his brother.

"It was my honor to help your mother," I said, taking his hand and squeezing it.

He nodded and his mouth lifted on one side in an almost smile.

"Well, uh, have a nice dinner," he said, squeezing by us and popping the white things back into his ears.

Gideon snaked his hand around my waist, and I looked at him. His face was calm, but I could feel the wave of emotion through the bond. Love and pride.

He grinned at me. "You're a miracle worker. A hug and an almost smile from Leo are probably greater feats than healing Mom."

I shook my head. "He's very sweet. But what are those white things in his ears?"

His brows lifted. "Earbuds. Like little speakers. He's listening to music with them."

"Wow," I said, the word drawn out. "I'd like to try that!"

His grin widened, and he chuckled. "You will. I promise."

In the dining room, I was pleased to see Diane sitting next to Finn. Even I had to marvel over the fact that I had completely healed her. She smiled, her eyes brimming with unshed tears, as she embraced me. I was getting a lot of unexpected hugs today. Her floral perfume reminded me of my mother on a day when she might dress up, even if the scent wasn't exactly the same.

"I can't ever possibly thank you," she whispered. "It is nice to officially meet you, Luna Eris. I could not be prouder that my son was deemed worthy to be gifted such an extraordinary mate. What a blessing you are."

I blushed under her praise, shaking my head. "It was nothing, really. I am honored to have helped you."

She waved away my humility and continued, "Nonsense. It's a miracle. I had the pleasure of meeting your mother and father several times, dear. They were outstanding leaders and kind people. They would be so proud, honey, really."

That got me. I slammed my eyes shut to stop the tears from welling, and I swallowed to temper the emotion that gathered in my throat. She grabbed my hands and squeezed them while Gideon laced his arm around my waist.

When I'd collected myself, she resumed, "Now, we need to plan your Luna ceremony for as soon as possible. This pack has been without for far too long. If it's okay with you, I'd like to organize it. Henry's mother did the same for me when she handed down the title. As I've heard, you also have a lot going on otherwise."

"I would be honored for you to plan the ceremony. Relieved, really. I wouldn't know what to do, anyway. I've never planned a party," I said, sniffling and shrugging my shoulders.

She beamed, clapping her hands. "Then excuse me. I've got a lot to do!"

Gideon interjected, feigning hurt. "Well, hello Mother, nice to see you, too."

She laughed and hugged him. "I'm sorry! I was so excited to meet Eris. I am just so happy to see you happy," she said, choking up a bit at the end. "Now if we can find mates for both your brothers, my life will be complete, and I can die happy and be with my Henry."

"Gods, Mom," Finn scolded. "We just got you back. Don't say that!"

She shrugged and said, "You'll understand someday, Finnic!"

"Mom," he groaned, drawing out the word.

"I can call you Finnic if I want. I'm your mother," she sang as she walked out of the room.

"You brought her back with plenty of spice," he said to me, and I shrugged, smiling.

River and Enid were at the end of the table. Gideon and I sat down, but Enid glanced at me, toying with Hades' ear. She was nervous about something, and she rarely got ruffled.

"What is it?" I asked, the old panic returning.

She looked at River, who gave her an encouraging nod, and then back at me. "Eris, they just started school a few weeks ago. Leo was telling me about it." She looked down at her hands, still fidgeting. "I'd really like to go."

I stiffened, and the, "No," was rushing up my throat to answer. Strangling it before it emerged, I looked at River. "Do you think it's a good idea?"

River nodded. "I don't see why not. She's a little behind because of your time in the cabin, but she's well-read, and I think she'll catch right up."

'Do you think it's safe?' I linked Gideon, and his hand found mine under the table.

'Yes. I would let her go. She should at least try to have somewhat of a normal childhood before she has to save the entire world. I can increase security at the school if it will make you feel better.'

Calli chimed in with her two cents. *'Let her go. She's only a young girl. She deserves to have some fun.'*

I painted on a smile and tried to sound upbeat even though my gut felt like a lead weight had dropped into it. "Yeah, of course you can go! Just try it and see if you like it? If you don't, you don't have to keep going, you know?"

She laughed. "I think I'll like it."

"Well. I'm just saying. Just in case you don't..." I added, and she rolled her eyes, giggling and standing to hug me.

She left, and River was behind her, but Finn said, "Before you leave, River. I have something to share." He pulled a paper out of his pocket. "I received this by messenger early this morning. It's the Fae King's daughter."

He spread it on the table. It was a missing poster.

Gideon read it and looked up at Finn. "You think the dragon took her?"

Finn shrugged. "He could've. I mean, they kept it hush-hush, but we've heard those rumors that she possesses powers unusual for a fae. That would make her desirable to a dragon, right?"

We all looked at River. Her face was drawn in a tight frown. "I would say that I don't believe in coincidences."

CHAPTER 21

ERIS

T HE NEXT FEW DAYS went by in a blur while the pack prepared for my Luna ceremony. Diane was like a tornado, planning and organizing at an unbelievable pace. Her efficiency and people skills intimidated me, and I was aware I was stepping into big shoes.

The day finally arrived, and after living in a one-room cabin for the last four years, it was still odd to be subjected to such pampering. Manicure and pedicure, followed by a full treatment at the spa and a trip to a salon. The stylist curled my long hair and secured it in a half-up twist. She decorated it with gold and diamond pins, and my makeup was done to match, complete with genuine diamonds glued next to my eyes. The look was finished as I slipped into a golden off-the-shoulder tulle gown.

They brought me to a mirror, and I gasped, staring at the unrecognizable woman looking back at me. The surrounding ladies swooned, and I flashed back to the girl wearing hand-stitched clothes who had stared at me in the mirror less than two weeks ago.

'*Our mate won't know what to do with himself,*' Calli said, her wolfish grin flashing in my mind.

My eyes pricked with tears as I wondered how this was even real, and what I had done to deserve so much.

The make-up artist nearly fainted. "Oh no, no, no, Luna. Please try your best not to cry!"

I laughed, nodding my head and looking up at the ceiling to dry the tears. Diane put one arm around me, and we faced the mirror together. She had also been made-up. Her hair was pulled in a simple updo, and she wore a golden column gown beaded with silver accents.

"I have seen no one look as beautiful as you do right now. And for one of the rare times in my life, I can say the beauty I see on the outside mirrors the beauty inside here." She indicated my heart and then squeezed my shoulders. "You are going to be an incredible Luna."

"I will always do my best. I promise," I said, both to Diane and to the woman staring back at me in the mirror.

"Oh, I have no doubts about that." She clapped her hands once and ushered the ladies over to gather my things. "It's time!"

GIDEON

I fidgeted at the door of the ballroom, adjusting the collar on my tuxedo for the twentieth time. Finn stood next to me and clapped me on the shoulder.

'Relax, Brother,' he linked me. *'It's not like you're getting married today.'*

'That will come soon enough, and it will be a glorious day.'

Mom offered to have it be our wedding as well, but Eris and I decided to have that later as a private event. The Luna ceremony was a celebration for the entire pack to welcome their new Luna. We wanted our wedding to be more intimate. Eris did, anyway, and I was happy to let her choose. I would marry her in front of everyone or no one; it didn't matter to me as long as I was married to her.

'You doubled the patrols like I asked. You told the warriors I was sorry for them having to miss the ceremony? We just can't take any chances—'

'Yes, yes, yes,' Finn interjected, sighing next to me. *'Will you relax? I've handled everything.'*

"It's not me," I said aloud, looking at him.

"What?"

"It's her. She's nervous, and now our emotions mix so much it makes me nervous."

I took a deep breath and held it, trying to release my nerves with it when I exhaled. I pushed comforting feelings toward her and checked my watch.

"That sounds awful," he said, wrinkling his nose.

I felt her small rush of excitement in return and whispered, "It's not. It's wonderful."

He nodded and forced a smile, as if he understood.

I put my hand on his shoulder. "I pray for you every day, Finn, that you'll find her. Don't give up hope just yet. You're not nearly as old as I am."

His mouth dipped at the corner. "The hope is almost worse, though, than the despair, isn't it?"

I'd noticed he'd been drinking more lately, and I opened my mouth, searching for words of comfort.

The elevator dinged, saving me from offering empty words to my brother. Leo stepped off, and like Finn, he wore a tuxedo to match mine. Black with golden embellishments, of course. Leo was my future Gamma, regardless of whether he liked it, so he was required to be up here, too. I chuckled when I noticed Mom had made him style his hair. He fidgeted in his suit, looking like he would rather be anywhere else in the world right now.

That seemed to change when Enid and Thad arrived, a small smile fighting its way onto Leo's face. We all made our way into the ballroom and up onto the stage. Enid was Eris' only living family member, and Eris had asked if Thad could stand with her on behalf of her mother. The burly man had fought hard to hold back tears at the time of her gesture, and he beamed today, his back straight and his chest forward.

'Look at him. Gods,' Finn linked, his humor floating on the words.

I knew he meant Leo, and I observed my youngest brother, his face flushing a bright red while he tried to stare at anything except Enid in her formal wear. They had an interesting relationship, where she talked endlessly to him, not noticing he could barely form a sentence in her presence. It was Finn's newest way of tormenting our poor baby brother, harassing Leo through the link anytime he had it open.

Enid maintained her usual grace, looking serene with Hades The Living Fur Stole on her shoulders. Her dress slightly offset the rest of us. It was a long-sleeved, emerald-green gown with golden embellishments.

Ivailo interjected into my thoughts, sighing dreamily. *'Our Luna has arrived.'*

He could always sense her before I could, but with my next inhale, I smelled that sweet vanilla. My heart quickened. There were nearly a thousand shifters gathered here, and I could pick her scent out as if it glowed. The large double doors opened at the other side of the room, and everyone quieted to whispers, all craning their necks to get a look at their new Luna.

She was escorted by my mother, as was tradition. Something we wouldn't be able to honor today if my incredible mate hadn't given Mom her life back.

My breath hitched seeing her in the gown, and I still thought that she must be a goddess. Her nerves were thick in the bond, but she smiled as she walked towards the stage. Her flushed cheeks only made her more beautiful, and I pressed my feelings toward her.

I was proud. Presenting yourself to a thousand people is not a simple thing to do, especially when you were living the life of a hermit in the woods a fortnight ago. She held her chin up, and her eyes focused on me.

Mom offered me Eris's hand, and I kissed my mother's cheek. I couldn't help but to lean over and kiss Eris on her cheek, too. I was struck by the moment. The years of waiting to find her seemed like a distant memory. It was so powerful that I had to pause and collect myself before I started my speech. We turned to everyone, and I smiled at the hundreds of beaming faces looking back at us.

I projected my voice so everyone could hear, broadcasting the message in the pack link at the same time. "My friends—my pack. As you already know, I was blessed by the Goddess to find my mate and our Luna."

Deafening cheers erupted through the ballroom, and I smiled broader, holding my hand up to quiet everyone. "At twenty-eight years old, I had given up hope of ever discovering her. But I can guarantee that she was well worth the wait, and she is a special and gifted wolf. A true blessing for us all!"

Cheers again, and I waited for them to calm.

"With that being said..." I turned to Eris and took her hands. "I, Gideon Greenwood, accept you, Eris Oakenfire, daughter of the Ice Moon, as my mate and Luna."

Her voice was quieter than mine, but it did not waver. "I, Eris Oakenfire, accept you, Gideon Greenwood, son of the Gold Moon, as my mate and Alpha."

Energy coursed through me as the ceremony was completed. I heard gasps from the crowd as they, too, felt Eris' powerful presence added to the pack bond. Everyone erupted into cheers, and Finn threw back his head, howling. A chorus of joyous howls answered, and before she knew what I was doing, I grabbed her and dipped her, kissing her in front of everyone.

The after-party was rowdy, as expected. There was plenty of alcohol on tap and the DJ, a high school kid with an mp3 player, was doing his job well.

"This music is so different," Eris shouted, leaning close to my ear. "There's so many sounds in the world now!"

"Yes, you wouldn't believe how many songs exist," I agreed, sure she only ever heard the small band in her pack and the traditional sounds of fae folk music in Snowwhistle. "You should give heavy metal a try. I have a feeling you'd like it."

"Metal? Why?"

"It's feral, like you," I said, winking.

She punched my shoulder, looking anything but feral in her formal wear.

We sat at the head table while pack members approached to introduce themselves and offer congratulations. Everyone was joyous, but I noticed them all giving sideways glances to Enid, who sat on Eris' right. They were wary of her, and I was sure they could feel her stifling aura.

Enid didn't seem to care and chatted animatedly with Leo, who stared at her, nodding intermittently with his mouth half-open.

'I'm going to accept Enid as a pack member,' I linked to Eris. *'They need to understand that she's one of us.'*

I felt her relief through the bond. *'I would like that very much.'*

Standing, I caught the DJ's attention. He lowered the music so I could address the room. "My friends, I have one more order of business to attend to tonight."

I gestured for Enid to stand, and she did, her smile bright. "This is Enid. She is Luna Eris's younger sister, and she is a special, powerful wolf."

The room was quiet, people observing her with pensive looks.

Unaware of the repercussions, I turned to Enid and put my hand on her shoulder. "I, Alpha Gideon Greenwood, accept you, Enid Oakenfire, as a member of the Gold Moon pack."

Power exploded into the pack bond, ripping through my body like fire. Almost everyone cried out, and many fell to their knees, grabbing their heads. I gripped the table, steadying myself, and stared at Enid. She glanced around, her brow knit and her mouth ajar in a horrified "o."

Ivailo said slowly, *'This little thing...she is more than we can comprehend.'*

Her wide eyes turned to me. "Have I harmed them, Alpha? I'm sorry."

There was stunned silence in the room as everyone recovered, staring at her.

"I don't think so, Enid. Don't be sorry. You've done nothing wrong."

The pain in my temple ebbed and a new power buzzed through our pack bond. People laughed, intoxicated by it. I sat, giggling like an idiot, and signaled the DJ to continue.

"Well, that was a humbling experience," Finn said, his eyes and smile wide. I nodded my agreement.

The party went from wild to downright crazy after that, with everyone energized like we'd been struck by a bolt of lightning. Eris and I were two of the last to retire in the early hours.

In the morning twilight, we helped each other undress, taking a lot longer than I expected because I had to pull what felt like a million tiny golden pins out of her hair. Under the covers, I held her while she drew small circles on my chest, the sparks dancing where she touched. Sleep beckoned me, and I hugged her closer.

"You shine so brightly. I cannot believe my fortune, and I am so *proud* to be your mate."

She leaned up and kissed my lips. "I love you, my Alpha. I'm the lucky one."

CHAPTER 22

ERIS

I T HAD BEEN SIX weeks since the Luna ceremony, and I was fulfilling my role. The work piled up when Diane fell ill, so I was fighting through an expansive backlog on pack member housing, event planning, and education budgets. Not to mention having to learn how to use all of this new, horrible technology. If I had to see the words "printer error" on my screen one more time, I was going to throw the blasted thing out of the window.

I dropped my pen and rubbed my eyes, grabbing the unrelated file from my desk and flipping through it for the hundredth time. It was full of missing persons' posters for the supernatural realms. I was trying to pinpoint any besides the Fae King's daughter that may have been taken by the dragon. There were hundreds of them and none of them disclosed if the person had special powers or not.

I tossed it down, sighing. Enid turned fifteen last week and I could hardly celebrate, plagued by the feeling that the older she got, the closer we were to this ultimate reckoning.

River hadn't heard from Rhia in over three weeks and, although she hid it well, I could tell she was worried. I was, too. If Rhia didn't locate Dragonsbane, we didn't have any hope of victory.

My office door opened, and Gideon stepped in, asking, "What's wrong, Luna? I can feel your worrying down the hall."

"I hate this evil machine."

He smiled, but said, "That is an awful lot of distress over a printer."

"I'm worried about Rhia. I'm worried about everything. I'm a worrier... that's what I do."

He nodded and walked around my desk, kneeling in front of my chair and placing a hand on each of my knees. I tilted my head, pretending to be unaffected when he slid them dangerously high up my thighs, parting my legs so he could rest between them.

"Well, lucky for you, Luna, I'm a fixer. I fix things."

It was true. I'd watched him these last weeks, and there was never an issue he shied away from. He believed every problem had a solution

"And when I don't have the fix just yet, I can be a great distraction," he added, kissing my neck.

"Well, let's see. I was going to go check on Ollie in the stables. Would you like to join me?"

Gideon gave me freedom on the budget to build Ollie a stable, and the gelding lived in the lap of luxury. We also bought three more horses to keep him company. My little bay had gotten his fairytale ending, too.

He arched his eyebrow at me, grinning mischievously. "The stables? A literal roll in the hay? We haven't tried there yet."

Over the last six weeks, we'd enjoyed a game of making love in as many places as possible. My office, his office, the stage in the ballroom where we stood during the Luna ceremony. Even once in the kitchen late at night. We'd nearly been caught that time.

He stood and took my hand, pulling me. "Why are you still sitting?"

We walked hand in hand towards the stables, the gravel crunching under our feet. His desire pulsed through the bond, but there was doubt nagging it.

"What's wrong?" I asked, stopping to look at him.

He sighed and ran his hand through his hair. "The Pack Conclave is scheduled for two weekends from now. I just got the notification this morning of the location."

I knitted my eyebrows together. "And?"

"It's at Ruby Moon," he said, his guilt heavy between us.

"Of course it is. Why wouldn't it be hosted by the pack where your ex-fiancé is?"

"We could opt out of this year. If you don't want to go."

"Absolutely not. The Conclave is an important event. Besides, what do I care what she thinks, or if she's there?"

"I think you'd kick her ass if she tried anything," he said.

My brows lifted, and I grinned over at him. "I think you'd like that a little too much."

His boyish smile appeared, and he pulled me into him, kissing me. We laughed, stumbling towards the stables and pulling at our clothes, when a sudden sound stopped us.

Someone was already inside. We heard muffled voices and then a guitar strummed. Gideon put a finger to his lips and cracked the door as the song picked up and a man started to sing.

We couldn't see inside, but I realized it was Leo singing, and that he was amazing. He had a beautiful, deep voice.

When he stopped, he chuckled, and I could hear his nerves hiding in the laugh.

"So yeah, that's as far as I've gotten. I mean, obviously the original isn't played on an acoustic guitar, but, you know, that's the gist of it. I've never sung in front of anyone, either, so... yeah. Sorry if it sucked."

The anxiety in his voice was painful, and I felt for him. Gideon was smiling at his brother's distress, both of us trying to stay quiet.

"What did you say the song was called? It was beautiful, Leo. You are so very talented. I would love to be able to do that."

My eyebrows shot up in surprise when I recognized my sister's voice. Gideon's head whipped over at me, his mouth in a hilarious "O," and I had to cover my mouth to keep from giggling.

Leo was mumbling now. "Uh, the song is called *Another Life*. And, well, I could teach you. I mean, I know you're really busy with learning to save the world and all that, but, uh, if you wanted, I could show you some stuff."

She exclaimed, "Okay!"

We heard feet moving, and the bang of the guitar.

Leo stuttered, "Oh. Okay. Now? You're sitting... right here... okay," as things shuffled. He cleared his throat and instructed her on the chords.

'My baby brother has more game than I expected. He would probably die if he knew we were standing here,' Gideon linked, his humor pulsing through the bond.

Not wanting to intrude any more on the private moment, I said, *'Unfortunately, my love, we'll have to find somewhere else.'*

Gideon sighed. *'Yeah, that's too bad. I guess we'll have to check the stables off the list some other time. But, there is this old watchtower in the northern woods... it's been on my mind.'*

I grinned, and we snuck away to make sure we didn't get caught eavesdropping.

CHAPTER 23

GIDEON

F INN AND I PACKED the bags into the car while Eris hugged Enid goodbye. She was worried about leaving her, but Enid insisted she would be okay. At least River was here to keep watch. I looked at Lucien, who was acting as Gamma until Leo was older.

He bowed his head. "I'll keep everything running smoothly, Alpha."

My mother was next to him, and she nodded her head in agreement. "Don't worry, Son. We've got it handled. Have fun."

"Just call me if anything happens. We can be right back over here."

We shared our northeastern border with Ruby Moon, so it wasn't a long drive. The Pack Conclave was an important yearly event where all the pack's Alphas met to discuss mergers and other important business. Everyone was invited and even the smallest packs usually showed up.

It was unfortunate, more like awkward, that Ruby Moon had been selected to host, but I wasn't worried about Eris. She'd killed three vampires by herself. I didn't think Sophia had a chance.

Finn hopped in the back, and Eris joined me in the front. I grabbed her hand, and we discussed the mergers we expected to see happen this year. She was a competent Luna, having been trained to take over the Alpha position of Ice Moon. I was proud, and I couldn't wait to present her as my mate to the other packs. I'd been the lone Alpha for too long.

We pulled up to the pack house, and I handed the keys to a valet. Another hosting shifter escorted us to a room with the other Alphas, Lunas, and Betas that had already arrived. There was always a casual mixer on Friday night so everyone could socialize before business started Saturday morning.

I searched the crowd and found my friend Rudy, short for Rudolph, a name he despised. Many of us that were now Alphas had attended the Conclave with our parents when we were children and teenagers. It was an important learning experience, and we could meet the other future Alphas. Someday, Eris and I would bring our children.

Rudy was my favorite person to see at any of these Alpha events. He was a brick of a man, much shorter than the rest of the Alphas here, but ungodly strong. He had coal black hair that held a wild curl, but he kept it cut short. Rudy found his Luna the day after his nineteenth birthday, something I had envied for years, and she was about four inches taller than him. Waif-like, but sassy to compensate.

"Rudy! Beth!" I shouted to get their attention, practically dragging Eris with me.

They turned and their faces lit up.

"Gideon!" he roared, grinning. His dark chocolate eyes creased until they almost disappeared when he smiled. We shared a rough embrace, where he slapped my back hard enough to force the air from my lungs. "This is her? Our long-lost Gold Moon Luna?"

"Yes. This is Eris. Eris, this is my best friend Rudy and his Luna, Beth."

"Best friend? That stings," Finn said next to me, and Rudy laughed, hugging him, too.

Eris smiled and held out her hand, which Rudy pushed aside before crushing her in an embrace, followed by Beth. Eris wasn't a hugger, but I felt a small burst of happiness from her.

"Oh, congratulations to you both. We just knew it would happen for you," Beth said, beaming.

Beth had flawless sable skin and eyes so dark it was hard to tell where her pupils started. She kept her hair shaved close to her head. Being the Luna of Emerald Moon, she wore dark green and had her makeup styled to match. Like Rudy, she was kind and made friends with little effort. Their mate bond was flawless, and they could make anyone feel comfortable in their presence.

"Well, if it isn't the luckiest man alive," an unfortunately familiar voice hissed behind me.

I painted on a smile, determined that nothing—and no one—would ruin this for me. In fact, I may enjoy this interaction the most.

"Lyrion, so good to see you. This is my Luna, Eris."

I knew my smile was smug, and I hoped it annoyed the Diamond Moon Alpha. His tense sneer indicated I was getting my wish.

As the world shifted into the modern age, the tiny packs like Eris's were all dying out and being forced to integrate with the larger. Two years ago, a small pack that used to divide our borders backed out of a merger with Diamond Moon. It would have brought their numbers closer to ours. They'd chosen to merge with Gold Moon, instead, and Lyrion had turned downright hateful.

The only thing he'd had to hang over my head was that he had a mate, and I didn't. Although, he'd rejected his true bond with an omega in favor of marrying a girl with alpha blood. A calculated political move so he could produce pureblood alpha children. His mate was a sweet, bubbly woman named Natasha, but I noticed that every year she seemed to withdraw further into herself. The Caine effect on women. Lyrion's father, Royce, was twice as insufferable as his son, and his browbeaten wife hardly left their pack house.

With the sneer still tight on his face, Lyrion said, "Yes, I heard. Not only do you get an alpha mate, but a healer."

His cold blue eyes were piercing as they assessed Eris. Finn and I called him Jack Frost in private because his long, straight hair was platinum blonde. Nearly white. His icy look matched his frigid personality.

Lyrion, Rudy, and I had been friends growing up, but as time went on, he became more like his predecessor. Cold and entitled. His jealousy over the success of Gold Moon had driven our friendship toward hateful acquaintances.

"We heard you healed the Luna Mother Diane. We heard you are a miracle sent by the Goddess herself!" Natasha gushed to Eris, grabbing her hand.

Lyrion growled at her under his breath, and she dropped Eris's hand, looking at the floor. Eris bristled, and I felt her anger pulse into our bond. He was a "lead by fear" Alpha, and still had the audacity to wonder why no one wanted to merge with him. Omegas weren't treated equally in Diamond Moon, an archaic bias that most of the other packs had abandoned. I could not imagine a world where my father had taught me to treat folks like Berta and Claude as lesser.

"Our wonderful mates are all blessings," I said to Natasha, not trying to hide the disdain I held for her husband's behavior.

Lyrion opened his mouth to answer, but Alpha Owen's voice boomed across the room, "Greetings to all! I am pleased to welcome everyone to the Conclave and to Ruby Moon. Let's all eat, drink, and be merry! Don't drink too much though, because we've got a lot of business to get through tomorrow and it's rough if you've got a hangover, trust me."

People chuckled, and he signaled for everyone to continue. When I turned back around, Lyrion had thankfully moved on.

Beth grabbed Eris's hand. "Come on! These things are actually fun if you can avoid the incorrigibles. I want you to meet Emma. There she is! Emma!"

Eris looked back at me and made a face while Beth dragged her towards a giggling group of Lunas.

'*Good luck,*' I linked her, smiling.

The rest of the evening was a dream. Eris was accepted and there was, luckily, no sign of Sophia.

ERIS

The summit was going well despite the tension we faced the first evening. Gideon made sure the Diamond Moon Alpha paid for it by expertly negotiating the two smallest packs in the Union into different mergers. One would join Emerald Moon, and one would join Ruby Moon.

My heart pinched as the realm moved more toward modernization. All the minor packs like mine were gone now, leaving the thirteen major packs in the Union. I doubted there would be any more mergers for a long while.

Gideon was addressing the room right now, and quickly received the positive vote he was asking for on the mergers. Lyrion wanted at least one pack for himself, and he was the only dissenter. I was glad the mergers had passed, but I felt terrible for Natasha. She was pale, staring down at her hands.

'She will pay the price for his failures today, I'm sure. Only the weakest men harm those they are tasked to protect,' Calli spat. *'Count your blessings, child. Our mate is perfect.'*

'I know,' I said, and turned my head up to watch him speak, barely hearing what he said.

He was a leader. Kind, compassionate, and determined. His attitude of no one left behind was uncommon for shifters, where the alpha mentality often led to intense selfishness.

I loved him beyond the mate bond.

When Gideon sat down, I pushed my desire to him and he arched an eyebrow, a small smile pulling up one side of his mouth.

'I wonder if Ruby Moon has any stables?' he joked, adding a husky growl.

I covered my mouth to hide a smile. *'You're still upset about that?'*

'No. Just eager to check it off the list.'

'We've got lots of time. It's not like I'm going anywhere.'

'That's true. We'll have to settle for our room this time. Those nice velvety ruby sheets.'

'I can deal with that,' I said while he ran his hand up my bare leg under my skirt, touching me.

I strangled a gasp of surprise as desire blossomed in my core, my heart fluttering. He frowned, lowering his hand to my thigh. Jealousy pulsed through our bond for the first time since our joining.

'You smell too sweet,' he said, looking around to see if any of the other men here noticed.

'Sorry, Alpha. I'll try to be a good girl.'

He squeezed my leg. *'You better be. For about two more hours,'* he said, checking the clock. *'Then I expect you to be as naughty as you'd like.'*

We made it back to the room three hours later, after having to bear some meaningless small talk. I hadn't heard a word of it, only plastered a smile on my face while we both tried to drown each other with our desire in the bond.

I was still trying to get the door closed, and he was on me, pressing my back into the wall and capturing my lips. Impatient, he extended a claw and shredded my blouse and bra with one slice before ripping at his suit jacket.

'I liked that shirt.'

'I'll buy you another one. I'll buy a hundred of them. You'll have everything you want for the rest of your life.'

"I have everything I want for the rest of my life, right here," I said aloud, jumping and wrapping my legs around his waist.

My back met those red velvet sheets, and his mouth traveled down to my breasts, taking one of my nipples into his mouth. It was a race to get his clothes off, and I yanked at his tie before starting with the buttons. He helped, peeling his shirt away. He didn't toss it like I expected, but started wrapping it around my wrists, tying them together.

We made eye contact, and he asked through our bond, *'Do you like that?'*

My thighs tightened, the desire thrumming hot between us. *'Yes, Alpha.'*

When we'd finished our second session, I rolled under him and he collapsed on top of me, his face relaxing into the crook of my neck while we caught our breath. Resting his forehead against mine, he whispered, "Goddess, help me. Every time I think this can't get better, it does."

CHAPTER 24

GIDEON

WE MADE IT TO the ballroom just in time, sitting down at a table with Finn, Rudy, and Beth. During dinner, I held a half-hearted conversation with Rudy about politics, but I spent most of the time watching her. Eris in her golden ball gown. She talked animatedly to Beth, and it was so striking to compare her to the woman I'd taken from that hut in the woods only weeks ago. She was blossoming before my eyes, and I was lucky enough to witness it.

A song that I liked started, and I stood. "Excuse me. Luna, would you like to dance?"

"Well, I can't let Romeo show me up, can I?" Rudy said, offering his hand to Beth.

I glanced back at my brother and watched him drain his champagne. He pushed away from the table and walked towards the bar. I knew how he felt. I was that guy for a long time. Eris followed my eyes.

'He'll find his mate,' she said, squeezing my hand. *'Probably sooner than we expect.'*

I smiled and wrapped my hand around her waist, swinging her slowly around the dance floor. It was another one of those moments where the world melted away and we existed as two halves of one soul. Each song seemed more romantic than the last, so we danced to several before we returned to our table.

I noticed her empty glass. "Do you want more champagne? I'm going to get another drink."

"Yes, but I need to use the restroom first."

I glanced around, finding Rudy and Beth at the dessert bar. "Do you want me to get Beth to go with you?"

Eris tilted her head, chuckling. "I think I can handle a trip to the restroom."

I kissed her on the forehead and brushed my thumb down her cheek. "I know. I love you."

She grabbed my hand and pressed her cheek into it, smiling. "I love you, too."

ERIS

I stepped out of the stall, jumping when I found Sophia leaning against the sinks waiting for me.

"It's all yours," I said, indicating the stall behind me, even though there were several empty ones available.

Her expression darkened, and she crossed her arms over her chest. "Save your flippancy, you stupid bitch."

"Excuse me," I said, and I tried to push past her to the door. There had to be another sink somewhere else to wash my hands. Sophia blocked my path and Calli came to my defense, pushing forward so we growled a warning.

'Does she really want to do this?' Calli asked, amused. *'Because if she does, I'm not opposed. We'll mop the floor with that pretty face.'*

I met Sophia's steely-gray glare and slipped the golden bracelet off of my wrist, setting it on the counter. It was Diane's, and I would be horrified to see it broken. "Are we doing this?"

She grinned, the tight smile stretching her face. "Oh, no, I'm not an idiot. He's got something for you, though!"

Sophia shoved me backwards into the arms of her waiting accomplice. I felt a sharp pain in my neck while the smell of decay filled my nostrils. Blackness clouded my vision, and Sophia's delighted sneer was the last thing I saw.

GIDEON

The bar was packed, and it took me longer than expected to get the drinks. I was surprised when I arrived back at the table and Eris wasn't there. Rudy and Beth were, and I asked them if they'd seen her.

"We haven't," Rudy said, scanning the dancefloor. "She should be easy to spot in that golden gown."

'Eris, are you still in the restroom?'

When she didn't answer, Ivailo whimpered, *'Something's wrong. The link is severed.'*

'She blocked us for some privacy in the bathroom. That's it,' I reasoned, but turned to my friends.

"Beth? Would you do me a favor and see if Eris is in the ladies' room? I can't seem to link her, and it's been a while."

"Oh, yes, of course. I hope she's not feeling sick. This champagne packs more of a punch than you think!"

Beth left the table, and I followed close on her heels, joined by Rudy. The knot in my stomach rolled in on itself as we approached the door. Beth was gone for less than ten seconds. When she returned, her face was drained of color.

"Oh Goddess, Gideon, no one is in there, but I smell..." She trailed off and looked at Rudy. When she looked back at me, her eyes were glassy. "I'm pretty sure I smell a vampire in there."

It felt like a rock hit the bottom of my stomach, and I yelled, "What?"

Rudy pulled Beth out of my way, and I threw the bathroom door open, checking every stall in a panic even though I knew she wasn't here. When I turned out of the last, I spotted the bracelet shining against the white marble counter. It was my mother's, given to her decades ago by my father, and loaned to Eris to wear this evening.

I snatched it, shouting, *'ERIS!'* into our link, but it went nowhere, lost to the blackness on the other end.

With a sharp inhale, I concluded Beth was right. The scent of rot and decay mixed with Eris's. Something was off, and I sniffed again, smelling a third scent. Flowers, sickly sweet like a funeral. I'd smelled it before. I knew who it belonged to, and I knew where she was sitting.

I pushed past Beth and Rudy back towards the party, running into the ballroom. The panic constricted my chest. I couldn't breathe. Not my Eris; not my heart. I got comfortable, and he grabbed her. I knew it, but I couldn't accept it.

Sophia was sitting at the head table next to her father. Ivailo was snarling in my head, as crazed as he'd ever been. He wanted me to shift and let him take control.

'Kill her! Rip her guts out and strangle her with them until she tells us where our mate is!'

Rudy was saying my name behind me, trying to grab my shoulder, but I ignored him. I stalked over and picked up the entire table, throwing it so it landed with an enormous clatter.

Everything in the great hall screeched to a halt. The music cut and there was silence, the entire room stopping into the echo of shattered plates.

I grabbed Sophia's shoulders. "You did this! WHERE IS SHE?"

The chandelier above us shook and the other Alphas in the room bristled, especially Owen. He growled a warning at me, and I answered in kind, sending him back into his chair.

"What is this?" he demanded, his wide eyes searching for an answer.

I gritted my teeth. "Vampires came into your pack and kidnapped my mate, and this vindictive bitch in front of me has something to do with it!"

Voices erupted behind me.

"A Luna kidnapped from the Conclave? It can't be."

"Did you hear that? Vampires have taken Luna Eris!"

"We have to find her!"

Owen stood up. "Gideon, please release my daughter. I know Sophia wouldn't do this. Eris is here somewhere. Maybe she's just lost her way or is sick outside."

I let her go, and he sighed in relief.

"Then compel her."

"What?" he asked, as if he didn't understand.

"You're her Alpha. If she has nothing to hide, then COMPEL HER TO TELL THE TRUTH!" Quieter and darker, I added, "Right now, or I'll tear her to pieces to find it, and there's nothing you or anyone else will do to stop me."

He nodded and leveled his gaze at his daughter, commanding her with his Alpha tone, "Tell us if you were involved in the kidnapping of Luna Eris."

She squirmed in her chair, fighting the command, but no pack member could resist such an order from their Alpha.

"Yes," she hissed through gritted teeth.

Owen gasped. "What have you done, you foolish girl?"

She smirked at me, enjoying herself. "Some guy contacted me and asked me if I wanted my revenge on Alpha Gideon for how he treated me. I, of course, said yes." Ivailo clawed at my mind, desperate to get out. I tried taking steadying breaths while she continued, "He said all I had to do was help get someone through the pack's defenses and signal them when she went somewhere alone."

"My gods, girl, *why?* We talked about this, and you said you understood! It's his mate, for fate's sake!" Owen said, and his wife sobbed next to him, starting a prayer to the Moon Goddess for Eris's safe return.

Sophia sneered at me. "No one does what you did to me and gets away with it."

My blood flared to boiling, and I started to shift. Ivailo was going to tear her limb from limb, and I didn't think I could stop him. I didn't think I wanted to.

The Luna of Ruby Moon, Emma, threw herself over Sophia. "Please, Alpha! Spare her! She's our only pup!"

The ballroom doors banged open, saving Sophia's life.

Finn shouted, "Gideon! They've got their scent, headed southwest into the forest!"

I shifted, running after my brother and tracking her scent.

Ivailo lost her in a clearing. From the broken trees, it was obvious something big had landed here. Big like a dragon. Ivailo kept sniffing, running around in a panic, only to find the overwhelming odor of cinders.

An older Alpha named Brutus had joined as his wolf, and he shifted back, turning to me. From the look on his face, I knew the news would not be good. "We can't find the scent past here. She's gone, Gideon. I'm sorry."

Ivailo searched for anything and whined when he couldn't pick up a scent. There wasn't one on the ground, and we couldn't follow them in the air. Throwing back his head, he howled. It was a low, woeful sound, begging the Goddess to bring back our mate. He forced the shift back to my human form, and I fell to my knees at the spot where her scent disappeared and stared at my hands. Just minutes ago, these hands held her. I could still taste her on my lips.

Questions whirled in my head.

How could I have been such a fool?

Would I see her again?

What would he do to her?

The possible answers to the last question sent me over the edge. Despair cracked my chest, letting my shocked heart bleed free. I stood, grabbing the nearest tree and ripping it from the ground, then throwing it as far as I could. I did the same to several others, trashing the small clearing.

When there weren't any trees left to destroy, I bellowed, "This *can't* be!" to no one in particular.

By this time, a crowd of Alphas stood behind me, watching me slump to my knees. They stared at me, their faces a blur of pity. Even Lyrion looked upset, his mouth pulled in a tight frown.

He glared at Alpha Owen, and his venomous tongue snapped like a viper. "Your daughter should be executed! Now! Facilitating the kidnap of a Luna? Allowing vampires into the conclave? It's treason!"

"Please," Owen begged. "She's my only pup."

"That means nothing!" an Alpha named Amos yelled. "She's guilty. We all heard her!"

Owen growled, and the tension in the clearing escalated toward violence.

"Enough!" Brutus quieted the crowd. "Right now, we need to focus on helping Alpha Gideon find his mate. I'll take the girl back to my pack and lock her in my dungeon until her fate is decided. Everyone else returns home and searches their pack lands, every inch of them. Look for vampires. Try to capture them alive and question them. Just look for anything suspicious at all."

"Question them about a dragon," Finn added, and there were gasps. We hadn't shared the information with the other packs yet.

"A dragon?" Brutus asked. "Impossible. There's been no dragons for centuries."

Finn shook his head. "I wish it was, but we've heard rumors there's a dragon in the realm. The Fae King's daughter is missing as well. How do you think they took Luna Eris without leaving a trail?"

"By air," Rudy said, and he kneeled next to me, his hand on my shoulder.

"Why have you said nothing of this threat?" Lyrion demanded. "Something this monumental should've been shared with the other packs!"

"We had nothing substantial. It's just a rumor," Finn lied, protecting the truth about Enid.

Lyrion snapped, "You still should have told us! Imperialist Gold Moon hoarding everything, even vital information!"

He wanted to start a fight, but Brutus said, "A dragon, then. Let's find him and kill the bastard!"

There were grunts of agreement, and I heard several people shifting, returning to collect their Lunas. My heart cleaved because my mate was not with them where she should be.

A hand fell on my shoulder, and I said, "Finn, we should... Finn, we need to... Finn...I...can't breathe," unable to form a rational thought. I rubbed my chest, trying to draw a breath.

"We'll find her, Brother," he vowed. "We won't stop until we do."

"Aye," Rudy said. "And she's a tough cookie. That dragon doesn't know what he's in for."

CHAPTER 25

ERIS

M Y BURNING THROAT WAS the first sensation as the drug-induced sleep lifted. I tried to open my eyes, but I couldn't. They felt as if they were filled with dry cotton. My hand moved to rub at them, but a chain rattled, followed by a burning sensation around my wrist.

The pain roused me, making me gasp, and I bolted awake, my heart leaping up into my throat. I was sitting up, and I blinked, pressing my back into the wall I was propped against. It was stone, as was the floor beneath my feet.

My blood ran cold. He had me. I knew he did. The red-haired dragon. I'd been so worried he was after Enid; I didn't even consider myself. Surely, my miraculous healing of Diane had generated talk in the realm. I tried to move, stopped by the silver cuffs on my wrists, and by a chained collar around my neck. In a panic, I flailed against them. Pain seared where they dug into my skin.

"Hey, hey, girl, calm down! Don't pull on them. It just hurts like a bitch."

The voice was kind, a young woman, but I didn't recognize it, and I sniffed, trying to understand who was here. I could hardly smell anything.

'Calli! Where are we?'

I searched for my wolf, but I could barely feel her, like she was in a deep slumber.

'Calli!' I tried again, but I couldn't rouse her, and I knew I'd been drugged with wolfsbane.

The kind voice confirmed my thoughts. "You're a wolf shifter, right? He'll keep you drugged so you can't use your wolf."

I followed the sound of the voice to find a woman on my right. She sat cross-legged and watched me. Her almond-shaped, chestnut brown eyes were filled with a deep sadness, and she, too, wore chains on her neck and wrists. Without thinking, I got up and crawled to her, needing to be sure she was real.

She mirrored me, crawling to meet me in the middle. The chains stopped me before I could reach her, and hers did the same. With both of our chains fully extended, we were about three feet apart.

I looked at my fellow prisoner, searching her face. Her accent told me she was from the United States, like me. Her long ebony hair spilled around her, easily touching the floor as she sat cross-legged again. She was a living portrait, her arms and legs covered with swirling tattoos, and she wore a sheer white dress, the material so translucent I could see the outline of her nipples and the tattoos on her abdomen.

Looking down, I realized I was wearing the same thing. My stomach rolled at the thought of my clothing being changed while I was unconscious.

"Who are you?" I asked, not recognizing her from any of the missing posters. My voice croaked like a bullfrog.

"I'm Kat."

"Eris," I answered, finally catching my bearings. We were in a stone chamber. A throne room.

On my other side, another girl sat against the wall, her knees pulled up to her chest and her forehead resting on them. Her skin was ochre brown, like earthy clay, and she had a shock of purple hair plaited into several long braids. She only had one chain around her ankle, and it looked like iron instead of silver. I recognized her from the missing poster Finn showed us in the dining room weeks ago. The Fae King's daughter.

I whispered, "Aster? Your father is looking for—"

The girl's head shot up at her name, and I recoiled when I saw her face, scooting back and wincing when I pulled my chains again. Bile rose in my throat, courtesy of my churning gut. I couldn't help but raise my hand and cover my mouth. Large iron stitches had been sewn into her lips, preventing her from opening them. A single tear slid down her cheek, her eyes shining with pain.

I choked out, "Oh, my *gods*."

"Yeah," Kat said behind me. "Welcome to the freak show."

GIDEON

I stared at the ceiling, waiting for my alarm to go off. Why I set it, I didn't know. It wasn't as if I slept anymore. One week. Today marked one week since Eris was taken from me. One week of Goddess-knows-what happening to her while I searched out dead end after dead end.

None of the Alphas found anything in their pack lands. I didn't think they would. I imagined the dragon was too smart and well hidden. River and Rhia counseled that they often sought the help of dark witches, who were excellent at sneaking in the shadows. Finn had contacted the Fae King earlier in the week and he agreed to search his expansive lands as well, especially after we told him the dragon could have his daughter. It could take weeks for that search to conclude, and I couldn't wait that long.

"I'm a fixer," I whispered, remembering that day in her office. "How do I fix this?"

There was a new sense of hopelessness today. I thought I'd have her back by now. One, maybe two days, and she'd be back with me where she belonged. I turned over and grabbed her pillow, shoving my face into it. Her scent filled my nose, and fresh tears pricked my eyes. The pinch in my heart never ceased, and I had cried more in the last week than in the rest of my life combined. Not in front of the others, but in this bed where she and I had existed for that short time in bliss, I wept. The others saw only my anger.

I reached out through our bond and searched for her, but it was the same black void I had encountered since that night at the Conclave ball. I assumed she was being drugged. She wasn't dead because if she died, I would die, too, right? Could I live without her? I didn't think so, and I was still here, painfully alive, so she was alive, too. I refused to accept otherwise.

'Gideon, we need you in your office,' Finn linked.

'Why? Have you found something?'

'Rhia has returned.'

I bolted up and, still in my clothes from yesterday, took the stairs two at a time. In my office, Finn, River, and Rhia waited. Rhia looked haggard, and I knew her quest had not been easy.

A spark of hope, even if I didn't know where this dragon was. Yet. If she succeeded, I could find him, and I'd have something to kill him with.

"What is it? Did you find it?"

Rhia spoke, a rarity, and her melodic voice filled the room. "I'm sorry, Alpha. Dragonsbane was destroyed many years ago."

My heart sank, and I gripped the door frame until it splintered in my hands. Finn sighed. I had become quite destructive in the last week as my moods swung between rage and despair.

"I could only recover this piece," she finished.

My head snapped up, and I stared at her as she pulled a bundle out of her pack. She handed it to me, and I tore the velvet open, discarding it. The broken piece of sword was slightly smaller than my hand. There was a strange shimmering pattern in the metal, and it hummed with magical energy.

"You could've started with that," Finn scolded her. "The carpenters are getting a bonus this month, that's for sure."

Ignoring his budget concerns, I said, "Find me a blacksmith. The best money can buy."

CHAPTER 26

ERIS

IT HAD BEEN ABOUT a week since the Conclave. I could see the sun rise and set from the light that came in through the open windows at the top of the walls. The room we were in was massive. It had to be part of some kind of castle, built with stone blocks.

A throne sat at the head of the room, and the walls were adorned with tapestries showing a red dragon fighting a knight. Behind the throne, gold coins, chalices, and precious gems all twinkled in the morning light, a show of immense wealth.

We were on the right of the throne in a large semicircle area. Six of us altogether. Kat was a hybrid mix of a kitsune and a werewolf. When she wasn't drugged with wolfsbane and bound by silver, she could shift to either form. Kitsune were private, rare supernaturals. They preferred to live among humans, and she was from a place called Los Angeles.

Kitsune and wolf shifters were natural enemies because kitsune hated all species of canine, making her impossibly unique, like oil and water forced to exist in the same vessel. She was, to our combined knowledge, the only hybrid of her kind. The tattoos on her thighs represented her kitsune and her wolf. On her left, a white fox was surrounded by the sun. On her right, a dark-colored wolf howled at the moon.

Then there was poor Aster. She usually sat with her head resting on her knees. Her pain had to be unbearable. Kat told me she had the power to compel people to do anything she wanted, but only once. She could speak to someone and make them do anything she said, but once she did, it didn't work on that person ever again. When she'd first arrived, she'd compelled one vampire to release her, and she'd almost escaped. Her lips had been sewn shut as punishment.

To Aster's left was a sixteen-year-old boy named Darowyn. The girls all called him Daro. He was the only male in the group, and he had beautiful ebony skin, offset by white hair and eyes that were so bright blue they looked white as well. The small lump on his forehead was the only indicator of his species.

Kat confirmed he was a unicorn, the only one I had ever seen. I wasn't even sure they still existed before I met him. They were the subject of genocide at the hands of dark witches, who coveted their crystal horns, which could purify anything they touched. Everything I had ever read about unicorns made them sound proud, regal, and so-phisticated. Daro didn't quite live up to that depiction, always chatting and being silly. It was welcome, as spirits were often low among us.

The woman on his left was a harpy named Wren. Another rare supernatural that kept to themselves and lived on the outskirts of big human cities. They liked to play tricks on humans and steal food from them, which she said was their "kink."

She wasn't exactly ugly, but she wasn't beautiful. Her skin was paper white, and she had black feathers on her head instead of hair. Not surprisingly, she had bird-like qualities; a sharp, beak-like nose and piercing black eyes. On her back, she had waist-length black wings that were bound with silver wire. Harpies were normally robust creatures, but whoever bound their wings owned that strength.

She and Daro bantered a lot. Wren's humor was desert dry, and she "roasted" the unicorn, as Kat called it, every chance she got. She called him *Twilight Sparkle*, which Kat explained to me was from a human show for little girls. He gave as good as he got though, and I was learning all kinds of pop-culture references. When I got home, I would share them with Gideon. He could show me these things my new friends spoke of.

The last girl on Kat's right was a rare type of fae called a sprite. Her name was Pia, and she was the size of a small child. She told me that her season was autumn, and I believed her because if autumn were a person, it would look like her. She had short blood-red hair, honey-brown skin, and bright orange eyes that were a little unsettling at first. Most nights, if Daro begged enough, she would sing us songs in the fae language. That's what had landed her in this horrible place. The dragon had heard her singing at a creek, and driven by his insatiable lust to hoard beauty, he'd taken her.

We would all sit and watch the stars out of the high windows while she harmonized for us. Aster enjoyed this time the most, leaning her head back against the wall and letting tears slide down her cheeks. I guessed the songs meant more to her than they did to the rest of us, as she understood the words.

I hadn't even seen the dragon yet, who I now knew was named Xeron. It was strange knowing his name after all this time of him being the red-haired man. His vampires cared for us, bringing us disgusting food that I choked down, knowing I needed to keep my strength up. Poor Aster had hers blended up and given to her in a large syringe, which she had to stick in past the stitches and shoot into her mouth.

All of us, even Daro, wore the same white dress. If you could call it a dress. It was so sheer that everyone's nipples and private areas showed through. A thin piece of material ran down the front from a necklace collar, barely covering our breasts, and the ankle-length skirt was slit so far up the side that you had to be careful not to flash everyone by accident. We were not offered underwear or bras. Captivity and humiliation were the ongoing themes of our lives.

I rolled over and started my morning workout. Push-ups first.

Daro asked, "Why do you do that, Wolfie? There's literally no point. We're totally screwed."

'Well, so much for upbeat,' I said to Calli, even though I wasn't sure if she could even hear me.

"Gideon will come, and I need to be ready to fight," I told him for the thousandth time. "He will come for me, and he will save us all."

I gritted my teeth and mumbled, "And I will kill that fucking dragon. Mark my words."

Everyone sighed. The new girl who just didn't get it yet. But I knew Gideon would come for me. Even if it took a year, or five years, or ten. He would come and save me, and I was, by the Goddess, going to be ready for that day.

A cackle floated through the chamber, and it was as if the air was sucked from the room. I watched my companions shrink, all of them retreating to their walls.

"I hope Gideon comes! I'm due for some fun!"

The voice was cheery, but cold, and so horribly familiar. I'd heard it in my nightmares for years. He was finally here to see his new prize. He had come in through the doors, around an edge that we couldn't see past, and he stalked to his throne.

"So sorry to keep you waiting, pet. I was out of the country on business. Doomsday prepping, if you will." He cackled at his own joke and then sat, fixing me with the predator eyes that had haunted me every waking and sleeping hour since he stole the lives of everyone I cared for. He looked around as if no one was paying attention to him, and we all jumped when he bellowed, "Well, bring her up here and let me see her, you fiends!"

The vampires sprang into action, detaching my chains from the wall and using them to drag me to the base of the throne. They shoved me to my knees in front of him, and he yanked my hair, pulling my head up so I was looking at him. I growled, and he giggled excitedly.

"Oh, I do love a wolf, so sassy!"

I glared at him but couldn't stop my traitorous body from quaking. The hand in my hair had ripped my mother's head from her body.

"Your mother was saucy, too!" My eyes widened when he mentioned her, and he grinned a cat's smile. "Did you even know she was so special? Probably not. I bet they were waiting to have that talk with the pups." He laughed again, his cackle wild and grating. His moods snapped from one to the next, and he stuck his nose in my neck and sniffed, moaning into my hair. "I hear you're special, as well. The realm is abuzz with talk of the wolf girl that can heal with a song."

My eyes squeezed shut, and I pictured I was back at the hut with Enid, watching her click the last piece of her puzzle into place.

Xeron continued, sighing dramatically as he said, "Healing that Alpha's mama for him, how romantic. Albeit, curious. That's much different from your mother. She could compel people as long as she was touching them. Incredible. Much like our little Aster over there! Isn't that right, Aster?" When she didn't answer, obviously, he guffawed, laughing for nearly half a minute. "Oh, yeah! Our dumb mute."

"You killed my mother because she bit you. You lost a prize to satisfy your own pride!" I gritted my teeth, wincing when his hand tightened in my hair.

He frowned, his eyes flashing. "I didn't kill her because she bit me!" Leaning close enough I could smell his breath, like sweet cinder, he purred, "Sweetheart, I love a little bite, trust me." I swallowed, and he sighed. "No, really, if she hadn't been such a cunt, this would be a proper little family reunion. She'd be here. One of my keepsakes."

I tried to pull away, but his hand tightened in my hair.

"I killed your mother because she was compelling me. She was telling me to take my claw," he extended his fingernail into a long black talon and held it under my chin, "and slit my own throat." He laughed, but I refused to flinch, staring up into his dead yellow eyes. "Can you believe that? I almost did it, too. That's why I had to pop her head off like a little daisy."

He made a gesture with his thumb like you would if you popped the head off of a flower, his lips making a *pop* sound. I kept my expression neutral, not even blinking. "I didn't want her dead!" he roared in my face, rage burning in his fiery eyes. I jumped, stunned again by the sudden shift in his mood. The roar changed to a whine, him saying, "I wanted her *here*," while he indicated the semicircle where the others were chained.

Gnashing my teeth, I hissed, "I've never been so proud."

"Really?" He leaned in close to my face, his vile breath fanning my nausea. "Because that little bitch made it home with me, anyway."

His eyes floated toward the wall on his right, the one I couldn't see from where I was usually chained. I followed his gaze and choked on the bile that ripped up my throat. A white wolf's pelt hung on the wall, next to other mounts and furs. I closed my eyes to save myself.

"Don't worry! I'm not a bad guy. Daro's papa keeps her plenty of company up there!"

I opened my eyes again and saw a black stallion head with a white crystal horn and a white mane mounted next to my mother's pelt.

"Killing her was unfortunate, yes, but *her blood*," he closed his eyes and groaned, "my gods, her blood. It was finger-lickin' good. I've been chasing that high for four years."

"You're sick," I gritted through my clenched teeth, rage roiling in my gut.

Xeron grinned. His teeth were white and perfect, and they were inches from my face. "Oh, honey, you haven't seen sick yet."

He moved so fast, pressing his lips to mine. I tried to recoil, but he held my head, and I snatched his lower lip with my teeth, biting down as hard as I could. His blood gushed into my mouth. It tasted like licking a burned log, and I gagged but held on, determined to rip his entire lip off.

Xeron snarled, his right fist connecting with my jaw, and the stars flashed behind my eyelids. He punched me again, and this time I felt and heard my eye socket fracture. I yelped, falling onto my side, and he stood and kicked me three times in my gut, stealing my wind.

I gasped for air, trying to curl into a ball, but he grabbed my hair, pulling me up to his face again. His lip was already healing, but blood had gushed down his chin. "Do something like that again, you little bitch, and you'll end up like Aster!"

I spat at him, a mixture of my blood and his. "Fuck you."

He growled, throwing me nearly twenty feet with a flick of his wrist. My head bounced off the stone floor, and my ears were still ringing when he barked the order, "Twenty lashes with the silver whip, and she doesn't get food for three days."

The vampires grabbed me, setting me back up on my knees, and my head lolled back so I could see him. Xeron was grinning, but his yellow eyes blazed. "Every dog can be trained. You'll learn how to behave."

A smiling vampire unraveled a leather bullwhip with a silver tip and walked behind me. Pain seared through my back as the first blow landed. I gasped, but I clenched my teeth to strangle any further reaction. I would not cry out. Tears streamed down my face, but I closed my eyes and thought of Gideon. How he smelled. How his hands felt. Of his smile, the boyish one when he was mischievous.

When it was over, Xeron walked around behind me and ran his finger up my ruined back. I heard him pop his finger into his mouth, and then his lips smack like he was sampling wine.

"That's a delightful blend," he sneered. "Maybe even better than Mama."

I was dragged back to my spot and chained. Facing the wall, I set my forehead against the stone and tried to breathe. On top of the lashings, my jaw, eye socket, and ribs were broken. Without Calli, my wounds would take more time to heal than normal. It was quiet until Xeron's loud footfalls left the room.

Daro muttered, "Damn, Wolfie." He had a full view of my back, which I knew was a mess.

I couldn't speak, so I retreated into my mind, finding comfort in my memories. Merciful blackness took me, and it all faded away.

CHAPTER 27

GIDEON

"*WHERE IS SHE?*" I bellowed, slamming my fist down on the map on my desk and breaking the entire desk in half.

I picked up one half and turned around, throwing it through the plate-glass window. It landed three stories down on the grass with a crash.

Finn started, "We still have—"

I cut him off, not wanting any more toxic positivity spewed my way. "We have nothing!"

Finn nodded, and he and Lucien stared at the floor. We had exhausted every avenue. Every possible lead. After the pack lands and the fae kingdom were cleared, we searched the entire realm, risking life and limb to venture into the shadow kingdom where the vampires and dark elves dominated. We'd tortured vampires and turned up nothing. I had called all around the world to other supernatural realms and was most often laughed at for even suggesting a dragon existed.

We could go there. I had a plane. It would take a long time to search the entire world, but I would do it. However, I had a nagging feeling that they were close. Just within my reach if I looked in the right spot.

I sat in my chair and put my head in my hands. It had been three weeks since Eris had been taken, and every day I lost more of myself. As my control slipped through my fingers, it led to more violent outbursts. I couldn't eat or sleep. My pack members were wrought with anxiety, and Mom had to take over running things so Finn and I could focus on Eris.

"What do I do?" I asked, clearing the emotion from my throat and looking at my brother.

His appearance was as haggard as mine. I knew he'd had as little sleep as I had, and he had also led many of the searches himself.

"We just keep looking for our Luna," he answered, but he had a hopelessness in his tone that made my heart cleave. "We never stop. I can call the hangar. We can go up to Canada first."

There was a small knock on the door, and Enid stepped in. Her eyes were brimmed with red, like she'd been crying.

She eyed the broken window and sighed. "I guess there's nothing new to report today?"

I shook my head and sat back heavily in my chair, listening to it whine under my weight. New tears swam in her eyes and my heart sank. She came every day and asked, but I never had anything good to tell her. Enid turned to leave when the door burst open, and River and Rhia rushed in past her.

"Alpha! We think we've got it!" River said, more excited than I'd ever seen her, and I shot back up.

"What? What's going on?"

"We've been working on a spell. A locating spell."

My heart quickened. "What? Why didn't you tell me?"

She shrugged. "We didn't want to get your hopes up. It's a very complex spell. That's why it took us so long to finish it. We didn't know if it would work at all."

Dangerous hope bloomed in my chest. "Are you telling me you've found her?"

"Not exactly," she said. "We've tried it twice ourselves and it gives us a pretty broad area. We think we need the energy of someone closer to Eris to push the spell towards a more accurate location."

"What do you need from me? I'll do anything," I said, desperation in my voice.

"Not just you," she said. "Enid as well. We've built the spell around the four elements because Enid's affinity to them is... intense."

River walked towards the desk with her supplies before she realized it was broken in half. Frowning, she turned to a table off to the side of my office and set everything down.

They arranged various things for a few seconds. A jar of water, a candle, a jar of dirt, and a stick of incense were placed at different corners on the map. Rhia lit the candle and the incense, and River pulled a reddish-black crystal out of her pocket. It had a feather, and some hair attached to it, as well as a long leather string.

"What is it?" Enid asked. Hades was here as well, of course. He watched the witches carefully from his perch on Enid's shoulders.

"The crystal is chalcopyrite. Attached is a magpie's feather and some of Eris's hair. Root intact is best if you're doing this kind of spell."

'Well, that's not creepy at all,' Finn linked me.

So, it was a little weird. I wasn't about to ask how they got Eris's hair, and I didn't really care as long as it worked.

The witches joined hands, holding the leather string at the same time, so the crystal pointed down to the middle of a map of our realm. They looked at Enid and I expectantly, and I placed my hand on top of both of theirs. Enid rested hers on top of mine.

"Okay, Alpha and Enid," River said, her eyes drifting shut and her voice a melodic chant. "Close your eyes and bring Eris to the forefront of your mind. Clear your mind of everything else."

I almost scoffed. My mind had held nothing else for the last three weeks.

I closed my eyes and pulled forward images of Eris. The first time I saw her in the fae market, how she looked sitting at her desk in her office, her in that dress the night of her Luna celebration; her smile, her laugh, the way her lips felt when she kissed me, the way her body felt underneath mine.

As I brought forth these memories, the witches chanted.

"Earth, Fire, Water and Air
Sacred four elements, we call you here
Please, our Mother, your help we need
Use our crystal to help us see.

Lost at present, location unknown
Spin the crystal until she's shown
We seek her now; we must know fast
Find her crystal, show us at last."

The acidic scent of witch's magic filled my office, but I kept my eyes closed, happy to stay here in my memories.

After several long moments, River instructed, "Okay, Alpha and Enid, you can open your eyes but don't remove your hand. It's working!"

I opened my eyes, and my mouth dropped open. The crystal was moving on its own, swinging in rapid, perfect circles over the map. Slowly, the circles shrank, becoming more concentrated as the crystal pulled toward a specific spot. It seemed it would work, but then it got wild again, and River frowned.

"No, hold true," she begged, and my heart sank.

Hades leaped from Enid's shoulders and smacked the crystal with his paw. It righted, spinning in a perfect pattern again, the circles shrinking.

River nodded and said, "Excellent work, sir."

We all watched it spin, including the cat, and when the circles couldn't get any smaller, the crystal broke free from its leather binding. Everyone jumped in surprise, watching the crystal whirl like a spinning top in one spot until it burned a hole in the paper of the map and finally stopped, falling on its side.

River smirked. "Now, that's what I call precise."

I glared at my brother. He was staring at the map, his brows knit. "That's impossible. We searched there. *I* searched there."

The crystal showed that Eris was in the forest by her old pack, now owned by none other than, drum roll please, Gold Moon.

My anger boiled over, and I shouted, "She's been *here* all along? In our own pack lands?"

He held up his hands. "We searched that area! Twice! There must've been an oversight."

"An oversight," I hissed, and then my anger exploded. "An *oversight?* We could've found her weeks ago!"

I grabbed his shirt and growled in his face. He growled back and shoved me off of him. Finn may be Beta by title, but he was still an alpha wolf, and he was the only person in the pack who could fight me if he wanted to. He wouldn't win, but he could fight me.

His face blossomed cherry red. "Well, I'm sorry! Maybe you could act more like an Alpha and actually do something! I am organizing all the searches and taking part in them. I'm talking to the other Alphas; I'm talking to the Fae King. You're just sitting here feeling sorry for yourself and breaking all the fucking furniture!"

"You have no idea what I'm going through! You don't even have a mate!"

His brows lifted, and he recoiled as if I'd struck him. He stalked to the door and stopped, looking back. "I may not have a mate, but I'm sure working my ass off to find yours."

It was awkward in the office, guilt already clawing through my anger.

River broke the quiet. "Gamma Lucien. Was there a witch with anyone when they searched?"

He shifted on his feet, glancing at me like he might be next to set me off. "No, ma'am. There wasn't."

"As I thought, and as I told you, Alpha. Dragons and dark witches enjoy each other's company. I wouldn't be surprised if this location is heavily warded with magic based on how difficult it was to find with this spell. That's probably why Beta Finn's searches failed."

Enid interjected, "Who cares why they failed? We need to go right now and find Eris."

I nodded, but stopped, looking at her. "You're not going anywhere, Enid. We'll go find her."

I didn't even want to know what Eris would do to me if I showed up to fight a dragon and a horde of vampires with her teenaged sister.

"I need to be there," she said, crossing her arms, and she looked more like her sister at that moment than she ever had.

"You're not coming with me. It's far too dangerous. You don't have your wolf."

River took my side. "He's correct. You are too important."

Enid glared at us and opened her mouth to argue, but I cut her off using my alpha tone. "End of discussion."

Her pale face flushed bright red, and she tightened her jaw, turning on her heel and stalking out of the room. I was doing a great job of pissing everyone off today.

I turned to River. "When can we leave? I'm assuming you two are coming with us?"

"We will be ready within the hour, Alpha," she said, bowing her head.

I took my new weapon from its place on the wall. An expert fae blacksmith had crafted the broken piece of Dragonsbane into a spear-head. It was attached to a retractable handle so it could pose as a spear or a dagger based on what the person wielding it desired.

Ivailo had been silent since we lost Eris and Calli, and he finally spoke. *'Now, we go get her, and we kill every single fiend that dared lay a hand on her.'*

'Or we die trying,' I agreed, feeling his aggression flood my veins.

'I'm coming for you, my Luna.' I pushed the thought through the bond, knowing she couldn't hear it, and hoping she somehow did.

CHAPTER 28

ERIS

I WAS DREAMING AGAIN. Gideon was here with me, holding me. Rain and mint danced on the breeze while we kissed. He ran his hand down my breasts and over my stomach, breaking the kiss to look at me.

"I miss you," I said, feeling a lump rise in my throat. "I want to stay here with you. Please."

He smiled, tucking a strand of my hair behind my ear. Like he often did, he pressed his forehead to mine. "Don't worry," he whispered. "I'm coming for you, my Luna."

I bolted up, my chains rattling in the silence. That familiar despair set in when I realized what I already knew. I was still in the castle, but that dream had been too authentic. His scent still lingered in my nose, and his voice echoed in my ears. I rested my head back against the wall and blew out a puff of air, blinking the budding tears away.

"Whatever dreams you're having, send them my way," Kat joked, receiving snickers from the others.

"Yeah, Gideon must be *amazing*," Wren teased, waggling her eyebrows at me.

"He is," I said, my whisper broken, and Wren's smile fell.

"Don't tease her," Pia said, and I glanced over. Her wide, orange eyes watched me, sharp with concern. "Wolf shifters experience physical pain and weakness when they're kept from their mate for too long. Are you okay, Eris?"

I shrugged. "Are any of us?"

The effect of being away from my mate was wearing on me, making me feel weak and listless. My chest was always hollow and cold. I slept more and more because he was always there with me. Luckily for me, there was plenty of time for napping. I expected many horrors of captivity, but one surprise was how extraordinarily boring it was.

Everyone was quiet, with Wren muttering an apology that I waved away. Kat moved closer to me, and I crawled to her, sitting as close as I could. We would spend hours like this, sometimes just sitting. Other times, she'd tell me about the human world, and I'd tell her about the realm. About wolves and the pack. For someone who was half wolf herself, she knew almost nothing about us.

I watched Daro and Wren playing one of their games, probably tic-tac-toe. We didn't have writing utensils, so they'd prick their fingers and write on the stone with their blood. It drove the vampires crazy, which was moderately entertaining. They couldn't drink from us, or Xeron would kill them. The game was a little morbid, maybe, but everyone did what we had to do to stay sane.

The boredom was better than the alternative, when Xeron was here. He stopped in every once in a while to torture us, physically and emotionally. Aster, unfortunately for her, was his favorite. He'd take her away from the room for several hours, and when they returned, the light in her eyes would be ever duller.

I shouldn't have thought about him. It was like I summoned him, with the door banging open. We all stiffened, Kat and I looking at each other.

"Look what I found today," he sang, and walked to Aster, uncrumpling a paper and showing it to her.

It was another missing poster. Updated to include the information of a dragon in the realm, and an accurate sketch of his face. I knew in my heart that my sister had provided the details of his appearance. The reward for any information that saved Aster was astronomical.

The dragon leaned close to her face, and she stared forward as if she didn't see him. "Your father is smarter than I expected. He's causing problems for me, and I don't like problems."

He was smiling, but he was angry, and he started unfastening her chain from the wall. I couldn't bear to think of what she was about to endure. Again.

"Can't you choose someone else, you monster?" I hissed.

The words bubbled up my throat and spilled out before I could stop them. I didn't regret them, though, even if I knew what it might cost me. If it spared Aster one time, it was worth it.

He froze, looking over at me, and tilting his head. "What, *you*? I don't fuck dogs. Or children," he said, looking at Pia, and then curling his lip in disgust at Wren. "Or ugly scarecrows."

Turning back to Aster, he touched her cheek. She stared forward, not reacting. "Fae are the loveliest of all. The epitome of beauty and grace." He finished unlocking her chain. "I'll tell you what, dog. Princess Aster is going to have an extra special time today because you can't hold your tongue. How's that sound?"

My heart sank, and I looked at her, trying to apologize with my eyes. She just stared at the wall, her feet dragging as he pulled her by her arm to follow him out of the room. I swallowed, tears brimming in my eyes, and rested my forehead on my knees.

"It's okay, Eris," Kat said. "That was so brave."

"For sure, for sure, Wolfie," Daro added, and Pia and Wren agreed.

I muttered something, and Kat said, "What?"

My glassy eyes floated up, finding each of them, and I didn't care if the vampires heard, too.

"I said, I'm going to kill that dragon. And I'm going to make sure he suffers."

Their brows all lifted, and Daro said, "Yeah, we know. Of course you are, Wolfie."

They didn't believe me. Well, I believed me, and that's all that mattered. I wasn't going to just escape this place. I was going to make him pay.

It was hours before Xeron returned with Aster. She hugged herself, her neck bleeding where he'd bitten her. It ran down and stained her sheer white dress.

He handed her off to a vampire and said, "Take our princess to the privy and let her clean herself up. Don't touch her or I'll kill you." As an afterthought, he added, "You can have the dress, though."

The vampire grinned his toothy smile, and Aster was taken to the bathing area.

Xeron wasn't done yet. "The harpy. Bring her."

Wren tensed but steeled her jaw as she was led up to the throne area. He made her get down on all fours and kiss the floor, and then he rested his feet on her back. Her body shook, and her wings blossomed with fresh blood where the chains dug into them with his weight. I said nothing this time.

Xeron drank wine, read through some papers, and studied a map, keeping his feet on her for well over an hour while we all sat in silence. Aster was returned in a fresh dress and showered, and she lay on her side, curling into a ball and facing the stone wall.

"You all look so dour today," he said, frowning at us. "You shouldn't! Everything is going flawlessly according to plan!"

One benefit of Xeron thinking we would never be rescued was that he never shut up about his plans. He was not the only dragon to escape his prison beneath the earth, and they together were hatching a scheme to bring about some kind of apocalyptic event. He'd gone so far to tell us they needed three artifacts to complete the ritual, and he bragged they had already acquired the first one. I held my breath whenever he spoke of it, but he never mentioned Enid.

Wren was a tough cookie, and she held out until he finally removed his feet. She was returned to her spot, shaken, but unharmed.

Xerox gathered his things. "Well, I must bid you all adieu. Try not to miss me too much while I'm out."

He left, and it was like the oxygen returned to the room.

"What're you thinking about?" Kat asked as she took her usual spot next to me.

"My sister."

She smirked. "It would've been cool to have a little sister. I was the little sister, and I gotta tell you, you older sisters can be pretty bossy."

I nodded my head and sighed. "I'm sure Enid would agree."

"Really? I can't imagine *that*. You're so docile," she teased, and I smiled.

"Is that what Celia is like?"

"No, she's definitely nicer than you," she teased, and we chuckled. Kat rested her head against the wall. "No, she's, you know, perfect. Beautiful. Smart. Preppy and bubbly. We're opposites. My parents love her way more than they love me."

My brows knit, and I looked at her, trying to see if she was still joking. I couldn't always tell with Kat. She wasn't, and I said, "I'm sure that's not true, Kat."

"Oh, but it is. They are probably glad I was taken. I doubt they've even looked for me. I'm a freak. The abomination. All of that fun stuff. I bring shame to the family."

"Why do you think that?"

She shrugged. "If ignoring me was an Olympic sport, my parents would have all gold. They clothed me and made sure I had food to eat, and that's about it." She frowned. "You know, I would bet that I've shared less than a hundred authentic words with my father. I just don't exist to him."

"What is an Olympic sport? Like the Greeks?"

She glanced at me and sighed. "Sorry, I forgot that you're so sheltered, Wolfie. But, yeah, it comes from Greek culture. It's a human thing. A worldwide sporting event that tons of different countries compete in. If you win, you're, like, the best in the world."

I nodded my head. "Oh, I see."

I searched for words to comfort her, but I wasn't skilled in the art of friendship. She sighed and went on, "I didn't ask to be born, you know. To be...what I am."

She would have already mentioned it, but I clarified, "So Celia isn't a hybrid?"

Her head snapped towards me. "What? No, of course not. She's a kitsune like my parents."

"Wait, your dad isn't a wolf shifter? How did that happen?"

"Well, that would be nice to know," she muttered, and I sensed, for the first time since we'd met, she was holding something back. A truth she didn't want to speak. "But we don't talk about it. We don't talk about me."

I glanced at Aster, then looked down at my hands, playing with my cuffs. "I'm sorry, Kat."

"I got so good at being the disappointment that I strived for it. What could I do next? So, I got a tattoo. Then another. Then I became an apprentice at a tattoo shop. That's when they booted me."

"They threw you out?"

"Yeah. I was homeless for a while. Kind of drifting from couch to couch. Celia helped when she could, but she's busy with school and stuff. A friend got me a job at a club for dancing, as a waitress at first. Then I figured out I could earn more on the stage, so I did."

"Oh, dancing? That sounds fun. Like ballet?"

Kat threw back her head and cackled, so everyone looked our way. She waited until they went back to themselves before she said, "You're like a child, Eris. It's so funny. No, not ballet. Exotic dancing. I take my clothes off and grubby old men and horny frat boys pay money to watch."

"Oh... and you like that job?"

"No," she muttered, "but it got me an apartment. No more sleeping under the slide at the park. Someday, I'll be an apprentice again, then a tattoo artist. I just have to keep focused and keep working hard." I nodded, but she was picking at her cuticle, and I watched a drop of blood swell where she pulled at a piece of skin. She hissed in a sharp breath, and sucked the wounded digit into her mouth, saying around it, "Sometimes I feel like I'm spinning my wheels. Like I'm stuck. You ever felt that way?"

She looked over at me, and her eyes were glassy. I nodded again, thinking of the cabin in the woods.

Kat sighed. "It doesn't help, either, that I basically have a dissociative identity disorder with these two in my head all the time. A fox and a wolf. They hate each other, and they argue nonstop. It's so annoying. It's almost been nice being drugged with the wolfsbane. With my wolf quiet, I don't feel like such a scatterbrain all the time." She glanced over at me. "But who am I to bitch about my crappy life to someone who had it so much worse? I'm the one who should be sorry, Eris."

I shook my head hard enough to rattle my chain. She had cried for me when I told her about what Xeron had done to my pack and my parents.

"The fact that I've faced a lot of trauma doesn't detract from your pain, Kat. I am always happy to listen if you need to talk about it. You're practically the first friend I've ever had besides my sister."

A sad smile lifted her lips. "Maybe someday we'll get out of here and I can meet her."

"We *will* get out of here, Kat. Gideon will be here soon."

"Man, I bet he's hot, huh? He must be with the way you talk about him."

I smiled. "Yes. He's very hot. You'll see."

CHAPTER 29

GIDEON

WE ASSEMBLED A FEW miles away from where we thought the dragon's lair was located. Every other pack, including Diamond Moon, had sent warriors to help us.

Rudy, Lyrion, and three other Alphas stood around the table. The Fae King himself was also here, accompanied by his king's guard and his queen's guard. There weren't many of them, but they were the most elite fighters in the realm. Together, we made a small but vicious army.

"We should attack now, Alpha," the Fae King said, and shifted on his feet, impatient. His name was Alderan, but I would never call him anything but His Majesty.

He was a tall, willowy man with smooth terra-cotta skin and jet-black hair that hung to his belt line. It was stick-straight and shined brilliantly even under the cover of our tent; I had a feeling a lot of women would kill for that head of hair. He always wore a silver diadem adorned with fine jewels, and his long, pointed ears stuck out of his fine hair to frame it. The fall air was icy today, and he wore a fine fur coat embellished with the royal insignia—a mermaid. His amethyst eyes were sharp, studying me. Fae were notoriously carefree. They loved to party and have fun. He did not fit the bill, but, of course, his daughter was missing.

It was uncomfortable to tell him no, but I said, "We have to wait until the witches get back and report about this magical ward."

"We're losing daylight as we speak. It will be dusk by then."

"Exactly, Your Majesty."

He arched an eyebrow at me. "We're waiting until nightfall to attack a regiment of vampires? Surely now would be better?"

I placed my hands on the map table and nodded. "Normally I would agree, but they're probably in a structure, or possibly a cave. If we attack during the day, they will all have to stay out of the sun and inside. We'll have to fight our way in. We should have a better time if we can draw them out into the open. They won't be able to resist the prospect of fresh blood. They'll come out, and we can spread their numbers amongst our warriors, making it easier to defeat them."

"I see... You are right, Alpha. Your logic is sound. I am just eager to get started."

I nodded, understanding. "Trust me, Your Majesty, so am I."

We discussed the positions and the strengths of each group of fighters until River and Rhia arrived.

They bowed, saying, "Your Majesty. Alphas."

"Have you found them?" the King asked. "Did you see Aster?"

River shook her head. "We did not enter, but we were correct in assuming there is some kind of ward in place. It's a Ward of Confusion. Anyone who gets too close suddenly becomes confused as to why they're there. The closer one gets, the more intense the feeling, until the person turns around and leaves. Based on the complexity and power of it, we assume he must have at least one, maybe two, dark witches helping him."

"Can you remove it?" Rudy asked.

"Yes, we can take it down. However, once we do, the caster of the spell will know. We'll lose any hope of any element of surprise."

I thought for a moment. "Can you get someone through without the caster knowing? Just one person."

River considered, pursing her lips, and then nodded. "Yes, we could. There is a weak spot that we could exploit for a few seconds and allow someone to pass."

"I should go in first," I said. "I can secure Eris and Aster so they can't be used as leverage. Then River and Rhia can bring the ward down and everyone else can enter."

"Why you?" the King asked.

"Because it's my mate."

"It's my daughter."

"You need to lead your army. My brother can stand in for me."

"I don't like it," he answered, shaking his head.

"I agree. This is risky, Gideon. If the dragon finds you, he'll kill you before we can get to you," Rudy said.

"If we don't get to them before he knows we're here, he'll just use them against us."

I looked for Finn to back me up, but he wasn't here. I had tried to find him to apologize before I left the pack, but he was avoiding me.

Rudy sighed. "I don't like this plan. But I know I can't talk you out of it."

The other alphas nodded, Lyrion saying, "I agree with Alpha Gideon."

Shocker. He probably believed it was reckless and hoped I would die.

The Fae King glared at me. "I will agree to this, Alpha, but if Aster is hurt because of it, I swear you will pay."

Under his glare, I saw the fear. The worry of losing his child.

I held my hand out to him, and he took it. "I promise I will do everything I can, Your Majesty."

"Then good luck, Alpha. The fae kingdom is counting on your success."

No pressure.

Outside the tent, Finn was talking to one of our warriors. I waited for them to finish and approached.

He gave me a look, and I lamely said, "You made it."

He scoffed. "Of course I did. You may be a dick and a shitty brother, but that doesn't mean I wouldn't come to help save our Luna."

I sighed. "The mate comment was uncalled for, and it was cruel. I'm sorry. I know you've worked harder than anybody to find Eris, and I appreciate that."

He raised an eyebrow at me as if he expected more.

I cleared my throat. "Uh. You're a fine Beta, and a better brother."

His expression didn't change.

"I, uh, love you, Finn. So much."

He grinned. "Alright, calm down, you sweet, mushy wolf. I forgive you. I know you're not yourself without Eris. You're a big baby."

"You want a freebie?" I asked, indicating my arm. It was a deal we'd had when we were little. If one of us was too rough playing, the other got a free hit.

I had been kidding, so I flinched when he hauled back and hit me.

It was a stinger, and I said, "Ouch."

He snickered. "You really must be weak right now if that little love tap hurt you."

I sighed. "Well, I'm going on a suicide mission, so take care of the pack in the probable event that things go awry."

"What kind of mission?"

"Solo, behind enemy lines. Cool stuff."

"What? What about me? You can't leave me behind."

"You're running point."

"Oh. That's kind of cool, I guess."

"Kind of."

We were joking, but he sighed and shook his head. "You're sure about this, Gid?"

"I need my mate back. I'm going to get her."

"That's so romantic," he crooned, holding his hands by his cheek and batting his eyes. "But I'm not sure if it's smart."

"You'll understand someday."

He shrugged. "Yeah, maybe."

I clapped his shoulder. "Don't worry, Brother. After we find my Eris, I swear we'll throw as many parties as we need to. We'll invite every she-wolf from all nine realms until we find your mate."

He grinned, waggling his eyebrows. "Now you're speaking my language. Parties? Every she-wolf from every realm? Like, French girls, even?"

"That's right."

He rubbed his hands together, chuckling before he slapped my back and gave me a shove. "Well, good luck! I don't know why you're still standing here! Bon voyage, Alpha."

CHAPTER 30

GIDEON

RIVER, RHIA, AND I made our way through the forest as the leaves of fall fluttered around us, leaving their perches in the trees and signifying winter was on its way. I was watching their backs and checking our surroundings when I stopped, furrowing my brow. Why was I out hiking in an aspen grove? I needed to go find Eris.

I stopped. "What are we doing out here? I want to go to camp. They're waiting for me to plan the attack. I'm trying to find my Luna."

Rhia snorted a dry laugh, and River said, "Okay, we're close enough now. Alpha, put this on."

She removed an amulet from her robes and put it around my neck. The confusion disappeared, and I remembered we were out here so I could squeeze through the barrier and into the dragon's keep.

"Thanks," I said. "Now what?"

She motioned for me to follow deeper into the grove of trees. Over a crest, in a small valley ahead, I spied the top spires of an old stone castle.

"Even with the amulet, you're going to feel confused if we continue," River said. "This is the weak spot in the ward." She had her hands braced against what looked like an invisible wall. "Rhia and I will hold this spot open, and you can pass through, but you need to hurry. It's difficult to hold, and if we drop it while you're still in the magical aura, you'll be fried like a moth in a flame."

"Oh. That's comforting."

"It'll be fast, at least," Rhia added, nodding like it might assuage my anxiety.

I nodded back, giving her a thumbs up.

River asked, "Ready, Alpha?"

"Let's do this, ladies."

The witches both put their hands on the invisible barrier. Their faces pinched in concentration, and after several seconds, River gritted, "Now!"

I went to sprint, but it was like hitting a wall. I lost the ability to breathe and felt as if I was walking through molasses. Panic threatened to overtake me, but I fought through it as quickly as I could, tripping when I burst through to the other side of the invisible force. I coughed, pausing on my hands and knees to catch my breath. There was no time to waste, and I hiked the incline at a sprint. Sweat dripped down my back and face despite the chilly air. My breath emerged in puffs of steam as I reached the highest point of the hill and looked down into a large valley. A shockingly well-hidden castle rose in front of me, boasting banners with a red dragon fighting a knight.

Here it was. We'd found him. Leaning against a tree, I surveyed the castle over my shoulder and checked my beltline to ensure the spear was still secured. The heavy metal was a comfort, and I wrapped my hand around it, spying a small wooden door near the back corner of the structure.

I made my way to it without incident, and I walked into a medieval kitchen. A sour rot struck my nose, and I put the back of my fist over my mouth to quell my nausea. Jars of blood sat around on counters and shelves. Vampires. Disgusting creatures. I prayed to the Goddess that none of this blood was Eris's.

Just as I placed my hand on the knob, voices echoed from the hallway. I stepped behind the door, shifting partially for Ivailo's strength, and I waited for them. Two vampires stepped in, both men, and I grabbed the one closest to me, digging my claws under his chin and ripping his head off before he knew what was happening.

The other one hissed and backed up, running into a shelf and causing several blood jars to crash to the floor. They shattered, and the caustic iron scent filled my nose.

I grabbed him by his shirt and lifted him until he was facing me. "There is a woman shifter being held here, right?"

He nodded.

"Take me to her, or you'll look like your friend over there."

ERIS

We were watching the stars and listening to Pia sing when a vampire came in. I scrambled to my feet, not believing my traitorous eyes. Another dream, but I really thought I was awake. Gideon was with him, holding him by the shoulder. I dug my fingernails into my hand, and when I felt the pinch of pain, I knew it was real.

The two vampires guarding us jumped up, snarling. Gideon ripped the head off the one he was holding and took a fighting stance. They attacked him, but he made it look easy. Within a few seconds, they both lay dead on the floor.

"Is that really you?" I choked out, stifling a sob.

Daro stood gaping as Gideon rushed past him. "Mr. Wet Dreams is here? No way!"

"Holy shit," Kat whispered.

Gideon ran to me, saying, "It's me. I'm here. I'm sorry it took so—" He threw his arms around me, picking me up, but I yelped when he squeezed the fresh whip marks on my back.

He set to my feet and spun me on the stone, studying my back. I said, "It's okay. It'll heal. We need to go."

His voice was dark, gravelly from the influence of his wolf. "He did this to you?"

It wasn't a question, but I nodded, holding up my wrists. "Get these off. Please!"

He grabbed them and swore when the silver burned his hands. When his eyes met mine, they were filled with burning rage.

"Is there a key?" he asked, looking around.

"Not that I've seen."

"He's got them," Wren whispered. "The dragon. He keeps the keys with him."

Gideon grabbed the collar around my neck and pulled at the seam where it clicked together, ignoring the burning in his hands. Everyone held their breath. Even Aster came to life, sitting up and pulling her chain to watch, her hands clasped in front of her like she was pleading for it to break.

Daro hissed, "Hurry, Mr. Wet Dreams! Come on!"

Gideon growled with effort, his arms shaking and his face red. The collar broke, finally snapping open with a clink, and I breathed a sigh of relief.

There were whispers of cheers from the others as he moved to my wrists, but we all jumped when a familiar cackle echoed through the chamber. "How absolutely romantic! You made it farther than I thought you would, Alpha. I'll give you that."

My blood iced, and I grabbed Gideon's face, making him look into my eyes. "Run, please. Just run!" I begged, tears falling over my lashes.

He pressed his forehead to mine, bringing his hand up to cup my cheek. "You know I can't do that. I'm no coward."

CHAPTER 31

GIDEON

I HELD ERIS, BREATHING in her scent and trying to calm my erratic heart.

"You don't understand. Don't. Don't!" she said, squeezing my wrists. "He's too strong. Run."

I lowered my voice as much as I could. "Finn is coming. I'm not leaving you."

"Don't you dare die!" she hissed.

I kissed her and turned, finally coming face-to-face with the monster. He stood in the middle of the throne room, arms out to me in a welcoming gesture.

'Oh... shit,' I said to my wolf, but he was so furious he didn't answer with words, only growls.

He was the biggest man I'd ever seen, several inches taller than me and probably two hundred pounds heavier. An absolute beast.

Ivailo snarled. *'Let me out!'*

At least he was feeling confident.

I linked Finn. *'What's the status? I've been caught and now I'm facing the dragon. I could probably use some backup. We're in a large throne room on the east side of the castle.'*

'The witches just brought the barrier down about thirty seconds ago. We're advancing now. We'll hurry as fast as we can. Just don't die.'

'Easier said than done.'

A deep horn sounded somewhere in the castle, alerting the vampires to the arrival of our armies.

The dragon arched his eyebrow at me. "You brought help. That's good. It's hard to find enough blood to feed these fucking ticks in my employment. It's nice to have dinner delivered."

'Let me out!' Ivailo howled.

'No offense, but my spear work is better than yours.'

He growled at me, but quieted. My hand rested on the spear at my belt. It was the only way.

The dragon hadn't moved, content to wait until I made the first move. I advanced until I was close, then circled him, trying to find any weaknesses. To my surprise, he let me. Not even turning when I was at his back.

"Looking for my weakness, Alpha?" he asked, chuckling. "I'll tell you. I don't have one."

His confidence was alarming, but I had to keep him busy until everyone else got here. If we all attacked together, I would go for the heart.

I lunged at his back, but he turned with a speed like I'd never seen before, easily blocking my blow. His right fist flew towards my cheek, and I leaned back, narrowly avoiding it and countering with a quick uppercut. I caught his jaw and then rolled away before he could get his hands on me. That was the worst-case scenario. He laughed while I shuffled back into a defensive position. With a sly grin on his face, he reached up and felt the trickle of blood dripping from the corner of his mouth.

"That was good. Caught me off guard. I'll admit it." He turned to Eris. "He's a good one! Strong. I should keep him, too. Then you can give me a pup that's even more powerful than its mother! I'm sure wolves are easier to train from infancy."

I clenched my teeth, aware that he was trying to goad me into making a mistake. I attacked again, and we became a blur of fists as we exchanged blows. No matter how hard I tried, or how well I executed my moves, I couldn't land another punch or kick. He laughed while delivering a harsh elbow to my ribs and a punch to my nose. We pushed apart again while I was holding onto his shirt, and it ripped off. His chest glowed. A small orange light on his left side showed me exactly where his heart must be.

Breathing hard, I wiped the blood from my face. *'Finn, I don't mean to pressure you, but I'm getting my ass kicked in here.'*

'Oh, sorry. There's just... an entire army... of vampires out here!'

He was strained, and I knew he was fighting, so I left him alone.

"You lied," I said, trying to buy time. "That looks like a weakness to me."

The dragon looked down at his chest. "Maybe it once was, but we took care of the problem."

I lunged again, executing one of my favorite moves in a hurry. He was giggling like a child, blocking the blows. I saw the opening and grabbed my spear, still in dagger form, and shoved it towards the glowing orange spot on his chest. I had it. The execution was perfect. My eyes widened when he grabbed the blade, stopping it. No one could be that fast. The tip pierced his chest skin, and he cried out, shoving me away.

"Dragonsbane?"

Showcasing his actual speed, he was suddenly in front of me, and picked me up, throwing me across the room. My wrist cracked against the stone, and the dagger flew from my hand. It skittered to a stop in the middle of the semicircle of kidnapped supernaturals.

"I am done playing with you, dog!" he snarled, stalking across the room.

I backed off, switching to a defensive strategy and focusing more on keeping away from his grasp than engaging him. He would kill me if he got his hands on me again.

Eris and the other captors were silent, watching with wide eyes. I needed to get back to the spear, but he blocked me every time. Once, I thought I might get it, but he picked up a raw emerald the size of a washing machine and threw it to impede me. I ducked it, and the massive gemstone went into the wall behind me, nearly crushing the black-haired girl chained next to Eris.

He was breathing hard, and roared, "Enough!" walking to Eris.

He stepped over Dragonsbane and grabbed her by her throat, slamming her into the wall. A spiderweb of cracks splintered the stone around her, and my vision blackened as I shifted, bounding towards them in a blind rage.

When I leaped at him, he turned and grabbed me by my throat.

"Love is the stupidest emotion," he sneered, and I knew I was going to die.

ERIS

My heart stopped when Xeron grabbed Gideon's wolf by the throat. The ringing in my ears was so loud, I didn't even hear what the dragon said before he lifted Ivailo over his head with both hands and bent him until I heard a sickly crack.

I clawed at the dragon's back, screaming, "No! No!" until my throat seared with pain.

He hurled Ivailo across the giant throne room, and I wailed when the black wolf was impaled on the sword of the knight's statue. He shifted to his human form and slid off the sword, landing with a sickening thump on the stone floor. I could see his chest still moving. He was alive. Barely.

Xeron turned to me, grinning. "Now you watch your mate die. Finally, I will break your spirit."

"No, no, please," I begged, sobbing. "I'll do anything. Anything you ask!"

I clung to the dragon, trying to hold him back. He flung me off, my back slamming into the hard stone. He sauntered towards Gideon, laughing.

"No! I'll kill you! I'll kill you!" I cried, pulling at the chains until they cut into my bone. The threats turned wordless, just wails that ripped from the bottom of my gut.

'Goddess! I pray! Give me a miracle!'

Xeron was about to stomp on Gideon when the doors flew open. The sound of the battle outside grew louder and a large brown wolf bounded in.

"Thad! Thad! Help him!" I screamed, my voice breaking.

Next to him entered a tall, beautiful fae man. Blood from the battle smeared his face, and he carried a heavy two-handed sword topped with a shining opal. Aster jumped to her feet, a muffled scream trying to escape her lips. The man looked at her, and his face paled, then eclipsed, becoming a shadow of rage. Xeron confronted their charge, and it was a flurry of movement as they erupted in a violent fight.

Kat streaked across the semicircle, running towards the vampires Gideon had killed. Stunned, I looked over and realized that the giant emerald Xeron had thrown earlier had crushed her chains enough that she could break away from the wall. She was digging in the vampire's pockets, looking for the key to take her cuffs off.

"They aren't there!" Wren said. "Find something little! Like... think bobby pin!"

Kat searched around, digging through the treasure. She growled in frustration and ran to his desk, digging until she held up a paper clip.

Wren jumped, screaming, "Yes! That's it! Bring it to me!"

Kat scurried over with it, placing it in Wren's steady hands. The harpy's tongue stuck out the side of her mouth while she unfurled the paper clip and dug in the keyhole with it. It felt like it took forever, but the lock on Kat's neck cuff clicked.

A roar pulled my attention back to the fight, and I watched Xeron overpower his opponents. Thad's wolf was limping, circling around behind the dragon while the fae faced him, his eyes searching like he was trying to figure out how to fight this monster. Aster fought her chain with a ferocity I had not seen from her, tears streaming down her cheeks.

A white streak caught my peripheral vision, and Daro cheered while a beautiful little fox joined the fray. She bit Xeron on the calf, tearing at the flesh. He roared and tried to grab her, but she avoided his hands, dodging with impressive agility.

"Yeah! Go Kit-Kat!" Daro screamed, jumping up and down with his fists in the air.

Wren was working on her own cuffs, but it was more difficult to maneuver on herself.

Kat, the fae warrior, and Thad moved in sync, battling Xeron with everything they had. It still wasn't enough. He was just too strong. There were no lies in the legends that painted dragons as infallible monsters.

Kat lunged at Xeron, and he smacked her, sending her flying back into the stone wall. She tried to get back up but yelped when her legs gave out. The fae warrior went down next, Xeron so fast in his execution of a move that it made my head spin. The dragon was raising a foot to crush his throat when Thad lunged at him. Xeron finished the kick, but it missed the fae's throat as he caught Thad's wolf by the scruff.

"Ah! No!" I screamed.

Thad struggled in his grip, snarling and snapping his teeth, but Xeron snapped his neck and tossed him aside like trash.

Fresh tears blazed a trail down my cheeks. "Thad!"

I could tell from the sickening angle his body lay at that he was already dead.

"You are insects!" Xeron bellowed, turning in a circle with his arms out. "You all locked dragons away and then forgot what power is!" He turned to look at me and the others. "Bend the knee, you pathetic worms. I am a god! None of you can stand against me!"

A small voice cracked through the chamber. "Maybe I can."

Everyone turned, mouths hanging open, and gawked at the petite girl in the doorway. Wearing a knit sweater with a kitten on it and a pleated skirt, she glared at the dragon, her green eyes swirling with intense hatred. Hades perched on her shoulder and hissed, growling in his throat.

Xeron backed up a step, and his face fell. "It can't be."

While I whispered, "Gods, no, Enid!"

CHAPTER 32

ERIS

THIS DRAGON WAS GOING to kill everyone I ever loved. My parents, my pack, my mate, and now my sister.

"Enid! Just run!"

Her eyes snapped to me, and relief flooded her features. She offered me her sweet, small smile, and I watched as she kneeled, her hands glowing green against the stone of the floor. Several of the stones started rumbling and then lifting, stacking on each other in a humanoid shape. Once stacked, a stone golem stood at least twelve feet tall. She placed her hands on it, and it lumbered forward with jerky motions, swinging at Xeron. He dodged, growled, and punched the top stone from the golem's shoulders. The stone flew and skittered to a stop, but rumbled and started rolling back towards the body, which picked it up and put it back in its place.

Behind that one, Enid had already created another, and it shuffled forward, ready to start its own attack. Xeron snarled and backed away, his face warping and bones cracking.

I felt my eyes widen, and I screamed, "He's shifting! Enid, watch out!"

We all watched open-mouthed, except Aster, of course, as wings sprouted from Xeron's back and black horns curled from his forehead. Scales, like perfect rubies, sprouted across his skin, glittering in the candlelight. They looked delicate, glasslike, but I knew they weren't. By the time he finished his transformation, the beast must've weighed eight tons and measured ten feet tall at the shoulder. Giant wings, bat-like and webbed with blood vessels, unfurled from his back, and stretched to the floor behind him.

Xeron threw back his head and let out a roar that shook the entire building. Dust rained down from the ceiling, and I covered my ears, looking over to see Aster doing the same. Enid flinched and Hades yowled again, the hair on his back lifting in a defiant line.

Answering the call of their master, more than a dozen vampires poured in from the door behind Enid and scurried for her.

"Enid! Look out! Oh Goddess, no!" I wailed, sobbing and watching through my fingers.

Hades dove from her shoulder, and rubbed against her leg, then looked up at her.

"You be careful, Mister," she said, and leaned down, touching her finger to his nose.

His body rolled in on itself and then grew. Before my eyes, the small black cat morphed into a giant panther, roaring and tearing into the vampires. He acted as a bodyguard, keeping them away from Enid while she turned back to the dragon.

I thought of a time when she and I had been together at the cabin, watching the summer sky on a moonless night. A blinding shooting star had blazed across the inky ether, glowing green and so bright that we'd had to shield our eyes. It was the same now, except Enid was the star, her eyes a blazing neon and her purple veins striking a stark contrast against her pale skin. The room filled with vibrations of power, making the hair on my arms stand at attention.

"My gods," I whispered, my heart catching while a tear streaked down my cheek.

Here she was. The Green Witch.

Xeron battled the golems, but no matter how many times he crushed them or broke them apart, they just put themselves back together again. He roared in frustration and swung his tail, smashing one into complete disarray. He did the same to the other, and while they were putting themselves back together, he advanced on Enid. The temperature of the room skyrocketed when he opened his mouth and blasted her with a stream of fire. She dropped to her knees and put her hands to the floor. Stones rushed to stack a protective wall in front of her. I could do nothing but stare into the inferno and pray she was still alive.

Enid stood, the ends of her hair singed, but otherwise intact. I cackled a wild laugh, unable to believe what I was seeing. All this time I'd spent worrying, and here she was, standing toe to toe with our nightmare.

Xeron roared as the golems, now put back together, advanced on him again. He started whipping at them with his tail, but Enid kneeled again and placed her hands on the floor. The ground rumbled, and giant vines—no—wet, white roots from the surrounding forest burst forth, shooting out between the cracks in the rocks. They started wrapping around the dragon's legs and tail, anchoring him in place.

His screech pierced my eardrums, and he pulled away from the tethers, breaking them and blasting them with fire. They just kept coming, growing faster than he could counter, and the golems were unrelenting, punching him in the chest and sides.

Wren and Pia cheered, and Daro was losing his mind, jumping around and pumping his fists, and shouting, "Who is this girl? Holy shit! Go blondie!"

Tiny roots snaked up out of the rocks around me, weaving into my cuffs. There was a moment of pause and then the cuffs clicked to signify they were unlocked. I shook them off, staring at my bare wrists. When I looked up, I saw that everyone else was uncuffed as well. Daro ripped at the chain on Wren's wings, and as soon as the chain dropped to the floor, she shifted to her full form. Like a raven, she was completely covered in rainbow-black feathers. She threw her head back with a shrill screech, and her powerful wings flapped once as she took off, flying into Xeron's face and clawing at his eyes.

The dragon roared and blew a stream of fire at her. She avoided it, doing a graceful barrel roll in the air. Daro went crazy, cheering on his friend. He was too young to shift and ran to help Aster and Pia towards an exit.

Between the golems, the vines, and Wren, Xeron couldn't stay oriented. He swung his tail and snapped his jaws with no actual target.

On his chest, there was one missing piece in his scaly ruby armor. Underneath, I could see the orange glow of his beating heart. The hair on my neck lifted, and my eyes dropped to the floor where Dragonsbane lay waiting only a few yards away.

The shine of the wicked spear called my name, saying, "*I am justice.*"

CHAPTER 33

ERIS

I TOOK ONE STEP, then another, nearly moaning with relief at the freedom from my chains. My feet kicked into action, and I didn't lose a step as I scooped the blade into my waiting hand. Dragonsbane. The spear had a presence, humming an ancient song into my flesh where I held it. Its own magical aura. It appeared a dagger but was actually a beautifully crafted spear. The smith was a fae; I could tell by the beauty of the blade. No other species could craft such perfection. I held the release of the weapon, flicking my wrist so it telescoped out to its full size. It was nearly as long as my body, but it was light and perfectly balanced, boasting a razor-sharp edge. I spun it once in my hand. Flawless.

Spear combat was a well-taught style in Alpha training, most likely why Gideon chose this presentation. He thought he'd be using it, but I didn't think fate meant it for him. My heart beat in perfect rhythm with my footfalls, and I realized every moment in my life had accumulated to this. I became an instant believer, knowing my Goddess had delivered me into this world to kill this vile dragon. Or maybe this was a gift from her. To end him like I'd dreamed of so often.

I surveyed the battle. Wren was incredible. Her agility and power in the air were like nothing I'd ever seen before. She attacked relentlessly, diving, clawing, and biting at Xeron's eyes while he screeched in agony. Enid's golems were still hitting him, and her roots sprouted like bony white fingers, trying to hold down his powerful tail. The dragon spun in circles to break them, roaring so the world shook around us.

Jets of fire spurted from his giant mouth. He kept shrieking, but no more vampires answered his calls. The battle outside was swaying in our favor.

I skirted around his right flank, dodging a swing from his powerful tail that was so close, I felt the wind rush against my skin. When I ran parallel to his head, I looked up at the side of his face and saw his yellow eye find me, widening when he realized what I carried in my hand. Xeron threw back his head and roared, shaking the stone beneath my feet. A giant stream of fire blasted in my direction, and the heat was unbearable, making it impossible to breathe as the hot air seared my lungs. His clawed foot swiped at me, and I dove, rolling beneath it. Xeron was too quick for something so massive, and I didn't see the other coming. The hot pad of his opposite foot pinned me, my back to the stone. The weight was immediate, crushing the air from my lungs. I barely had time to realize I was going to die. He wailed, and the weight was gone as soon as it had arrived. Xeron whirled, and I coughed, rolling to my side to see. It was Gideon, unsteady on his feet and bruised and bloodied. He had the sword from the knight's armor and had sliced a long line in Xeron's fleshy wing, the dragon's blood spraying in a fan and splattering the wall.

Gideon looked at me, our eyes meeting. The corner of his mouth lifted with that boyish smile, and then his eyes closed, his body going lax as the dragon's jaws closed around him.

"NO!" I tried to scream, searing my raw lungs. Xeron took Gideon in his mouth, chomping once, a sick squelch that spurted blood in every direction. He tossed him like a rag doll, and Gideon's body hit the back wall of the throne room, falling into the endless pile of treasure and out of my sight. "Ah! Ah!" I cried, grabbing the front of my dress. My heart pinched in my chest; a crack of pain so intense I believed it had split me open.

The world went silent for a few beats of my wailing heart, and then Wren screeched, starting a fresh assault on his face. The spear lay next to my hand, and rationality abandoned my thoughts. I picked it up and ran at the monster straight on. He saw me coming and shook out his scales as his maw opened. I saw the glow of flame in his throat. Maybe I would burn, but I would get this spear to his heart before I did.

The ground trembled beneath my feet as flames erupted from his mouth. A stone pillar shot me into the air, and I jumped with the momentum, my legs treading on nothing but fire as I leaped the stream, closing the gap between him and me. The vault brought me level with his horns, and his yellow eyes met mine, widening as my heartbeats passed like minutes. I dropped in front of him, rolling into a sprint, and his last effort was a swipe with his clawed foot. Falling to my knees, I let my momentum carry me under the attack. The stone tore at my skin, ripping it open, but I felt nothing as a shining black claw slid through the air, missing my nose by mere millimeters. My target appeared, glowing orange. I could feel the heat of his blood and see the movement of his rapidly beating heart through the translucent skin.

With a roar of my own making, I drew back my weapon and struck.

The spear hit true, finding its target, and burying itself into his chest. His heart was so powerful that the spear jumped in my hands with each beat, *thump-thump, thump-thump.*

Xeron screeched, flailing, so I was lifted off my feet, but I held fast, not willing to release the spear. He started shifting back and, in a few seconds, the red-haired man kneeled in front of me.

"Impossible," he choked out, his orange eyes wide, his hands gripping the handle of the spear.

I put my weight behind the weapon, pushing it deeper into his chest. He groaned, and his eyes rolled around the room, searching for someone who might help him.

I grabbed his hair like he had mine, and forced him to look at me, growling through gritted teeth, "What did I tell you, dragon? What did I promise you? That was for my mother, and this is for my mate!"

I twisted the spear, opening the fatal wound wider with a brutal pivot of my wrist. His mouth opened and closed like a dying fish, but he would never speak again. Blood poured out instead of words, and I watched the life fade from his yellow eyes. When his chest rattled its last bloody breath, I yanked my spear free. He flopped at my feet.

Silence. My heaving breaths. The beat of my heart.

Daro's voice boomed, "That is what I'm talking about, Wolfie! Fuck yes! Oh, my gods! She did it!"

Cheers erupted, filling the chamber, but not from me. I leaped over the body in front of me, running and tripping into the pile of treasure. It slipped and slid beneath my feet and hands, but I clawed over the ridges of cold coins, searching and afraid of what I'd find.

CHAPTER 34

ERIS

WHEN I FOUND HIM, a sound bubbled up from my gut, a weak wail. If I didn't know it was him, I wouldn't have known it. A pile of leaking flesh lay before me, blood seeping like red oil into the golden coins.

"Gideon," I moaned, my voice thick and unrecognizable. "I'm here."

I crawled around to his head, taking it into my lap. He coughed once, misting me with a spray of blood, and I watched the hole in his neck pulse with the beat of his heart, the failing organ working to expel the last of his life force.

"Don't worry, it's not so bad. I'll fix you," I said, and sang my mother's lullaby, my hands glowing white.

Without Calli, darkness almost immediately flooded my vision, and my head spun. I couldn't heal these massive wounds without her.

"No, no, no," I sobbed, feeling his life waning. "Don't you go! Don't you dare! I can be the fixer this time."

I tried again, but slumped forward, my body sagging as I nearly fell into the blackness.

'Calli, wake up! I need you,' I begged.

I could sense her stirring, trying to fight the cloud of wolfsbane that still ran through my veins. She couldn't get through. I couldn't tap into her power.

"No, no. Gideon. Stay. Stay here with me," I begged, taking his cheeks in my hands and pressing my forehead against his.

"He is not going anywhere."

I looked up through tears and saw my sister's face. She put her hand on my arm and closed her eyes, starting our lullaby and pushing her power into me. I gasped with the surge, feeling like hot metal ran through me. When I joined her song, the white glow in my hands erupted brighter than it ever had. I pulled at the pain in his blood, hearing the squelch of flesh mending and Gideon's bones snapping back into their proper places. After we'd done all we could, I sat with my eyes closed, listening to see if his heart still beat.

Gideon stirred, his eyelids fluttering and opening. I laughed out a sob, tears streaming down my cheeks while I brushed his hair off of his forehead.

"Eris? What happened? Is he dead, or are we?"

"You were as close as I've ever seen," I whispered, "but we win today."

He smiled and asked, "You killed him, didn't you?"

"Enid and Wren did most of it. I just wielded the spear."

He grabbed my wrists, running his thumbs over my hands. "And here I thought I was impressing you."

"Your form could use a little work," I whispered, and he grinned, trying to sit up.

I didn't let him, crawling on top of him and straddling his waist, scolding him, "Stay still. You need to rest, Alpha." His hands laced around my back, pulling me down to his kiss, and I let my fingers drift over his chest, checking to make sure he was whole. His skin was blood-caked, but healed, as if it had never happened.

"He's living up to his name, isn't he?" Wren said. "Nearly dead one second and trying to get laid the next. I would expect nothing less from Mr. Wet Dreams."

I laughed into the kiss, and Gideon muttered, "What does *that* mean?"

My voice was thick with tears again. "It means I missed you."

"I would never have stopped looking. I would've torn this world apart to find you."

"I know. I would've never stopped believing."

I heard the treasure sliding, and knew they were leaving us, and Gideon pushed me to my feet this time. I helped him stand, and he ripped a tapestry off the wall, wrapping it around his waist.

"Did we really just *do* that? Killed a dragon?" Wren asked, throwing her arms out.

"Yeah, you did! Yeah, you did!" Daro yelled and made a flying gesture with his flat hand. "You were like *vroom*, and *nroom*, and *sks-sks-sks!*" He made a scratching motion with his hands, and Wren laughed.

The fae man was up, and it appeared he was going to be okay. He stood with his hand on Pia's back and held Aster protectively at his side. She clung to him. Seeing them side-by-side, I knew he must be her father, the Fae King.

"Let's find something to cut those," Gideon said, looking around for anything that could rid her of those awful stitches.

As they approached us, I bowed my head with respect to the king. "Your Majesty"

He shook his head and bent at his waist, showing me the top of his head. Pia and Aster did the same.

His deep voice echoed in the chamber. "You will never bow to me, Eris Dragonslayer. I owe you my life and my daughter's life. The fae people are forever in your debt."

"It was my pleasure," I said, needing no accolades. The revenge was sweet enough.

Daro and Wren stood together talking a thousand miles an hour with each other. Daro was still raving about her role in Xeron's destruction. He commented something about "a sick move," and she laughed, hugging him and squeezing him to her chest. Gradually, their laughter turned to sobs as they held each other for the first time since they'd met. Free at last.

Things felt like they were moving slowly and quickly all around me, but I panicked when I no longer saw Enid. I quickly found her, her tiny shoulders shaking with sobs while she kneeled by the body of our sweet Thad.

I stumbled over and fell to my knees beside her, laying my head on hers as my own tears streamed down my cheeks. After years of suppressing emotions, it felt as though they all bombarded me at once, having no mercy.

"You should've seen how brave he was. He died trying to save me," I said, the guilt like a heavy stone in my chest.

"It's like the last part of Mother died with him," she whispered.

Hades was rubbing on her chin, catching her tears.

She sprang to her feet, and to my surprise, glowered at Gideon. "Never leave me behind again. I could've prevented this."

He held his hands up, and his face pinched with regret. "I'm so sorry, Enid. I-I couldn't have known how you... what you... I promise I'll never underestimate you again."

We were interrupted by Finn. He pushed through the growing crowd, yelling for me. "Eris! Luna! Help!"

His eyes were wild, an unconscious Kat cradled in his arms.

My heart dropped. "Oh, gods, Kat!"

Finn had taken down one of the red dragon banisters, wrapping it around her.

"Kat. Kat," he repeated in a whisper, stroking her face. "Please. Please save her."

Gideon asked, "Finn? You alright?" and he rested his hand on his brother's shoulder.

Finn ignored him, and his panicked eyes found mine. "Please! She's my mate."

Enid put her hand on my arm, and I put mine on Kat, singing the lullaby together again.

CHAPTER 35

GIDEON

IT HAD BEEN NINE days since we walked out of the dragon's keep, and the lives of every supernatural in every realm were impacted by what we had found. Xeron had only been the first clue in a puzzle that we were all trying to piece together. Dragons were back. That was a fact we knew for certain. Not just one or two, but several. They were planning something that would bring the world to its knees. In Xeron's office, there were letters, documents, maps, and other evidence of an ancient ritual they wanted to perform.

If successful, they would release a beast they referred to as the dark one. He or she would bring about the apocalypse; ending the world as we know it and casting us back into the dark ages, where dragons ruled without opposition.

To complete the ceremony, they needed three specific items: a chalice, a bell, and an athame, or a witches' blade. River explained that these three items must've been used centuries ago during the spell that placed the powerful ward on this apocalyptic beast, and that the exact three items would be needed to undo the spell.

According to Xeron's records, the chalice had already been located and acquired by his associates. It was beyond our reach. The locations of the other two items were unknown, but they had several possibilities lined up to be searched. Now it was a race. Dragons, vampires, and dark witches versus the rest of the supernatural world. We needed to find the items first and keep them out of the hands of the enemy or destroy them.

Unfortunately, there was discord among the packs about who should seek and keep these items. Lyrion had been present during the unveiling of this new information and had accused me of trying to make a power grab to further strengthen Gold Moon. He had convinced some of the other Alphas that it was unfair for Gold Moon to have Eris, Enid, and these powerful items. He claimed the balance of power was already tipped too far, and that I was going to take over as Alpha King if we were allowed to seize the items as well. They were unfounded and ridiculous accusations, but they had sprouted some contention amongst the packs. Things were tense and grew more so every day.

Eris and I were scheduled to attend an emergency pack meeting at Diamond Moon in two days to discuss our future actions. I didn't want to wait two days. We should already be seeking these items. Eris stirred against my chest, and I held her tighter, inhaling her scent and never wanting to let her go. The full moon shone in through our open balcony doors, and I thanked the Moon Goddess for the thousandth time for bringing her back to me.

I hadn't slept well since we'd come home, afraid that I would wake up and she'd be gone again. That it had all been a dream, and she was still captive in the dragon's keep.

I looked down at her neck, where the silver collar had burned its mark. The angry red welt was healing, and it may fade with time, but it would take a long while to disappear. Silver left scars. She would wear the cuff marks on her wrists and the whip slashes across her back for years. I wanted to be rid of the rage that burned in my chest and veins, but it always lingered, unable to bear what my mate had endured for those weeks in captivity.

'Our mate is unbreakable. She is the Dragonslayer. She will be okay,' Ivailo said, puffing with pride.

'Yes. I don't know if I will be okay, though.'

She was handling post-keep life better than I was. I was the one having issues, barely able to let her out of my sight for over five minutes at a time. I felt my throat tighten as I caressed her arm, treasuring the sparks of pleasure it sent through my fingers. People who had endured what she had been through would most likely shut down, hardened by the horror that exists in this world.

Kat had run from it. Finn's mate had disappeared into the night, leaving nothing but a note and him reeling. That was an entirely different issue to be reckoned with, but I didn't know how to fix it for him.

My mind was like a revolving door, returning to what had happened in the dragon's keep to Eris and Kat. I nuzzled my nose into Eris's neck and let her scent calm me.

She faced me and sleep clouded her voice, but concern drew her features. "What's wrong?"

"I'm sorry," I said, pressing my forehead to hers. "I didn't mean to wake you."

"It's okay." She sighed. She ran her hands up my chest. "I am awake now, though."

Catching the heat in her tone, I grinned down at her. We'd barely had time for each other these last nine days as we waded through the chaos. There was time now. It had been a relief to find out that he hadn't touched her, not sexually, anyway. There'd been one kiss, apparently. That alone was enough to make my ears ring, but she'd bitten him hard enough to draw blood.

Eris pulled herself up and kissed me. Soft at first, just the pillows of her lips like satin against mine. I pulled her closer to me, deepening our contact. Our movements increased, lust and longing pulsing through our bond. It was she this time that used her claws, shredding my pajamas and hers. I smiled into the kiss, and she giggled, pushing me back and climbing on top of me. We moaned together as she guided me to her entrance, and I squeezed her hips with my hands.

The sex was soft and sensual. An expression of our love. When we both finished, she relaxed onto my chest where I could feel the fierce beat of her heart against mine.

With little thought beyond the spark of the idea, I said, "Marry me tomorrow."

She leaned up to look at me. "Are you sure? With everything that's going on?"

I pushed her hair back, tucking it behind her ear. "Yes, I'm sure. I don't want to wait one more day. It doesn't have to be anything big. Just you and me."

She relaxed on my chest and whispered, "Okay. I don't want to wait either."

CHAPTER 36

ERIS

G IDEON'S CHEST STARTED RISING and falling in the rhythm of sleep, and I smiled. He had slept little since we'd gotten home. I almost felt guilty for how amazingly I'd coped. I felt free. Not just free because I wasn't chained to a wall anymore, but free from the black cloud that had been following me since the day my pack burned.

The dragon was dead, and I had the privilege of ending his life. I thought back to those moments. The way the spear felt in my hand, the heat of the flames, the thumps of his still-beating heart. My lips curled into a smile. I'd kill that dragon every day for the rest of my life if I could.

Father, Mother, Thad. They'd all died protecting me, and I'd delivered what justice I could. Enid and I brought Thad's body back to our old pack lands. We buried Mother's pelt next to where I had laid my father's head. We agreed to place Thad on her other side so they could all rest together for all time and eternity. They weren't there anyway, not really. I hoped they were all running together through the lush grass in the meadow of our Goddess.

Besides Thad, we had lost almost twenty warriors. Twenty shifters that would never return to their homes, just so I could return to mine. We'd had their funerals the third morning after my liberation, and it was the hardest thing I ever had to do. They were fathers, mothers, brothers, sisters, and mates. I could see their other halves in the crowd, their hollow expressions unchanging as their life and soul was buried in the cold ground.

Immediately after, one woman had walked into the woods and ended her life to join her mate. It had shocked no one, a common occurrence when mates were separated by death. Dying in battle was revered as the greatest honor among wolves. It was believed that all fallen warriors went to Elysium. Knowing that did little to soften the pain of their deaths.

There had been other casualties, too, amongst the other packs and the fae. New tears ran down my face, and I closed my eyes hard, trying to push away the images of their slain bodies out on the battlefield. Using our powers, Enid and I had saved five shifters and two fae from dying, and that comforted me in these dark hours.

'They are all heroes. We will never forget their sacrifice,' Calli said.

'I am afraid, in this changing world, that they are the first of many to succumb to this Dragon War.'

My thoughts drifted to my companions. The six of us who endured that torment together and came out alive. There was a bond between us that couldn't be explained, and I loved every one of them.

I had healed Aster that day after they cut the stitches out of her lips. They were made of lead, which is to fae what silver is to a shifter, so the scars might never fully heal. She had ten dots around her mouth now, five on top and five on bottom, and iron burns across her lips. The Fae King had even hugged me after that, which Gideon told me was highly unusual. Hearing Aster's voice for the first time had been surreal. It sounded like wind chimes, light and melodic.

Pia had assured us she would see us again someday, but that she needed to go home. The Fae King had spoken to her for a long time before she left, insisting that she become a diplomat between the sprites and the fae, who had suffered a falling out many years before. She promised him she would do her best. We all hugged her, holding her tightly, and thanked her for her beautiful songs that got us through the worst time in our lives. After that, she'd simply walked into the woods behind the castle and disappeared.

Wren returned to her flock outside a big human city called Seattle. She dearly missed her mother and sisters. I hoped they all learned how brave she was, taking on a dragon face to face and living to tell the tale. She gave all of us a phone number to reach her and promised that when the time came to battle for our lives at the end of days, her people would be there.

Daro came back with us to the pack house and stayed a few nights. He'd left to go home early one morning, hugging me and telling me I was "one badass lady" and promising to be in touch soon. I didn't doubt that because he was sweet on Enid. He had mercilessly laid the charm on my poor blushing sister the entire time he was in her presence.

Enid, after being told to stay home by Gideon, had recruited Leo into her rebellion. He had broken into Gideon's office with her and stolen the map they used during the locating spell. They'd wrecked a vehicle on the way, trying to drive it off-road into the trees in their haste. Enid wouldn't let Leo go any farther, though, as he didn't even have a wolf yet. Apparently, he'd been so insistent that she'd had to wrap the entire vehicle in those huge roots, trapping him inside until the battle concluded.

That left Kat. My sweet friend. Finn was her true mate, and it had sent her into a spiral. When her wolf finally recovered from the wolfsbane, she was ecstatic to have him. Her fox half hated him. Kat left in the middle of the following night. Not a word to anyone, but a note asking please not to follow, and that she'd call when she was ready. Finn was devastated, but I believed Kat when she said she'd come back. I hoped they could work everything out for my own selfish motives. If Kat was Finn's mate, she would live here at the pack house with us, and we could be best friends forever.

I snuggled into Gideon's chest and tried to relax into sleep, thankful to be alive, and thankful for the girl inside me who always found a way to survive. I lived through the murder of my entire pack, and I escaped the dragon's keep. Lying in bed with my mate, I promised all those who hadn't made it I would live every day for the rest of my life for them. I owed it to them to be happy, and I was going to do my best to honor that.

CHAPTER 37

ERIS

WE SLEPT IN THE next day, and I finally woke up when the strong afternoon sun beamed through the open window. The first snowfall of the season flurried outside, and a soft breeze was blowing several wayward flakes into our room.

I got up, pulling a blanket around me and trying not to wake Gideon. Intending to close the balcony doors, I ended up stepping out into the quiet winter. The flakes floated around me, and I closed my eyes, letting the cold air sink into my soul. I always liked the snow. The bright white cleaned away the drab brown of late fall. Nature's purifier. I let the flakes fall and melt on my face, imagining that they were cleansing me, too, and scrubbing away the horror of my three weeks in the dragon's keep.

The wind gusted, whipping my hair, and I wrapped my arms around myself, shuddering. Even for a shifter, the breeze was icy, and my thin sheet wasn't insulating. I was about to return when brawny arms wrapped around my shoulders, warming my blood. I let my head fall back against him and sighed.

"We'd better go tell Mother about the wedding today. She'll want to be there. And Leo and Enid. Finn... if he's up to it."

My heart skipped. I knew he was serious last night, but part of me wondered if he'd remember his midnight proposal.

Knowing Diane would want it to be perfect, I said, "She's going to freak out."

"Freak out, huh? Where'd you learn that?"

"Daro."

"Of course," he said, chuckling.

GIDEON

My mother did, indeed, freak out. She'd rushed Eris into town for a dress. I'd almost argued, anxiety rolling through me at the thought of not being with her, but I knew I had to let her go. As much as I wished to, I couldn't loiter by her side for the rest of our lives.

I sat at my desk, trying to catch up on work. I was fixated on the mate bond, ready to shift at the first sign of panic. Mostly, I felt some anxiety and sadness, followed by a light, happy feeling that calmed my worry.

I stared at the documents and maps in front of me. Everything we'd taken from Xeron's office. Finding the bell and the athame was going to be more difficult than I had expected. Some of the possible locations included the pyramid of Giza, the Smithsonian Museum, and somewhere in the middle of the Amazon jungle.

I *wanted* to assign this to Finn. He was the only person I would ever trust with something so important. Unfortunately, he was struggling with his mate, and I knew he wouldn't be able to focus. I scrubbed my hands down my face and sighed, thinking I might need to pursue the items myself.

There was a light knock on the door, and I was surprised to find Lucien escorting Daro and an elderly gentleman. The similarity between the two was uncanny; the same ebony skin, white hair, pastel-blue eyes, and small lump in the center of their foreheads. It was more than that, though. They shared the same jawline and bridge of their nose. It was obvious they were related, even with the deep wrinkles creasing the older man's forehead and around his eyes and mouth. Despite his age, he looked strong, standing proudly with broad shoulders and an air of confidence that only comes with the wisdom of age.

"Daro? I didn't expect you back so quickly," I said, standing and walking around the desk to greet them.

He put his fist over his heart in an official greeting. "Alpha. My grandfather insisted on returning immediately and meeting you and Eris."

I held my hand out to the man. "I am Gideon Greenwood. Alpha of this pack and mate to Eris."

He took it, his grip firm, and shook it. "I am Zekaiel. Stallion of our herd until my oldest grandson comes of age in a couple of months. He is young for the role, but we didn't expect his father to be taken so soon."

I remembered the mount on the wall at the dragon's keep and nodded my head in understanding. Daro looked at the floor, shame cracking across his features.

"So, Daro, you're next in line?" I asked.

He blanched and held his hands up. "Me? No, sir, of course not. I'm only sixteen. My older brother will be the next Stallion."

Sir? I almost laughed. Zekaiel probably didn't know how cheeky his grandson was when he was out of his presence.

"Please sit," I said, indicating the two chairs in front of my desk.

Returning to my spot, I continued, "I have to say I'm a little star-struck to have two unicorns in my office right now. Before we met Daro, we weren't sure that you even existed anymore."

Zekaiel stared at me, his sage eyes piercing. His gaze made me feel like a young pup under the scrutiny of a stern teacher. Unicorns were rumored to be proud and elegant beings, and Zekaiel rang that bell.

"As you probably know, Alpha, the horn of the unicorn is the most powerful purifier. The other supernaturals hunted us down, poached, and murdered us for it. My mother was taken this way while I squalled in her arms, only an infant."

I nodded, aware of this horrific practice from decades ago. Dark witches sought to possess the horns to purify their ingredients and spells, making them much more powerful. Vampires hunted them like bounties, always looking for ways to make blood money.

"Years ago, my father took our herd out of this realm and into the human world where we could live without fear for our lives. We existed so comfortably for so long that we became lax, no longer expecting that evil lurked around every corner. The day the dragon came for Daro, we were not ready. The consequence was the death of my only child, Daro's father."

"I am sorry for your loss," I said, adding, "Both of you," and looking at Daro. "I lost my father abruptly as well."

Daro looked at his hands and nodded. My heart went out to him. He was about the same age as Leo, and I understood how deeply he must have been affected.

Zekaiel continued, "I never want to feel unprepared again. That's why my grandson will stay here for the time being. My people need an ambassador to relay information about the situation involving the rise of the dragons. Daro insisted it must be him. At first, I was hesitant, but since his brother is the future Stallion, I see it is a noble task for the second son."

I looked at Daro, my brows lifting. He was so young to have such an important duty. But I trusted him, at least. More than I would anyone else they might send.

"I don't see a problem with that, but I would like to discuss it with Luna Eris if that is acceptable?"

"Yes, that would be ideal," he answered, nodding.

I linked Lucien to return.

"Please show these gentlemen to a guest room. Have food and fresh clothes delivered."

He nodded his understanding, and I addressed the unicorns again. "Anything you need, please let Lucien know. I would be happy to have someone show you the pack grounds or the town if you'd like."

Daro blurted, "Could Enid do it?"

My brows lifted again.

"Uh, it's for my grandfather. He'd like to meet her."

Zekaiel's expression shifted slightly toward confusion, but he didn't argue.

I had to stop myself from laughing. "She is at school, but she'll be free later."

Daro grinned, and Zekaiel bowed his head. "Thank you, Alpha. May the sun warm your path."

"And the moon light yours," I said, finishing the official acknowledgment.

Chapter 38

Eris

WHEN WE WERE DRIVING to see the seamstress, my gut was tight. It had only been a handful of days since the fight at the dragon's keep. Sighing, I stared out the window at the falling snow.

"What's wrong?" Diane asked, touching my arm.

Tears brimmed my lashes as I turned to her. "I really want to be married. I do. But our warriors just fought in a battle—for *me*. Some of them died. And now I'm here about to choose a wedding dress. Is that even appropriate?"

"They chose their role as warriors and died how they would consider most honorable."

"I know. I know that's what everyone... keeps telling me."

"You say they died for you, and they did. For their Luna and their pack. You and Gideon should be married. It signifies the strength of Gold Moon. We're not having a party today. It's a private ceremony. The way we honor those who fall is to continue in happiness the best we can."

I closed my eyes, and two tears rolled down my cheeks. "That's what I keep telling myself, but it's so hard to actually do it."

She squeezed my hand. "That's an unfortunate part of being an Alpha or Luna—or any leader, for that matter. You have to ask people to sacrifice for you. They may have been there to save you, but Gideon is the one who asked them to go, and they answered the call. The best we can do is honor them by trying to be as good of leaders as we can be."

I nodded my head and sighed again.

"Have you put any thought into your wedding dress?" she asked, still holding my hand.

"Yes, I'd like to wear something like my mother wore." In the sitting area of our home, a portrait of my mother and father on their wedding day had hung over the hearth. As a girl, I'd always pictured myself in that dress on my wedding day. "I'll admit it's probably simpler than what most Gold Moon Lunas would choose."

"Oh, probably. My dress was very extravagant." She sighed and smiled. "I'm just picturing how Henry looked that day. He's what I remember most. Him and the love I felt for him. That's what you need to focus on. You and Gideon, and this life you're starting. I'm not saying forget the others. Keep them with you and keep putting one foot in front of the other."

It was my turn to squeeze her hand, and she smiled at me, eyes glassy, as we pulled up to the shop and stepped out into the snow.

GIDEON

After being told by my mother that the event didn't warrant a tuxedo, I knotted the tie on my favorite black suit. A knock on the door drew my attention, and seconds later, Finn joined me in the bedroom. He looked worse than I'd ever seen him, even in his formal wear. Without glancing at me, he shuffled in and plopped down in a chair, sighing and leaning his head back, eyes closed.

"I'm dying," he croaked.

Those weeks away from Eris were the worst of my life. "Trust me, I know."

"I don't know how you survived three weeks. I understand why you were such a dick the whole time."

"Why are you here?" I asked.

"You're getting married."

"Not here in my room. Here, at the pack. Go get her, my gods."

"You don't understand."

"Understand what?"

"Kat doesn't want me. I could feel it in the bond. Part of her is disgusted even to speak to me."

"She's confused. I bet she never expected to find a mate. A wolf shifter, anyway."

From what I understood, Kat was more inclined to identify with her kitsune heritage.

"She *hates* me."

"Only half of her does."

"That's comforting, thank you," he said dryly.

"So, what are you going to do?"

He lifted his head and looked at me, arching an eyebrow. "What do you mean, 'what am I going to do?' I'll wait for her. When she returns, I'll convince her of my love for her. No matter how long it takes or how hard she makes it for me. She's my mate. Kat is mine."

"I hope she doesn't make it too hard on you, even though you deserve it after sleeping around so much."

He scoffed and ran his hands down his face. "And she doesn't even know about that yet."

I winced, not envious of his situation, and offered him my hand. He brushed it away and stood on his own, adjusting his suit and smoothing his hair.

He tried his best to smile, and he clapped me on the shoulder. "Come on, brother. Let's get you married."

Leo, Enid, Finn, River, and I walked together to a clearing just past the tree line. There was a small spring that still ran despite the ice that framed it. The winter's first snow covered the boughs of the trees and the forest floor like a white cotton blanket. It was calm. It was peaceful. My soul was in the same state; there were no nerves. Feeling the bond, I knew she was the same.

I heard the brush of her dress over the snow, and my heart jumped, ready to have her safely in my arms again.

When they, Eris and my mother, emerged from the tree line, the flurries had picked up again, dancing around her. The snowflakes were heavy, landing on her rosy cheeks and melting so her skin shimmered. Her wedding gown was traditional and modest, with a high lace collar and full sleeves. The snow gathered in her long hair, a curtain of wavy ash blonde decorated by a crown woven of white flowers.

My mom passed her hand to me and went to stand by Enid. They wore matching velvet dresses in gold. Enid was beaming, tears in her eyes. I was committing it all to memory, never wanting to forget any of the details. Eris dusted the snow that had gathered on my shoulder away, and River started the ceremony.

"We are gathered here today to unite two souls as one. Do you, Gideon, and you, Eris, join us here of your own free will, to acknowledge the eternal bond shared between you?"

We had little time to prepare vows, but I had a good idea of what I wanted to say.

"I, Gideon, choose you, Eris, to be my friend, my lover, mother of my children and my wife. I will take you in joy and I will take you in sadness. You are to me the whispering of the trees, the seduction of the summer's heat, and the purity of the spring's rain. I ask you to grow old and wise with me, as I will do with you."

She was smiling, and I would never forget it. How rosy-red her cheeks and lips were. How her eyelashes held onto two stubborn flakes, and how the golden honey of her eyes shone as she spoke.

"I, Eris, choose you, Gideon, to be my husband and one true love. I promise you always my deepest devotion and tenderest care through the pressures of the present and the uncertainty of the future. I give you my body, my love, and my spirit until our life may be done, for I am yours, and you are mine."

River concluded the ceremony. "Here, before witnesses, Gideon and Eris have sworn their vows to each other. Please exchange rings."

We did, just simple gold bands for now. River then draped a golden cord around our interlocked hands. "With this cord, I bind them. However, these binds are not tied so that neither partner is restricted by the other. The only true enforcement of love is the will to love. Now, you may kiss your bride."

River smiled, a rarity, and I took Eris in my arms, kissing her. Our little group cheered, and I heard several sniffles, including a couple from Finn.

'Gods, I love you,' I said through our bond, feeling like I was floating on the delicate happiness that pulsed through it.

'And, I love you, Gideon Greenwood.'

CHAPTER 39

GIDEON

E RIS' NERVES BUBBLED IN the bond as we pulled up to the Diamond Moon pack house. She and I were the only ones attending the emergency meeting, as Finn had taken off last night, desperate to find Kat.

He wouldn't have known where to look, but Eris knew the name of Kat's hometown. Somewhere just outside of Los Angeles. I gave him my blessing to go, of course, and hoped he could wrap it up quickly so we could focus on the artifacts.

The other Alphas and Lunas were milling around the conference room, waiting for the meeting to start. As soon as we walked in, all the ongoing conversations stopped, and everyone turned to look at us. The tension in the room was palpable. Alphas I'd regarded as friends my entire life stared at me with a new sense of distrust.

Ivailo confirmed their feelings. *'A lot of aggression in this room.'*

'It's worse than I expected,' Eris linked me, sensing the same.

'Agreed. Lyrion's been hard at work sowing the seeds of strife.'

"Alpha Gideon! Luna Eris Dragonslayer!" Rudy greeted us, his jubilance shattering the silence.

Beth hurried to us, wrapping Eris in a crushing hug. "Oh, my Goddess, be blessed. I am just so happy you're okay." Her eyes floated to the large scar on Eris's neck where her silver collar had burned her. "I can't imagine what you've been through."

Eris grabbed her hands and held them. "I am fine, Beth. Don't worry about me. There are more pressing matters to give our attention to."

The conference room door opened, and Lyrion walked in with his Luna. Poor Natasha.

His smile was irritatingly smug, and Eris linked me. *'He isn't taking this seriously, Gideon.'*

'His only concern lies in forwarding his own interests. He really thinks this is some kind of power grab.'

Sticking his arms out, Lyrion said, "Shall we begin, Alphas?"

ERIS

The strength of the annoyance coming through the bond from Gideon was stifling as we all took our seats around the enormous table. The Alpha called Brutus stood up and everyone quieted, giving him their attention.

"Before we begin the debate, we need to settle another issue first," he said. "The fate of the woman in my dungeon, guilty of treason."

Several eyes turned to Alpha Owen and his Luna, who both squirmed under the scrutiny of their peers. Luna Emma looked ready to burst into tears, and my heart hurt for her. Sophia may be awful, but she was their only pup.

Rudy spoke first. "She should be executed. Immediately. Her decision ultimately led to the loss of several wolves during the battle at the dragon's keep. Alpha Gideon was nearly killed, and Luna Eris was held in captivity and tortured."

There were several "ayes" of agreement, including Gideon. Brutus spoke again. "I think the decision should fall to Luna Eris."

Several eyes turned to me, and my heart jumped, racing.

'I don't want to be responsible for taking their only pup,' I linked Gideon.

'She is accountable for her own actions. Choose however you wish, and I support you.'

I cleared my throat. "Without her actions, as wrong as they were, we would've never found the dragon's keep and gained the valuable information we found there. I don't... wish for any more blood to spill, or for anymore sorrow. I vote for banishment, effective immediately."

Several people lifted their eyebrows, surprised by my leniency.

"While I disagree, Luna Eris, I respect your wishes and it will be done," Brutus said, sitting.

"Goddess bless you, Luna, for your mercy," Alpha Owen muttered, his face pale. His wife was trying to get control of the tears flowing down her cheeks.

Lyrion stood. "Moving on to the issue at hand." He looked directly at Gideon as if he were the issue. "We all know what was found at the dragon's keep and the impending consequences the world is facing if the bell and the athame fall into the hands of the dragons."

Everyone nodded, accompanied by several more, "Ayes."

Lyrion continued, "As dire as the situation is, I don't think it's appropriate for Gold Moon to shift the balance of power any further in their favor. They are threatening democracy, and the pillars of equality that the Union of Packs represents."

Gideon stood. "The balance of power has nothing to do with it. These artifacts have to be found and protected. We don't even know if these items have any usable power. We are the pack most able to protect them, so we should hold them."

Lyrion's face darkened, shadowed with anger. "Are you suggesting Diamond Moon cannot protect its own assets?"

Gideon tilted his head. "From dragons? Yes, that's what I'm suggesting. You did not see what I saw in that throne room. None of you did."

"How dare you?" Lyrion hissed.

"We are the only pack that has killed a dragon. We're the only pack that has the weapon to kill a dragon, and we're the only pack that has the Green Witch."

"So we should all just stand by and let you have everything? You already pose a serious threat to every pack here." He looked around at the others. "He could use that witch and overthrow us all. We saw her.

She's only a child, and we sensed the power! Don't let him fool you, brothers."

Several murmurs of agreement circled the table.

Gideon was struggling with his temper. "I don't want to be Alpha King! I just want to do what's best for everyone. I want to keep everyone safe."

"I don't believe that. You've been planning this for years. Stealing mergers from other packs and building your numbers. Tipping the scale in your favor one grain of rice at a time. This entire situation just gives you an excuse to exercise your power."

Other Alphas glared at Gideon, nodding their heads. One stood, I couldn't remember his name, and spoke, "Why can't Diamond Moon and Gold Moon both pursue the items? Wouldn't that make more sense? The more people we have looking, the better our chances are of finding the items before the dragons do."

There were murmurs of agreement, with Lyrion and Gideon still standing and glaring at each other across the table.

With several others agreeing to his plan, the Alpha spoke again. "Then I make the official proposal that any pack that wants to pursue the items is open to do so. Whoever finds it is responsible for protecting it."

"I vote nay," Gideon snapped before the last word was out of his mouth.

To my disappointment, several of the other Alpha's chimed in with "ayes." At the end of the vote, only Rudy, Brutus, and to my surprise Owen, voted with Gideon.

An older Alpha said, "Motion passes."

"You're an arrogant fool, Lyrion," Gideon hissed through clenched teeth. "Your selfishness is going to end with the loss of countless innocent lives. Mark my words."

Lyrion's smug smile dropped, and his wolf pushed forward, snarling, "*Fool?*"

"Enough!" the older Alpha, I thought his name was Amos, shouted. "Alpha Gideon, you are ordered to make copies of all the information regarding the location of the items and distribute it to every pack by the end of the week. If you do not comply or if you fail to include even one piece of documentation, Gold Moon will be found to be noncompliant, and action will be taken. Do you understand?"

Gideon stared at his hands spread on the table, and I sensed his inner turmoil. He wanted to object, but I knew, as did he, it would do no good.

"Alpha?" Amos asked again. "Do you—"

"Yes, I understand."

Sensing that he was ready to leave, I stood, as did several other Lunas. He grabbed my hand, and we stalked out without another word. We went straight to the car, his rage pulsing through the bond. I started to climb in, but a smug voice stopped me.

"Well, how's it feel not to have things go your way for the first time in your life?"

Gideon pivoted on his heel, turning to Lyrion. "You're letting your petty squabbles with me put every single life on this planet in danger. You're going to get your people killed!"

Lyrion's temper was boiling, and he shouted, "Diamond Moon is as capable as you are in every way, you arrogant prick!"

Gideon stabbed a finger into Lyrion's chest, making him bristle, and I thought there might be a fight. "How *dare* you accuse me of arrogance while blinded by your own hubris? You should pray Gold Moon finds those items before you do, because you'll rue the day a dragon comes knocking on your door."

With that, we got in the car, and Gideon slammed on the gas, leaving Lyrion fuming in a cloud of dust.

CHAPTER 40

ERIS

I WATCHED GIDEON DISMOUNT awkwardly from his horse.

"It wasn't bad for your first ride," I told him, smiling but trying not to laugh.

He looked at me as if I'd lost my mind. "It was awful!"

I giggled, still trying to keep it under control. I may have suggested he wasn't bold enough to learn to ride, and he'd taken it personally. We'd gone out today for a simple trail ride through the forest. It had been a pleasant, relaxing day for me; for Gideon, not so much.

"What did you think?" I asked, finally laughing as he rubbed his inner thighs and walked with the typical bow-legged stance of someone not used to the saddle.

"I think I'll stick to my wolf. I can't believe that's a leisure activity for you!" he said, making me laugh harder. "Gods, I used muscles today I didn't even know existed!"

We led our horses inside and removed their tack. I brushed Ollie, relaxing into the familiarity of the action. Life wasn't simple anymore, so we had to do simple things to balance the stress. I thought of the day Enid and I rode away from everything we ever knew, two orphans with nowhere to go. So many things had changed since then, but the horse was the same. I led Ollie to the pasture and let him off his lead while Gideon did the same with his horse. We returned to the stables, and while I was hanging my halter, familiar arms laced around my waist.

Gideon kissed down the back of my neck, stopping at my marking spot and nipping.

His breath tickled my ear with a whisper. "Well, Luna, here we are in the stables, *finally*, and no one is around."

I grinned, asking, "And what are we going to do about that, Alpha?" as I pushed my hips back into him.

He spun me, pressing my back to the wall. "You know what I want."

A month later, I sat in our bathroom and stared at the little stick in my hand as it processed, a flurry of emotions whirling in my gut.

Sure enough, a little pink plus sign appeared in the circle, confirming what I already knew. Calli yipped in my head, but shock clanged through me like a dropped bell.

To be shocked was silly because I knew what caused this, and Gideon and I had done plenty of that these last few weeks, but I'd felt I had been careful, tracking my cycle and taking extra precaution on my most fertile days.

He was sitting on our bed and shot to his feet. "Well? What does it say?"

"We both knew it was going to be positive," I said as I sat on the bed. Our wolves didn't need pregnancy tests to know, and they'd both told us already.

He sat by me, and we stared at the little pink plus. I could feel how happy he was, but my heart was slamming against the wall of my chest.

"Wow. A pup. Our pup," he whispered, and had his arm around my shoulder, holding me. "When will they be here?"

Shifter gestation was about six months, and I did the math in my head. "Late June? Beginning of July, maybe."

He hesitated. "Are you okay? Aren't you happy?"

"Of course I'm happy!" I shouted, and buried my face in his shirt, sobbing. "But I'm devastated!"

He was hugging me and kissed the top of my head. "Forgive me for being confused, but you're sending some conflicting signals."

I took a deep breath, trying to calm down, and looked up into his hazel eyes. "What kind of fools bring a pup into a world they know is ending?"

Understanding pulsed through the bond, and he pulled me closer. We sat quietly for a long while before he had an answer for me.

"Hopeful fools."

EPILOGUE

EDANA

I TOOK MY SEAT at the table and looked at my colleagues, trying to ignore the painfully empty seat next to me.

"Your stupid brother has complicated everything for us, Edana," Tirich hissed, glaring at me.

I knew he was right, but I snarled, "How dare you speak ill of Xeron!"

"Tirich speaks the truth. We've hidden our existence well for years, biding our time. Then, Xeron had to get greedy, kidnapping half a dozen supernaturals in less than six months, and now they know *everything!* That fool deserved to die," Nox said, curling his lip. "I wish I'd been the one to end him."

I hissed at him. Everyone glared at me, seeing my brother's foolishness as a strike against my competence.

"So, what do we do now? The dogs know our plan and have our research. I'm sure they will seek our items for themselves," Semele stated, concern darkening her features.

"We will find them first," Nox said. "My sweet crone is entering the Smithsonian Museum as we speak. If the athame or the bell is there, she will find it."

"And if it's not?" Tirich asked. "We need to send others right away to search the other locations. We cannot let them fall into the hands of the enemy."

"I can send my fiends," I volunteered, trying to prove I wasn't a fool like Xeron. That I was important to this cause.

They ignored me, and Semele said, "Maybe we should go person-ally. We must stop the wolves from—"

A giant fist smashed into the table, cutting her off, and we all jumped, cowering. Typhon stood, glaring at the room.

His deep voice rumbled in his barrel chest. "Why would it matter if these dogs get the items first? They are irrelevant specks. We should let them find the items for us. After that, it will be easy. Kill them all and then take our prize."

I swallowed but found my voice. "But, sir, you've heard the rumors. The Pythonissam Viridi—she lives. She's among them. She and the Maiden killed my brother!"

He leaned forward, getting too close to my face, and I felt the blood drain from my cheeks. His eyes, one yellow and one white with blindness, with a deep scar running through it, bore into me. "I hope you aren't suggesting that I could be killed as easily as your weak, simple-minded brother."

I shook my head vigorously, shrinking into my seat.

"This makes it easy for us," he said, smirking. "We sit back, and we wait while they secure the items for us. Then the fun starts. We end every single one of them, and take what's ours. If the Green Witch thinks she can stop us, I'll kill her myself, and then use her bones to pick my teeth."

Smiles curled around the table, and we glanced at each other, excited for the day to arrive.

THE BETA AND THE FOX
TEASER

Chapter 1

FINN

I UNBUTTONED MY CUFFS and rolled them up, still in my suit from Gideon and Eris' wedding. It was a beautiful ceremony, and I wanted to vomit. After downing a shot of whiskey, I tapped the bar, telling Pike I needed a refill. He obliged, once again attempting to engage me in a conversation about my mood. I ignored his questions. Usually, I was the life of the party, but now I felt like I could barely breathe.

'That's because we need our mate. Why are we sitting here, idiot?' my wolf, Shaw, asked.

I pulled the note out of my pocket and read it for the millionth time.

Finn,

I know we have to do something about this, but I can't stay. I don't understand where my mind is. Please don't follow me. It'll just complicate everything. I'll be back.

-Kat

This referred to our mate bond. She'd stayed for a week after her liberation from the dragon's keep. During that time, she'd championed the sport of avoiding me, and I'd championed the sport of stalking her. We'd barely had a conversation. Then she'd disappeared and left me with nothing but a hole in my chest and this shitty note.

'She doesn't want us to follow her. I'm trying to respect that.'

'That's stupid. You're so stupid,' Shaw snapped, rushing me with a wave of possessive desire. *'Someone could be with her now! What if it's another man?'*

The glass in my hand shattered, and I barely felt the cut in my palm.

I sighed and opened my hand, taking the rag Pike handed me. *'Will you shut up? She's not doing that!'*

'What if she is? She could be with him now. And you're sitting here! What if he marks her? Steals her?'

I swallowed and rubbed my temples, trying to find a buoy of rationality in the ocean of his jealousy.

'Do her emotions feel like she's enjoying a man right now?' I asked him, knowing that arguing with the stubborn brute was pointless.

She was so fucking sad. Her aching sorrow in our partially formed bond had been drowning me since the wedding started.

'That's because she needs us. Let's go!'

'Go where? We don't even know where she is!'

'Don't give me that! Your brother can find anyone with his fancy computer.'

I jumped because a hand landed on my shoulder.

"Finn! Look, Finn's here!"

A girl I'd partied with. Slept with.

I mumbled, "Just go," and shrugged her off, trying to temper my guilt so Kat wasn't affected by it.

"What? Come on—" she started, pulling on my jacket.

I erupted. "Just go! Get away from me!"

The bar quieted, everyone looking our way, and she spat, "Fine, asshole. What the fuck is your problem?"

I didn't answer, slumping in my seat and tapping the bar again. "Just bring the bottle, Pike."

I would've gone if Kat had asked. It didn't matter where we were going; I just wanted to be with her. I had a detailed daydream of meeting her parents and convincing them that wolf shifters weren't so bad. Showing them I could make Kat happy. We were fated to be together, and the Goddess never made mistakes. Blah, blah, blah;

all of that rhetoric fed to every wolf shifter from the moment they could toddle. It wasn't supposed to be this way. The mate bond was presumed to be the easiest choice a shifter ever made.

Kat had suggested meeting her parents was a terrible idea, assuring me they would never accept me. In the same conversation, she'd hinted she might never accept me either.

My kind and your kind, Finn... we just don't agree.

Shaw was relentless. *'It's the fox in her that hates us, but her wolf is mine! We can win her heart. You shouldn't have let her go without us. Feel her pain. She needs us. We need her.'*

'I didn't let her go! She left!'

He growled at me, not bothering with a response, and finally, thankfully, resorted to the silent treatment.

A hand fell on my shoulder, and I was shouting, "Does it look like I want company?" only to find Gideon. And Eris. Fucking awesome. Just the people I wanted to see. I took one look at their interlaced fingers and drank the rest of my whiskey in one gulp.

"Did you call him?" I asked Pike, and the wince on the bartender's face answered when he didn't.

My brother grabbed under my arm. "Let's go home, Finn."

He tried to pull me to my feet, but I didn't budge. "I'm good where I am. Thanks."

Before he could say anything else, Kat's despair ripped through the bond, making my chest roll into itself. I grabbed the front of my shirt, closing my eyes and hissing at the pain. "Fuck. What is that?"

"What's wrong?" Gideon asked.

"I don't know," I gritted through my clenched teeth. "She's in so much despair, it's painful."

Involuntary tears formed in my eyes as waves of her sorrow crashed through me. I blocked the bond so I could compose myself and stood, making a decision.

"I have to go. I have to find her," I said, searching my brother's eyes for disappointment.

We had a lot going on right now with the dragons, the end of the world, and the artifacts, but nothing mattered to me except Kat. I didn't know where to start, but I was going to find her. Katarina Kimura. I was sure I could dig something up.

He clapped me on the shoulder and smiled. "Be careful out there. Call me if you need anything. Try to hurry if you can."

I turned, jogging to the exit, but Eris spoke up. "Hey, Finn?" I turned back to her. "Kat told me she grew up in a little town called Ontario. It's just outside Los Angeles. If that helps."

I nodded and threw the door open. "Yes, it does. Thank you!"

I left my car. A jog to the pack house would sober me up, and I needed to buy a plane ticket.

'It's about time,' Shaw grumbled.

www.ingramcontent.com/pod-product-compliance
Lightning Source LLC
Chambersburg PA
CBHW022015170626
46808CB00001B/419